OLEANDER OATHS

STEEL ROSES MOTORCYCLE CLUB
BOOK 3

JENA DOYLE

DIRTY WORDS PUBLISHING LLC

For anyone who's ever had to fight off their inner monsters...
You are worthy of this life.
Keep fighting.

STEEL ROSES FAMILY TREE

* Member of Caputi Family Tree

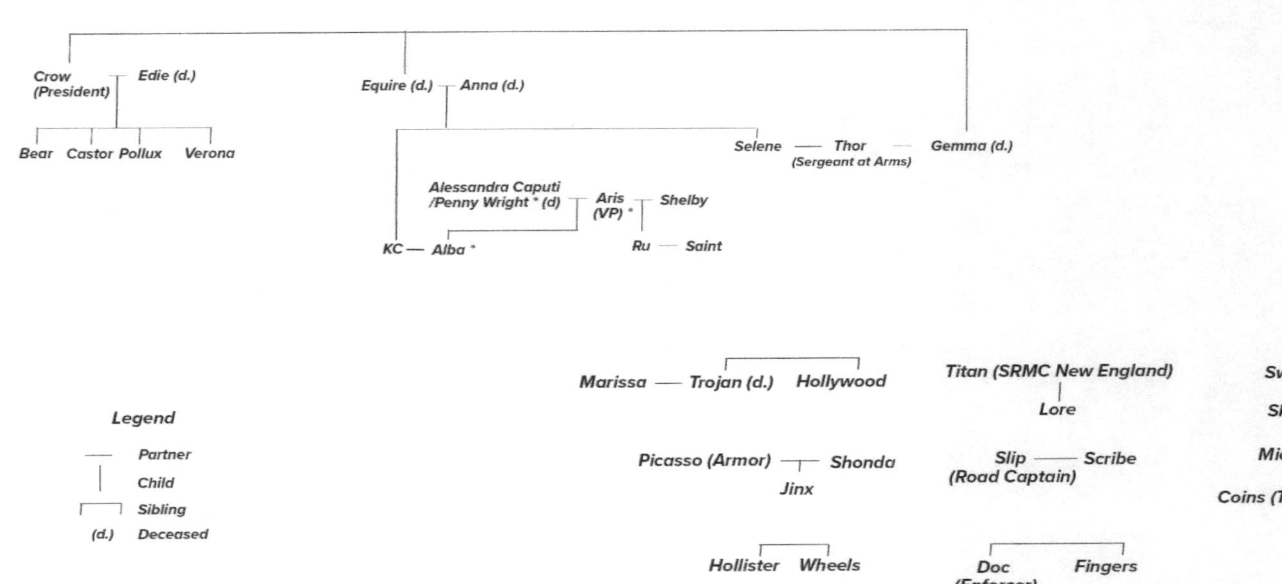

CAPUTI FAMILY TREE

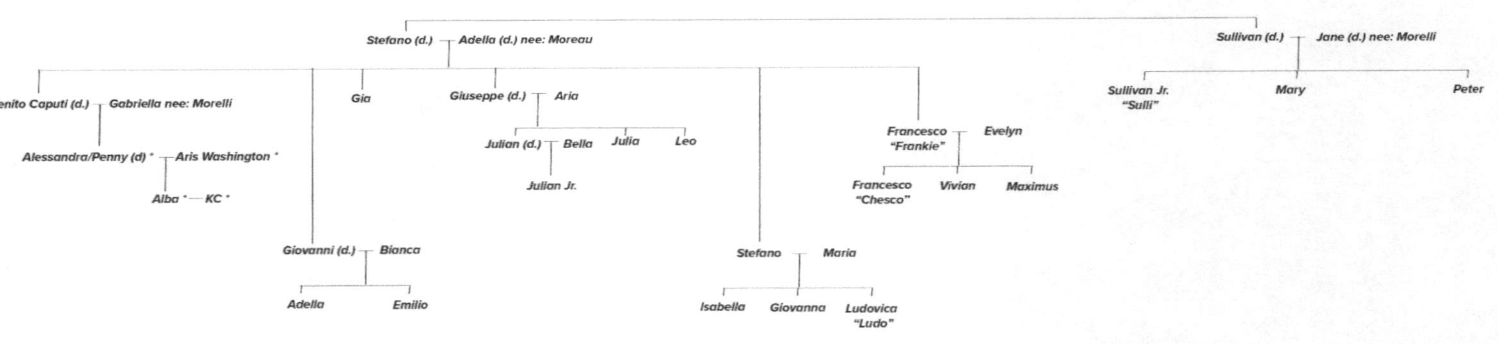

Legend

—	Partner
		Child
⌐	Sibling
(d.)	Deceased
nee.	Maiden Name

* Member of Steel Roses Family Tree

1

SELENE

Thanksgiving

I ducked out of the way before Thor's massive fist connected with my cheekbone, but I missed the cues indicating he'd swiped his foot out. When his leg connected with the back of my knees, I melted like ice cream on a hot summer day, landing on my back with a loud *oof.*

Fuck.

The air rushed out of my lungs, and I blinked up at the shadow of my mentor, holding out his hand for me so he could yank me to my feet. Grimacing, I shoved it away. I didn't need his help, not anymore.

"You're distracted," Thor said, his steel eyes twinkling in the sunlight.

I ignored his comment and peeled back the tape around my wrist to make it tighter before slapping it down again.

"Let's go." I held up my hands, ready for another round, but Thor only raised an eyebrow and smirked before picking up his water bottle. He tilted his head back to squirt some into his mouth while I stared at the drop that trickled down the side of his jaw and onto his neck. The muscles worked under his skin as he swallowed, and for the millionth time, I wondered what it might be like to lick that throat as he slid inside me.

Get your shit together, Montgomery. I shook my head to bring my attention back to reality. Not that there was ever a good time to lust after the man who'd married my aunt before her untimely death, but it was definitely the *wrong* time when my focus was supposed to be on hitting him in the face as hard as I could.

"Why don't you tell me what's on your mind?" Thor sat on a fallen log to take another long drink, tossing his bottle to the side so he could adjust his own wrappings.

Of all the people on this great earth, he would be the last person I spoke to about my dark, twisted secret. He'd do everything in his power to talk me down, to remind me it was Rose business, not mine. I didn't care.

The Steel Roses Motorcycle Club had been dragging their fucking feet for three months since my best friend, Ru, and her boyfriend, Saint, had gotten shot. As soon as the time was right, I would take action.

"I'm just tired."

He narrowed his gaze, tilting his head to the side while he waited for me to continue. It was always this battle of wills between us, who had the most patience, who had the courage to hold their tongue the longest. He read me like a book most of the time, and even when I tried to keep my walls up, he found a way to bring them crumbling to the ground.

"Are you having trouble sleeping?"

I chuckled softly, forcing a tight smile I knew looked fake. No, I wasn't sleeping. I hadn't slept in over a year, and he knew why. Nikki McNally, a woman I'd known since childhood, a woman that had dated my twin brother, Jericho, for over a decade, had defected to our enemies last July. Since then, the information she'd given to the Caputi crime family had led to the abduction and brutalization of multiple Roses, the shootout this August only being the latest. Ru had barely made it out alive, and as I stood over her hospital bed, debating with myself about the odds of her survival, I made a promise.

I wouldn't stand for this any longer.

The only problem was Nikki had *also* gone after the Roses by attacking Saint and the other brother in the vehicle, Hollywood. They claimed it was club business, that I wasn't a member of the MC so I had no reason to get involved.

What these fuckers failed to understand was the women of the club, people like me, Ru, and the hang-arounds, existed in a liminal space—not quite in, not quite out. Nikki had lived in that gray area *with me.* In here, the women of the SRMC took care of each other. We were the heartbeat of this family.

"I can't help you if—"

"I don't want your help," I snapped, shooting him a sharp look.

He sat up straighter and smiled, knowing he'd hit a nerve. There was only one person in the world I trusted beyond reason and logic, and he couldn't resist needling my temper.

"I know what you're thinking," he said.

Again, I glared at him, waiting for him to show his cards.

"If you go after her, Selene, so help me fucking Gods..." It came out as more of a growl than a calm, controlled statement.

Yes, yes, I knew what he planned to do. He'd come for me, just as he came for me all the times before. But I'd done my research, and I was good. I could get in and out without anyone knowing, and once Nikki was gone, the leak would be patched and she wouldn't be a threat any longer.

"Tell me that's not what you're planning, and I'll leave it alone." He stood and took a step toward me, raising his eyebrows in expectation of a response. "Be honest."

I cleared my throat and focused on the ground between us, unable to look him in the eyes because he'd see right through me. He always did.

"That's not what I'm planning," I lied, although technically, I wasn't planning to go after her *yet.* I wanted to be sure. I needed a solid plan, and until I had that, I had to keep up the great facade.

"Hmm." Thor didn't believe me. Why should he?

I'd spent the last three months trying to find her, calling in every favor I had. The information ultimately came from the most unlikely of places—an old friend of mine, Marissa. She'd been an old lady in the club for years until her husband, Trojan, died protecting Ru and Alba the first time the Caputis attacked. After that, Marissa had taken off to start a new life...until a few weeks ago, when she'd reached out from Buffalo, New York with pictures of my most favorite hang-around slung all over a biker from their local club, the Kings of Carnage. Marissa said she saw her in the bar with the same group of bikers almost every night, and up until now, Nikki hadn't recognized the former SRMC old lady. Or if she had, she hadn't been provoked by Marissa's appearance nor asked for a reunion. In the absence of a safety net, Nikki had done what she always had...infiltrated a group of men and found one to fall in love with her and protect her, the idiotic sap.

Once upon a time, Nikki and I had been kids together—running in between the sheds out behind the clubhouse, making mud pies until our clothes were filthy, playing hide-and-seek under the summer moonlight. Nikki's mother had been a hang-around that had taken up space at the clubhouse for as long as I could remember. Her father was one of the old-timers, a Rose who had likely already died or moved on to a different chapter. I might have even called her a friend until she dicked around with Jer's emotions for all those years. But I'd been willing to overlook that because she'd always been a part of the tribe. If she and her idiot husband hadn't gone all *Et tu, Brute*, she likely still would be.

Marissa should have reached out to Crow or Thor. She should have taken this to the club. But she came to me because she knew what it was to be a woman in an MC. She knew I'd handle it.

"How's Leo?" I asked, changing the subject.

"Pissed off and silent." Thor ran a thumb over his eyebrow.

After Nikki and the Caputis came after us, the Roses had wanted blood. In September, they had gone after the remaining Caputi heir, Leo, but he was only the kingpin because his uncle and elder brother had died. He'd never been cut out for the crown and preferred to snort his inheritance away instead of control it. By the time we'd gotten to him, he was so tweaked out that it was surprising he could hold his head up. The Roses had been sent there to kill him, to repay blood with blood, but Saint had a crisis of conscience and brought him back to the clubhouse, where Leo had been drying out ever since.

I'd been a big part of bringing him back to life, especially once he stopped eating. Now, he'd resigned himself to our food but hadn't uttered a word in over eight weeks. They were running out of ideas, and Leo was quickly losing his potential value.

"We shoulda killed him when we had the chance," I said.

Thor shrugged. "Jury's still out. He might talk."

"Would you?" I laughed out a sad noise.

He raised an eyebrow, running his tongue across his lips. "We don't have the right motivation."

"What are you suggesting?"

Thor shook his head, giving me a look that reminded me it was club business, and I should mind my own. Instead of answering, he held his fists up and nodded. "Again."

He went harder on me that time, quickly getting me in a choke-hold before twisting my legs out from under me so he could tumble me onto the undergrowth.

"You're thinking too much," he said. "You're up in your head."

"Yeah, no fucking shit." I climbed to my feet, but Thor was already there, tripping me up so I fell face first on the ground.

"Stop fucking around," he said, crouching so he was closer to eye level. "How are you going to go up against Nikki and the entire Caputi family if you can't even take me down?"

A raging fire built in my gut, part fury, part humiliation. He was right. I *was* distracted, and it had everything to do with this stupid, annoying thing between us. I hated that Thor could read me so well. I hated that I'd been forced to live with him for the last fifteen years. I hated that my brother had found his soulmate and moved out, leaving me to deal with Thor by myself.

I had nowhere else to hide anymore.

Maybe I never did.

"Get up, Montgomery." Thor pushed to his feet, moving his toned calves toward his water bottle again. Fuck him for being so beautifully made. At six four, he was practically a giant, and his long dark blond hair and gunmetal-gray eyes had contributed to his nickname.

Thor.

A fucking Viking God come to life, and I was the stupid human that had developed this ridiculous codependence on him. I couldn't live with him, but the thought of leaving him made me want to peel my skin off my body. Ru thought I was in love with him, but such a minuscule concept had never encompassed the depth of decadent vileness in our relationship.

I pushed to my feet and took a deep breath, focusing on the way the air circulated through my body. The trees rustled in the crisp autumn wind, whispering a soothing melody that brushed against my cheeks in a healing embrace. Curling burnt umber leaves rustled along the ground, reminding me of the world's cyclic nature. Everything around me was dying, long since wrestled into submission by the stillness of November and now preparing for the ultimate death of winter.

With my mind more focused, I looked at Thor and held my hands up. "Again."

This time, I kept up with him. I dodged his first few blows, backing away when he advanced. I was only five ten to his tall, muscular frame, so I had to use his momentum against him if I ever wanted to win. He was big, so he tired easily. I only had to block him for so long before he got slow, and despite having an impressive military background, Thor was ten years older than me, thirty-nine to my twenty-nine. He was still in amazing shape, but forty hit everyone like a ton of bricks.

Even so, he tripped me up with an ankle I didn't see coming, and when I couldn't maintain my balance, I tried to use his weight to throw my other leg up on his hip in an effort to bring him down. It didn't work. He caught me and slammed my back up against a tree.

I winced on impact, ignoring the sharp pain that shot down my spine. With my hands wrapped in his between our chests and our legs tangled together, we were at an impasse. I couldn't move without submitting to him, but he couldn't back away without me letting him go.

"Give," he snarled.

"No." I tried to pull away, but he tightened his grip.

"Give!" His breath hit me in the face, minty and warm and *him*, and I shivered at how close we were. His lips hovered centimeters from mine, his fiery molten irises burning into me, our hearts pounding in time against our combined embrace. He'd shoved his knee in between my legs, pressing his hard thigh firm against my leggings, rubbing my vulva in the best and worst way. We danced on precarious battleground, one minor slipup away from total disaster.

This wasn't the first time we'd sparred; Thor taught me everything I knew. He'd held me down in hundreds of sessions before, grabbed my hair and yelled in my face, but none of it had ever been as charged as this one moment. Trapped against a tree, nothing but our pride and our clothes between us, the mood shifted. My blood boiled and my skin shrank, making everything so fucking hot and untenable. I'd never been so aware of every inch of him, and I licked my dry lips, hoping to cool down. Thor dropped his gaze to the movement, and my heart pounded harder.

He was going to kiss me, and I desperately wanted him to. It was wrong, but for one moment, I imagined a world where a love like ours would be okay, where our relationship wasn't so damned unhealthy, regardless of the title society had put on us. We were toxic and possessive of each other in ways that should have made me uncomfortable, and the whole cycle had become so strangely addictive that I couldn't get away. He claimed not to want me, but no one else was allowed to have me, and everybody knew it.

"You live with monsters," he'd once told me. *"Don't be surprised if you turn out to be one."*

Yes, I was his little monster, and he'd made me this way.

Thor gripped my chin with his massive hand to hold me in place while he stared down at my frenzied state. Analyzing me. Regarding me. I tried to pull up my defenses, to file away all my errant thoughts before he could see them. But he knew me so fucking well. I could never hide from his calculating eyes.

"Training's done for the day." He took a step back, bent over to grab his water bottle, and walked away. "See you at the clubhouse."

My knees shook as I struggled to hold myself upright, cursing him with a one-finger salute as he walked away. For fifteen years, I'd danced around my attraction to him like it didn't exist, and any time someone came close to finding out my depraved little secret, I lied and pretended it was nothing, reminding the world he'd married my aunt so we could never cross that line.

Even if she'd died so long ago that I could barely remember her voice, Thor and I lived a life where a romance like ours would ultimately end in soul-shattering heartache, no matter what. If I didn't die caught up in the middle of this stupid war between the Roses and the Caputis, then he'd perish out there in the trenches, a measly piece of cannon fodder, and for what? Who could even remember anymore? They killed our people, we killed their people, and on and on it went.

Arbitrary words like uncle and love and broken hearts would never describe the relationship between Thor and me. He was there when even my brother wasn't. He'd done things for me that we swore we'd never speak of again. I'd confessed to him every dark, delicate secret I'd ever had, and he'd listened without judgment, only to convince me I wasn't a piece of shit for doing what I had to in order to protect the people I loved.

Thor always had been and would remain everything to me. And that made me so frustrated, I couldn't stand it.

2

—————

SELENE

I never said I was a good person. Just because I took some stupid oath to do no harm when I graduated medical school didn't mean I'd actually keep it or I'd never done such a thing *before* I took it. No, I'd been a monster since I came out of the womb, just as tainted and evil as the fuckers I lived with.

So deep was my rottenness that I often had to question how far would be too far for me. Would I eventually hit a limit? Would I find myself staring down the barrel of my M33 and be unable to pull the trigger, lacking the will to see it through? Maybe, but even I could admit I didn't know where that boundary was.

"Now, that's how to cut a turkey," Jer said, clapping the president of the SRMC, our dear Uncle Crow, on the shoulder while he sliced into the massive bird with an electric knife. The jolt nearly sent the tool straight through to the other side. Crow growled and straightened, glaring at my laughing brother as he held his hands up in surrender, lest the MC president take that blade to him.

"You better back the fuck up, KC," the VP, Aris, said, chuckling as his son-in-law got the look of death from Crow.

My brother had been born Jericho Montgomery, but once he joined the Steel Roses, he'd been given the nickname KC. It stood for

Killer Cock, which was an unfortunate story that made me groan. I refused to call him anything with the word 'cock' in it, so I stuck to the name I'd always used.

Jer and I were twins. Our parents had died when we were fourteen in a car bombing outside Annapolis, Maryland. My father, Esquire, had been the MC's lawyer until his death, but I'd always been closer with my mother. Jer and I both looked like her, with the same light-tanned skin, the same dark hair and bright blue eyes. The older I got, the more my facial features started to resemble her. Sometimes, when I stared in the mirror, I wondered if she was the one really staring out at me and what she would think of the life I'd made for myself.

It was my fault my parents were out that day, that we'd gone to Annapolis at all. I'd wanted to go to the annual pirate festival, and I had begged for months until they decided to make a day of it. We even brought my Aunt Edie, Crow's wife. They dropped Jer and me off while they went to find something to eat, and that was the last time we ever saw them. Sometimes I thought that if I could protect enough of the family I had left, save them from anything like that ever happening again, maybe Mom would forgive all the terrible things I'd done since. Maybe she wouldn't think I was too much of a monster.

Verona, the youngest of Crow's children, sat across from me with her face twisted in a horrified wince while she stared at Hollywood shoveling mashed potatoes into his mouth.

When he noticed, he froze and raised his eyebrows, blinking his pretty eyelashes and grinning in her direction. "Don't stare at me with those fuck-me eyes, Verona Marie. Everyone might get the wrong impression."

"I'd rather swim through hot garbage." She sneered, turning her nose up at his lurid tease.

"Such a flirt." He blew out a playful whistle and shook his head, going in for another bite.

She shoved him away and groaned, focusing her attention on her brothers, Castor and Pollux, on the other side of her, but I didn't miss the way her cheeks turned a bright rosy pink.

Twins ran in our family. Jer and I had come first, Castor and Pollux a few years later. They were currently roping their sister into a discussion about the next superhero movie while Ru, sitting on my left, added her opinion.

"Can't they find something else to write about?" she whined. "There's been like sixteen of those damn Revenger movies."

Saint chuckled and rubbed her back, making her lean farther into him so he could whisper something in her ear. He had once been Aris's best friend, but Ru and Saint's secret age-gap relationship put a damper on that. I glanced to the other side of Saint to see her father laughing with Doc, so perhaps things were on the mend. After his former lover died, Aris had taken a back seat at the MC's strip club, the Beacon. Ru and V had since renovated it and turned it into Madison County's first sex club.

Bear, Crow's eldest son, sat on my right. I was close to all my cousins, but especially him. He and Jer were like brothers growing up, which meant he'd become mine as well. Where Verona had inherited their father's dark hair and rare deep indigo eyes, Bear and his brothers took after their mother—darker olive skin tone, soft brunette curls, and big mahogany puppy dog irises. I didn't let that fool me. He made up for those adorable, boyish features with intellect and prowess. Bear was Crow's son in personality: calm, collected, strategic. He saw more than he let on.

"Have you been by to visit our special guest?" he murmured, taking a drink of his beer. He traced his eyes carefully over me, reading me as his father did. Neither one of them was as good as Thor, so I kept my shields up, shoving all signs of my secret project into the deepest, darkest recesses of my mind.

"No." I moved the turkey around on my plate, unable to eat, though I probably should. "Do you think I need to?"

He shrugged. "Might be worth your while."

When Saint had saved Leo Caputi two months ago, most of the club thought he'd made a mistake. It took getting Aris on his side to convince Crow, and after eight agonizing weeks, everyone was on edge about it. The longer they held on to him, the more of a liability he became. Bear's trigger finger grew itchier by the day.

That intrigued me. "Is he talking?"

Bear turned to face me so he could lean in closer. "His knee's fucked up. He can't walk."

I snorted, thinking he was joking, but when his features stayed serious, I scowled. "He probably needs surgery. Send Doc."

Bear shrugged, giving me a knowing look. "You have a...*kinder* touch."

Sure, that was true. The MC's enforcer sat at the far end of the table with his little sister, talking to a few of the other club members. He laughed, his green eyes twinkling, his skin sunburned from too much time outside. At thirty-five, Doc should have been at the height of his career at the hospital. Like me, he was a talented doctor, but he too had a dark side. That was how he'd gotten his nickname. Sitting here today, he was Doctor Jekyll, but when he let his inner demons out to play, he turned into Mr. Hyde. He'd been known to work wonders with a machete and scalpel alike.

"Why can't you do it?" Bear said. "You got something better going on?"

He was a walking, talking lie detector, so I had to play my cards right for him to leave me alone about this.

"No," I said. "I just don't like helping the fuckers that killed my family. If his leg rots, chop it off."

Bear took another drink of beer and raised an eyebrow, still not convinced. When Crow stepped down one day, everyone expected him to take up the mantle as president. I thought that was some antiquated, patriarchal bullshit. Why wouldn't the MC elect their new leader from the rest of the group? Why did it *have* to be Bear? Whatever. Like they loved to remind me, club business wasn't *my* business.

"Will you go see him tomorrow?"

Fuck no. I had no desire to help the bastard that tried to kill my family and maimed countless more. "I've got plans."

He scrunched up his face and grabbed an ear of corn to plop on his plate. "What plans?"

"I don't have to explain myself to you," I said, even though I had nothing special going on. After a long, boring day in the garage, I'd go to the Beacon's reopening where I'd watch a kink show that would undoubtedly leave me sexually frustrated and confused. After that, I'd go home alone and rub one out to fantasies of my uncle, who would probably be doing the same thing in his room on the floor below me.

"Leave her alone," Verona cut in. "She's fucking that guy from high school."

"What guy?" Bear asked, a scowl between his eyebrows.

"Yeah, what guy?" Jer said from his end of the table, attention focused on me. "I didn't know there was a guy."

"There's no guy," I insisted, glaring at my little cousin.

"What's his name? Marty?" Ru said.

"That's right," Verona added. "But it's been a while since you've mentioned him."

"That's because it's nothing." I playfully sneered at Verona. "Anyway, I'm not the one that keeps my relationships a secret for years at a time."

Ru gasped and turned to face me, mock outrage in her eyes. "How dare you?"

"It's true, though," Hollywood piped up, giving Ru one of his classic lady-killer smiles. Despite how attractive he was, he had never done anything out of line with any of the MC princesses. To us, he'd always been a brother, a lovable goofball that wore his heart on his sleeve.

"Guess we deserved that one, huh?" Saint kissed the tip of Ru's nose, drawing her attention from the laughter around her. The conversation carried on and any mention of my extracurricular activities, or lack thereof, died down.

But hot, angry pinpricks drilled into the side of my face, indicative of Thor's gaze boring jealous holes into me. I *had* hooked up with a guy from high school, even if it was nothing more than a one-night stand. I needed to blow off steam, and who could blame me?

I ignored those gunmetal eyes and nibbled on my dinner.

"So you'll go see him?" Bear continued. "As soon as you can?"

I nodded, knowing my cousin wouldn't drop the damn thing until I agreed. I had a million other things I'd rather do instead, so while I might add it to my list, I wouldn't make it a high priority. If he happened to die between now and then or if he could never use his leg again, well...I would've called that karma.

"Thanks, Sel." Bear smiled and nudged my shoulder with his own the way he'd done since we were children.

I watched the revelry carry on around me, Castor and Pollux having moved on to arguing with my brother about who was the best Ninja Turtle.

"You're fucking useless," Jer said.

"Michelangelo is *clearly* the best, and you fucking know it. He's hilarious, he looks great in orange, and he fights with nunchakus," Pollux said, counting on his fingers while he listed out the cartoon character's best qualities. "You're gonna tell me I'm wrong? *I'm* wrong? How are we even related?"

I chuckled, memorizing the familial warmth in the center of my chest. We were a motley bunch, the definition of a found family. That was the difference between us and the Caputis—they prided themselves on their genetics, believing the only real kin had been popped out of their purebred women. We picked our nearest and dearest based on loyalty, only letting someone in once they'd earned it.

Of course, we'd been stabbed in the back before, and the churning in the pit of my gut told me something terrible was about to happen again, some unknowable disaster lurking under the radar.

I sighed, my thoughts drifting to the research I had hanging up at home, and I reminded myself to call it early. The crew was gearing up for an epic Thanksgiving party, and if this were any other year, I'd be shooting 'em back with everyone else.

But I couldn't. I needed to stay focused and alert. I needed to protect my family. We couldn't afford to be blindsided again.

This is how I do no harm now. This is the only vow that ever mattered.

About an hour later, Verona found me coming out of Doc's pantry and asked to talk alone.

"Would you mind?" she said, wincing at her sternum where she'd gotten shot in June.

The healer in me sprang to life, and I nodded, forgetting everything else in favor of helping my cousin. We ducked into one of the rooms in the back so we'd have more privacy.

She closed the door behind her and lifted her shirt, revealing the ten-inch scar running between her breasts. It was angry and purple, but otherwise looked the same as the last time I'd seen it.

She'd been in the truck with Saint and Ru when the Caputis attacked. A bullet had gone through Hollywood's torso and lodged itself in her breastbone. If he hadn't been there, she would have died. If it had hit at any other angle, in any other way, they both would have died. We got incredibly lucky that day.

Still, that had been almost three months ago. Bone injuries were tough, but if she still had this much pain, something else was wrong.

"May I touch you?" I pursed my lips as I ran through the likely issues. Possibly inflammation? We were past the window for infection.

"Yeah, just be gentle." Verona looked over my head while I pushed and poked at areas around her scar. Despite being puffy and stiff, it reacted like normal muscle tissue. I ignored the necklace that hung low on her chest, a tiny glass jar containing a bullet fragment one of my old colleagues had pulled out of her body. I'd called in a few favors when she'd asked me to get it for her, and now she wore it around like a tribute to the night she'd almost died. She'd never told me the reason she wanted it, but I'd never asked.

"It doesn't feel any better?"

"No, it...it's getting worse." She shook her head as I stepped back, lowering her black Led Zeppelin shirt so she could tuck it into her skirt, concealing her necklace once again. "I wake up in the middle of the night with stabbing pains. It's like I'm there again, like I'm rolling out of the truck and screaming for help, nearly on the verge of passing out." She took a deep breath and winced, her hand going to the spot over her heart where it evidently ached the most. "Something didn't heal right."

"Chest injuries are difficult. Your ribs never stop moving, and those muscles support your balance every time you walk." I crossed my arms, deciding she better check it out just to be sure. "Have you had your follow-ups at the hospital?"

She nodded. "Last week. The scans were fine, but it doesn't *feel* fine."

I thought about other options, hearing what she wasn't saying as loudly as what she was. Shortly after the ordeal, she had proposed we move in together. I needed a break from Thor, and she wanted to get out of her brothers' house. After telling Thor, he had opted to move into Jer's old room in the basement, leaving the primary suite for me and my old room for Verona. So far, the arrangement had worked. She counterbalanced the awkward energy between Thor and me, and I appreciated the help with the bills.

However, it had made me painfully aware of her habits. Like how many times she got out of bed to pace down the hallway and back up in the middle of the night. Or the soft glow of the television in her room sneaking in through the cracks around my door when she thought the rest of the house was asleep. She hadn't had a solid eight hours in weeks and likely long before that.

"You need rest, V," I said. "You've been running around these last few weeks, helping Ru with the reopening and moving into my old room. When was the last time you slept a full night?"

"I can't get comfortable," she said. "The pain meds don't work anymore, and I never liked them anyway. Opioids make me itchy."

"Have you talked to someone?" I raised an eyebrow.

She gestured between us, indicating *this* was her doing that.

"No." I laughed and ran a finger over my eyebrow. "I mean...a therapist."

"I can't afford that." She rolled her eyes. "That's why I'm here with you."

"Well, I'm a surgeon, not a shrink."

She grumbled to herself and gave me a sidelong look. "Why'd you come back here, anyway? Weren't you one of the top people at TW Hospital?"

I bit my bottom lip and tried not to fidget. She was right. I'd graduated college, gone to the most prestigious medical school in Virginia, and damn near completed my residency at the learning hospital. I had been expected to become one of the best trauma surgeons in my generation. I'd like to say I flew too close to the sun and careened back to earth in some epic display of malpractice, but the truth was so much more fucked up.

The lie came naturally. "I burned out. By the time I got where I wanted to be, I was too tired to be there."

She narrowed her eyes, suspicion radiating out of them. Not only had I known her since she was born, but we were also related. The family resemblance was too uncanny, and she knew how it sounded when Montgomerys kept things back, when we didn't tell the entire truth.

"Besides, Jer was fucked up over Nikki. He needed me." I cleared my throat.

She nodded, swallowing in acceptance even if she could tell there was more to the story. Only two people in this world knew the truth about that, and I aimed to keep it that way. It was one of those skeletons I locked in the back of my heart, gathering dust, never to see the light of day again.

"But he's okay now." Verona nodded toward the front of the clubhouse. "Jer...and Thor."

She was right. Jer was happily married to Alba. Thor was...well, still Thor. It was unlikely he'd ever change. Ru was with Saint, finally revealing their torrid affair to her father. My family was surviving, and I didn't trust it. Somehow, someway, the other shoe was about to drop. I knew it in my bones the way some people knew it was about to rain. I needed to stay alert, on my game, prepared to act.

"So when do you get what you need?" Verona raised her dark eyebrows and pursed her matching lips.

I snorted, gesturing at the Thanksgiving Day revelry happening on the other side of the wall. "What do you mean? Can't you see I'm overjoyed with gratitude?"

"Right." She chuckled in obvious disbelief. "I live with the two of you, Sel. I see those yearning looks. I hear the hushed conversations. Be out with it already. Like Saint and Ru. Fuck what everyone else thinks."

"It's not—It's never been like that." I shifted uncomfortably, a brick forming in my gut that I had no desire to explain. "He's our uncle." He'd married her aunt, too.

Verona sighed. "If he's our uncle, then I'm the queen of the fucking world."

She drove her point home with one more snarky look before turning to head back to the front, the chains on her skirt jingling while she walked. When she opened the door, Thor stood on the other side of the hallway, leaning against the wall while a dark-haired hang-around smiled up at him with hearts in her baby blue eyes.

The fucking menace.

"Hiya, *Uncle* Thor." Verona gave me one last look over her shoulder before hissing at the hang-around loud enough to make the poor girl jump. She backed away from Thor as he sighed.

"Knock it off, V." Then he looked inside the room and saw me standing there.

Our eyes locked for one heartbreaking second before the door shut and separated us again.

The urge to throw it open, grab that bitch by her filthy hair, and drag her down the hall to stomp her stupid face in rattled through my body. But how could I blame him? Hadn't I done the same thing? Marty hadn't been anything more than a night of sex before he went home four states away, but I realized how screwed I was. I'd wanted to like it, but every time I had closed my eyes, I'd seen an angry gunmetal stare, and the fun had stopped.

Thor tried to hide his possessiveness, but he hadn't been very good at it. Maybe it was my turn to mope around and slam doors and throw wrenches in the garage. Instead, I stood there, pretending the sight of him with someone else didn't sting. I closed my eyes, swallowing the rising anguish in my throat, breathing down the chemicals ricocheting through the neural pathways in my brain.

I don't love him. Not like that. I don't. I swear I don't.

I should have been ashamed of myself. Not that I'd ever gotten along with Aunt Gemma, but she would beat the living fuck out of me if she knew I felt this way, that I wanted the things I did about her husband.

She's dead, a dark voice whispered. *Dead people don't have opinions.*

I went to my safe space—my mental library. Here, no one could touch me. Here, no stupid alpha assholes could hurt me. This had been a trick my father had taught me when I was a child, how to compartmentalize the things that happened to me. It had gotten me through the trauma of his death and the horrific experience of adolescence as an orphan. Now, I filed away this memory with the rest.

I found the mental book where I contained the things related to my dead aunt's husband. It rattled on an upper shelf, thick and leather bound, the same gunmetal color as his eyes. I opened the cover and dumped everything from today inside, all the pain, all the desperation, all the years of fucked-up yearning. Yes, he was *technically* my uncle, and yes, I shouldn't *technically* want him the way I did, but fuck, none of that soothed the ache in my chest. I hated myself because of it.

If he wanted to fuck a hang-around, he should, part of me said.

I forced that voice in there, too, and watched the images of our time together play out on the pages like a movie screen, like I was removed from it, like it had happened to a famous actor instead of me. Just like that, the tension in my chest cleared. My brain fog dissipated. I could breathe again.

More focused, I opened the door, expecting to see Thor and the girl making out, but they must have already found a different room because the hallway was empty. His book rattled harder. I ignored it and walked through the chaos of the clubhouse, out into the fresh autumn air.

By the time I got home, I was exhausted, but I still had a few things to do before I went to sleep. Thor and Verona would be at the clubhouse until the wee hours of the morning, so I had the place to myself. After I showered and grabbed a bottle of expensive whiskey, I put on a pair of gym shorts and a white tank top and went to my closet, sliding all my clothes to one side so I could go through my research again. I'd printed out everything I had on Nikki and pinned it up so I could see the bird's-eye view.

Drinking down three full swallows, I winced against the burn and sighed at the warmth settling in my gut. My attention caught on the most recent picture of Nikki at a bar, hanging all over her new boyfriend and throwing down hundreds like she was made of money. Where the hell was she getting the cash from? And where was her child? She should be toting around a one-year-old. New Guy was knee deep in some bullshit he didn't even know he was swimming in, which made this even more dangerous. She was hiding in a wolf's den, those assholes having opened up their trust to her for some god-awful reason.

And where were the Caputis? Were they still after her? They had given her a test of loyalty that night—kill Ru. Kill Verona. Kill them all. She'd run instead. If I were Gabriella Caputi, I'd be out for her fucking guts. And yet, there she was, living her best life out in the open, not bothering to keep a low profile. If I found her, certainly the Roses and the Caputis had, too.

What about this lucky Judas had made her so indestructible?

A book on a mental shelf I tried not to visit rumbled, one I'd let grow dusty and decay with age. No, I didn't go down that aisle anymore, not in a long time. But in my weakest moments, I wondered if it was that screaming book that had kept me from going after her up until now. I pointed my finger at the Roses and screamed cowardice, but I'd had a few weeks to settle it myself, and I hadn't.

Taking another swig of whiskey, I cursed the side of me that delicately held my bleeding heart.

3

THOR

"**B**rothers," Crow said, standing at the head of the table. "The time has come to make a decision. I know it's Thanksgiving, but the Caputi cocksuckers wait for no one."

I sat in my normal spot next to Aris, watching as the rest of the club milled around in the background, lazy from the big dinner but looking forward to the revelry after the meeting. KC, Bear, and Hollywood stood in a corner toward the back with Saint, their arms crossed and their serious scowls set between their eyebrows.

"We know what brought us here is a war that has shaped damn near every part of our lives," Crow continued. "We've lost brothers and old ladies, good men and women that this war didn't need to steal from us."

I cleared my throat as a memory of my best friend, Trojan, passed through my mind. He'd given his life to protect KC's old lady last year, and I missed him every fucking day.

"Gabriella Caputi is coming undone," Crow said. Last year, KC had killed the kingpin, Benito Caputi, Gabriella's husband and Leo's uncle, leaving a huge void for someone in the Caputi family to fill. Leo and Gabriella had been fighting for it until we'd abducted the drugged-up psycho a few months ago. "Those that were loyal to Leo are reluctant to fall in line with her, and her own faction is fraying. She's desperate, which will make her reckless. We need to be on high alert."

"What's the plan for our houseguest?" one of the brothers, Wheels, shouted from the back.

"He still isn't talking," Doc said, rubbing at his dark beard before leaning forward to rest his forearms on the table. "Despite receiving...*excessive*...medical treatment."

"Leave Leo Caputi to me," Crow snapped, shooting a glare at Doc. "I know how to get through to him."

"And after that?" Wheels continued. "Are we just going to keep him around?"

"That depends on what he has to say," Aris said, effectively shutting up the peanut gallery.

"I know you want your vengeance," Crow added, glancing around at the gathered members of his family, the proverbial king before his peerage. "You've gotten restless, but I'm only asking for a few more weeks. If we're patient, we might be able to use him to our advantage."

Murmurs rose from within the group. "*Waited long enough*" and "*slit their fucking throats*" and "*if he's this weak now...*"

"If there's dissent, speak it loud enough for me to hear it," I growled, forcing myself to my feet. My presence kept everyone in line, reminding them we had a hierarchical order here for a reason. If they had an opinion, they made it known or they shut their fucking mouths. Crow's hesitation had fuck all to do with being weak. If anything, his restraint might be one of the strongest things about him. He'd lost a lot in this war, too—a wife, both siblings, and nearly his daughter. We'd all lost people. I understood their bloodlust, but I wouldn't have them sowing the seeds of mutiny in dark corners. Best to show their damn faces so we could deal with them now.

"We should have killed him already, Prez," someone said. "This is getting old."

"I agree," said Doc, giving a noncommittal shrug.

"Gabriella thought she could get ahead of us by making a deal with the Canadians, but after the one I made with the cartel, she's got no supplies to sell," Aris said. "She's up shit's creek with no life raft. If she needs Leo to calm things down, then we need him to create chaos."

That got a hum of approval.

"I want to hear what our informant has to say," said our treasurer, Coins, glancing at Saint. For over a year now, the quiet brother had been in contact with someone inside the Caputi network, and the knowledge they'd given to us had proved instrumental in laying siege to Gabriella's plans.

Saint took a step closer and cleared his throat. "She's close to Leo. She wants confirmation he's alive and healthy before she'll tell us anything else."

"Fuck," KC murmured, running his hand over the back of his neck.

"Give it to her. Take a picture, I don't care." Crow ran his fingers through his dark hair, the bags under his eyes heavy and pronounced. The stress wore us all down, but none more so than him, the patriarch, the link holding it all together. "Then find out what's going on."

The room fell silent, but at least some of the tension had eased.

After we'd discussed the rest of the topics on the agenda, including the upcoming charity drive for Christmas, Aris banged his rings on the table to announce the end of the session. "All right, you fuckers. Church is over. But don't forget about the Beacon's grand reopening tomorrow. Y'all better fucking be there to support my little girl."

Some of the older brothers had an issue with watching the younger MC princesses own their sexuality, especially knowing Alba and Ru ran a cam site and V had started working at the Beacon when it was still a strip club. In a life where any of us could be killed any second, flashing a little tits and ass seemed like a stupid thing to worry about. I was proud of them for what they'd done, and I couldn't wait to see what they'd go on to do. So, hell fucking yeah, my ass would be planted at the bar for Ru and V's big night.

Aris didn't wait around to talk to anyone, just barreled toward the back rooms, laughing as two hang-arounds met him at one of the doors and dragged him behind it. I took a deep breath and let it out through my nose, shifting my focus to Saint. He'd already said his goodbyes to his buddies and found Ru out front, wrapping his arms around her torso so he could lean down to whisper in her ear. Whatever he said made her giggle and turn toward him to kiss him.

I might have to say something soon.

I filed that away for later dissection. If my suspicions about Selene were true, then we had to pull the trigger on Nikki sooner rather than later. She hadn't come up in conversation in a while, largely due to Leo's massive presence, but I knew Selene better than anyone else on this planet. She would only wait so long before she took matters into her own hands. Being more stubborn than a fucking mule ran in her family after all, and Crow would know that best.

"We need to talk about Nikki," I cut in, leaning forward so I could put my elbows on the table and keeping my voice low.

"What about her?" Crow raised his eyebrows.

"It's time we took care of it." I cleared my throat, meeting the MC president in the eye. "We can't keep putting it off. She's a rat and we need an exterminator."

Crow waved a hand and shook his head. "She's on the run."

"She's still a threat." Slip twirled a cigar around between his forefinger and thumb before sucking back on it, making the ember tip burn a bright tangerine orange. When Crow's gaze cut to him, Slip shrugged and pursed his lips. "Just saying."

"Castor's on it," Crow said. "She's running from the Caputis, hiding out with an MC in Buffalo."

"That doesn't negate the fact she knows a lot of our secrets," I argued. "She grew up around us. She's been around this clubhouse since she was in pigtails. Fuck, she's the reason Trojan is in a fucking urn instead of sitting at this table."

"What are you suggesting?" Crow raised his eyebrows. "I can barely spare the manpower to watch Leo, much less send a hit squad after a fucking snitch."

"Hey," I cut in, holding up my hands lest the alpha start growling in my direction. "No one said wearing the crown would be easy. That's why I'm not the fucking president."

"If she's fucking one of the members, I can't ask them to hand her over. That will start another war." Crow pinched the bridge of his nose, rubbing his fingers over his tired eyes before letting out a deep sigh. "I agree that we have to do something, but until I have a solid plan, I can't bring it to the club."

"I know you feel some sort of way because of the baby." Slip sighed, shifting uncomfortably in his seat. "Trust me, I do, too. I hate to make anyone an orphan, especially so young."

"There's no saying we have to kill her," I said. "She and Leo were close. Maybe we can use her against him."

"Stop," Crow cut in. "Just...stop. I know she's gotta go, okay? Let me think of the right way to do it."

Sure that he would follow through on his word, I gave him a firm nod and finished my drink before placing the tumbler back on the table.

"Hey, get the fuck out of here, yeah?" Crow nodded to the festivities going on around us. Some of the hang-arounds had started dancing in the open space out front, and Bear currently had two girls on his lap, one on either leg, leaning in and whispering in his ears. "It's Thanksgiving. Go make merry and all that shit."

I barked out a laugh and pushed to my feet, shaming myself over the fact the only merry I'd get tonight would be when I went home and blatantly ignored the one person that held my attention these days.

For fifteen long years, I'd told myself that Selene was off-limits, and not just because she was Gemma's niece. Yeah, it walked a special line of fucked up that I'd developed this whatever-it-was with someone so closely related to my dead wife, but I was a fucking idiot in so many other unique ways, too.

In fact, protecting Selene had been one of my main reasons for agreeing to the marriage in the first place. Gemma and I hadn't been in love, and we didn't have any dedicated commitment to each other.

It was another item in a long list of things I'd done for the club. When Crow asked me if I'd be willing to move in with his sister to guard her and his family, Selene's bright blue gaze had been the only thing flickering through my mind when I said yes. KC had the rest of the club to keep him safe, and Gemma had her parade of lovers. Who looked after Selene? Who protected her?

The day I'd decided it would be me, I let myself into Gemma's place at her request to pick up Selene and bring her to the clubhouse, but I stumbled into a nightmare. Selene was sixteen at the time, angry at the world for stealing her parents from her too soon. She'd been dating some piece of shit loser named Billy that beat the hell out of her at least once that I knew about. KC had promised to decapitate him if he put his hands on his sister again, but even the threat of the Roses had not deterred him. When I walked in, the sounds of Selene's screaming reverberated from the back.

Fire in my blood, I raced through the hallway to discover Billy holding her down while he rutted in between her legs. She shoved at him, but it was no good. He outweighed her by at least eighty pounds.

I didn't think. Just reacted.

I had him under me, pounding my fists into his face, before I could process my actions. Then, I dragged him outside, grabbed my sledgehammer from the bed of my pickup, and brought it down on his skull in a sickening crunch, only to bring it back up and do it again. Over and over and over. I only stopped to realize the consequences of my actions when my hands trembled and I was covered in his blood. I'd all but made good on KC's threat, except I'd beat his fucking head in with the reason I got my nickname.

"Please," Selene had whispered, her bruised eyes almost swollen shut, her lips bloody and cracked, streaks of her assault running down her legs. "Please don't tell them."

As we hauled his disgusting body into my truck and drove him to the farm, I decided I couldn't turn my back on her. Killing Billy to save her had marked her as mine in some twisted, fucked-up way, and I would protect her until she could do it herself. I'd teach her how to fight, how to shoot, how to track her kill until the most opportune time to pounce. I'd teach her patience and control, what it took to be a soldier, so she'd never again find herself in the position of having to grit her teeth and bear the torture just because she didn't know how to stop it.

This, of course, had backfired on me. Selene was incredibly intelligent, perhaps the smartest person I knew. She was a teacher's wet dream, and when she surpassed me in skill, I told myself it spoke to my acumen as an instructor, rather than my lack thereof as a soldier myself. I'd spent ten years as a Navy SEAL. I could hit a quarter from five hundred yards away. Once upon a time, I'd been the most skilled sniper in my quadrant.

Now, when she called herself my secret weapon, she wasn't being facetious. Every word smacked of the truth.

WHEN I GOT HOME, I focused on the light at the far end of the hallway, a soft hazy orange echoing from under her door. I told myself to go downstairs and forget this morning's sparring session had ever happened. But that look in her eyes when I pinned her against the tree haunted me—hunger laced with desire, a wanton fury that bloomed to life when we touched. I couldn't have her. I could *never* have her, but fuck, what I wouldn't give to make her look at me like that while I was buried deep inside her.

She probably thought I was fucking that hang-around, and maybe it was better that she did. Maybe she should run off and be with that Marty fuck, whoever the hell he was. As long as he didn't abuse her, as long as she was happy. I swallowed back the raging envy that slithered up my throat and forced myself to unclench my hands.

She's Gemma's niece. She's Crow's niece. She's your niece. Back the fuck off, Erickson.

Ah fuck, maybe I was a masochist, because I walked down that hallway regardless of the reasons I drew a big fucking line between us.

Heart pounding, I took a deep breath and knocked twice on her door.

"Sel?" I put my hands on the doorjamb above my head to give them something to do while I waited. I was afraid if I let them hang, they'd take it upon themselves to twist open the handle and storm inside.

She didn't answer, but the floorboards creaked as she tiptoed closer, the shadows of her body moving in the light below the door.

"I didn't—" I cut myself off and cleared my throat, my voice low and gravelly, giving away how carefully I wanted to word my sentence. "I'm not fucking the hang-around."

"I don't care," she said, an obvious lie. I'd seen the hint of betrayal in her wide gaze as the door closed. "Fuck who you want."

I laughed and rolled my eyes at her indignant response. That was our fucking game, wasn't it? We lived to torment each other.

"Open the door." It came out more like a command than I intended, but I held my ground, waiting to see if she would deny me.

Slowly, the handle twisted and the door cracked open, revealing my gorgeous wildcat leaning up against the wall, sliding her sultry gaze over me. Gods, she was beautiful—big blue eyes and long dark hair she kept up in a messy bun. Tonight, she wore a tank top and a pair of tiny shorts that barely counted as more than underwear. I didn't give a fuck what she called them—I wanted to rip them off and sink my teeth into the juicy flesh underneath.

Fuck. Stay focused, Erickson.

She tilted her chin up, staring at me with rebellion echoing in her eyes, and I'd swear that was one of the things I admired the most about her. She never backed down from me, and I never wanted her to.

"Yes?" she said, her voice cracking at the end of the syllable.

She tried so hard to be strong and tough in front of me, but I saw down to the shaking, terrified woman underneath. She'd been hiding something for the better part of the last month, and even though I suspected it had to do with Nikki, I didn't know exactly what it was.

I intended to find out.

Amused by her attempted nonchalance, I raised an eyebrow and tried to step forward, hoping to use my presence to move her back. She didn't budge, and that too delighted me because it said something about her. Whatever she wanted to keep to herself, whatever she was planning to do about Nikki, she already had it figured out. It was in this room somewhere—probably her closet or her underwear drawer.

Staring up at me with such defiance in her eyes, she looked like a fuzzy little kitten, like something that would swat at me with her tiny claws but barely draw blood. But I knew the truth. She was a lion—sharp, vicious, and terrifying. I'd trained her that way.

"I just thought you should know," I said, dropping down to almost a whisper.

She laughed out a sardonic noise. "Why? You've never cared how I felt about who you fucked before."

"Maybe I care now." I brushed a stray piece of her delicate hair behind her ear. Gods, was there anyone more radiant on this fucking earth? If there was, I'd never seen them. Fire burst to life in her cheeks, and I pretended like that response had nothing to do with my touch. No, she was definitely hiding something. I picked up the scent of her bullshit a mile away.

"Yeah, right." She shoved my chest, perhaps thinking I was fucking with her.

I wasn't, and I grabbed her wrists to haul her closer to me, her soap mixing with her fresh feminine scent to assault my nose. Fuck, she always smelled so good—like flowers in the moonlight and fresh citrus.

She gasped and glanced up to meet my gaze with a startled one of her own.

I used her surprise against her. "Or maybe I wanted to watch you squirm with jealousy because it gives me sick pleasure."

Selene struggled against me, not putting in much of a fight, just enough to tell me she was serious when she said, "Fuck off, Erickson."

That got my attention, and I widened my gaze, curling my lips into a knowing grin. "Make me, Montgomery."

Fuck yeah. I loved when she fought back.

She clenched her jaw as the ways she planned to defend herself echoed behind her gaze. She'd knee me in the gut and run, but she knew I'd chase her. Oh, I always chased her. I fucking *lived* to chase her.

"What do you want?" she murmured, the words entirely too soft and vulnerable for how hard she could fight.

A small burst of happiness hit me in the chest when she relented, and I pushed us so we were in her room before kicking the door closed behind me. She jumped when it slammed shut, her heart rate kicking even higher.

"We need to talk." Sobering, I let her go and took a step back, my smile still in place while I glanced around, looking for any clues. I'd trained her to be good about cleaning up after herself, but everyone made mistakes.

"About?" Her hands trembled so fucking hard, it must have vibrated her molars, and she clenched her fingers into fists to hide it.

I turned to face her. "I think you know."

She trained her facial expression into a cool, stoic calmness, one that meant she'd compartmentalized whatever it was that I'd interrupted. She knew where this conversation was heading and had prepared herself to lie through it.

I see you, Montgomery. I see you.

"Why have you been so distracted at training?" Using my height against her, I put my hands behind my back and took a step forward. She hadn't moved from her spot by the door, still a shivering little thing waiting to be devoured by the big bad wolf.

"Oh, I don't know. Maybe my best friend almost getting murdered after my brother's wedding had a lingering effect," she said. "Or the fact we haven't killed the person responsible. Or maybe it's because I'm still expected to treat him like a human despite all the horrible shit he's done to my family."

Those were flimsy excuses. She had survived worse with much

less complaint, but I could see how these things might pile up, one after the other. It could be stressful. Perhaps I had underestimated how much she could take. Perhaps the things I'd been seeing were signs of stress rather that an ill-advised revenge plot to take off after a woman who'd betrayed us.

I took another step closer and assessed her. "Do you need a break?"

"It'll pass." She ran her fingers over her face, rubbing in exhaustion as she moved away.

Crowding her against the door, I grabbed her wrists to pull them away. I needed to see her eyes when she responded. "That's not an answer."

"No," she said, gritting her teeth and blinking quickly. "I don't need a break."

"Then what's going on with you?" The more she lied, the harder her pulse pounded against my hand, damn near smacking me in the face with her dishonesty. We didn't keep secrets from each other, not like this. We reveled in the filth together ever since she watched me beat Billy's face in.

"It doesn't concern you," she growled.

"Bullshit." I closed the distance between us, lowering my forehead to hers so I could breathe her in deep, memorizing every damn note. "Your heart's fluttering like a hummingbird's. You're lying." I gripped her harder, making her wince. "Tell me the truth."

She didn't say anything, just stared back at me with that haunted look in her gaze. Heat radiated off her tanned skin, her body flushed up against mine, reminding me of how I'd tucked my thigh up against her precious pussy earlier today. I'd stared down at her mouth, just like I was doing now, and I'd wanted to tear and taste and *take*. I'd wanted to rip open her leggings, drop my gym shorts to my ankles, and plunge myself so far inside her that I'd forget my own name.

Standing there with her between me and the bedroom door, I found myself wanting those same things again. I couldn't want them. I *shouldn't* want them. She was so much younger than me (*only ten years*) and she was my dead wife's niece (*a dead wife is still dead*). There were a thousand reasons why it was fucked up and wrong, but none of those things stopped the moan from barreling over my tongue when she pushed up on her toes and collided her lips with mine.

Time froze.

All thoughts in my head came to a stop. The touch sizzled down my spine and up the back of my head, warming every nerve in my body. My heart pounded against my rib cage in a paralyzing rhythm that sent a jolt of lust straight to my balls. With my fingers itching to bury themselves between her legs, I groaned against the scent of her wet cunt as it surged up between us, making my mouth water.

Fuck.

I bucked my hips against her, my cock jerking to life, desperate for more attention. I'd whacked off to fantasies that started like this more times than I'd ever admit. The worst part of me, the beast that I kept muzzled and locked away, stretched awake, raking its claws down every last bit of restraint I had left.

This is a distraction. I smacked my beast back into place. I couldn't give in, and I couldn't lose focus. In place of telling me the truth or lying to me again, she'd kissed me. I should be furious. I should be so Gods damned angry with her that I couldn't see straight. But, for the same sick reason I'd been denying for years, I wanted more.

4

SELENE

I prided myself on my alcohol tolerance, and four swallows of whiskey would hardly make me inebriated, but combined with the exhaustion of trying to stay away from him, I couldn't lie anymore. Trembling and unable to say anything without revealing myself, I fell back on the stupidest advice I'd ever heard.

A woman's best asset is the one between her legs.

For the rest of my life, this would be my biggest regret. I'd always imagined that the first time I kissed Thor with any real desire would be romantic and passionate, born out of finally giving into the obvious chemistry between us. But as I pushed myself to my toes and crushed my mouth to his, I lamented that I'd done it to throw him off.

He would be furious about this, and I would deserve it.

A moan poured out of him and down my throat, curling my toes as the vibration ricocheted through my bloodstream. I could smell how much I wanted him, how wet I was getting, and I trembled knowing that he could, too.

What are you doing?! The logical side of me thrashed and screamed, mortification taking over. Any second, he would end this. He would push me down and step away, giving me the same look of disapproval he did when I fucked up during a sparring session. My cheeks burned, and I slid my hands up his chest to his neck, wrapping my arms around him to pull him closer.

That seemed to break him out of his trance. He grabbed my elbows and unhooked himself from my embrace, ending the kiss so he could stare down at me. But there wasn't disapproval in his gray stare.

No, I saw the brutal side of him, the same man that had killed for me, that'd taught me how to kill for myself. Fingers shaking and heart thumping, I waited for him to react, waited for him to storm out of my room and chide me for daring to break the unspoken rule between us.

He shot his hand to my throat, startling me enough to make me jump, and pushed me back against the wall, rubbing his thumb against my thundering pulse in a caress that echoed through my body to the throbbing ache in my cunt. Thor chuckled darkly, an obvious threat. He was on to me, and now that I'd revealed myself in such a sloppy display of desperation, he planned to take advantage of it.

"What the fuck do you think you're doing?" He shook his head and tsked, twisting his lips into a dangerous smile. I'd seen this look before, right before he sank his sledgehammer into someone who needed killing. I'd truly fucked up, and for the first time, I was almost scared of him. Thor would never hurt me permanently, but our entire relationship had been built on a never-ending cycle of mind-numbing pain mixed with all-consuming angst. I didn't know what would happen next, and a part of me, the nasty fuck, thrummed with excitement.

"Do you think you can kiss me and I'll forget about all the weird shit you've been up to? Hmm?" Thor narrowed his eyes, now fiery with his aggression. "Hiding in your room. Sneaking around in Doc's pantry."

I opened my mouth to argue, but he gripped my throat tighter, nearly cutting off my oxygen. I'd seen what those giant palms could do, and the fighter in me giggled with glee. Getting Thor worked up had always been one of my favorite activities, and now that I had the beast looking out at me with pure hedonistic attention, I'd never been more thrilled.

"I'm not some brainless fuck that thinks with his dick." His scowl hinted at the fury burrowed just under his skin, and I used it to my advantage.

I shoved my arms up and brought them down on his elbows, breaking his hold on me enough that I could duck under his body and run. Thor had always been quicker to react, and he snaked an arm around my stomach, lifting me off the ground, my back to his chest. I kicked my legs and struggled against him until he slammed my torso down on the vanity in the far corner. Ignoring the shock that went through the right side of my face and into my stomach, I shoved at the wood, trying to right myself, but he overwhelmed me with a palm on my back, pinning me in place.

Glaring up at him in the mirror, I snarled, "What are you doing?"

"You wanted a fight." His pupils had blown out, making the molten gray disappear completely in the dim light of my room. "Now you've got one."

I pushed against the tabletop again, but he wrestled me down, grabbing my wrists and twisting them behind me so he held them together on my lower back. He had me trapped and panting, nearly naked, in my own room, and I didn't know whether I was more upset or turned on. Possibly both.

A sharp sting zigzagged through my scalp when he gripped my hair and forced me to arch farther into him, my eyes meeting his in the reflection.

"Go on," he snarled. "Distract me again."

He adjusted his stance behind me, making his thick, hard cock brush up against my ass, telling me how much I turned him on. It surprised me, and I sucked in a breath as my cunt clenched so hard that my stomach hurt. Should I be pleased or astonished that he was handling me like this? Fuck it, I wanted more, he wanted more, and the lines between us had blurred so much, I couldn't tell where we'd once drawn them.

I opened my mouth to talk, but a sharp, burning slice went

through the right side of my ass cheek as a loud, fleshy slap sounded through the room.

He spanked me.

My knees nearly gave out, suddenly trembling too hard to hold me up, and my tank top twisted under me, so tight and suffocating. I wanted it off. I wanted to be naked for him.

"What was that?" he said. "Were you about to tell me the truth?"

My entire body shook. I didn't know what to do or say. I'd never been spanked before, not by my parents, not by a lover, and certainly never by Thor. I should have been outraged at the degradation, but I wasn't. No, I warred with myself over how much I wanted him to do it again. It was fucked up, but Christ, nothing had ever felt so fucking good.

"No? Nothing?" He raised his hand again, this time bringing it down harder, making me wince and nearly lose my balance. I pushed up on my toes, presenting my best parts for him, yearning for more.

"Fuck," I whispered, grimacing at the scalding arousal puddling in my underwear. I was absolutely dripping for him.

Another spank, this time on the other cheek, pushed all the air out of my lungs, and he followed that up by spearing his fingers straight down the center of my vulva.

I wilted like an overwatered orchid, my entire body turning into a sopping mess on that vanity. My hips dug into the wood, and there'd be bruises later, but fuck, the way his eyes shimmered with feral possession held me there, captivated. Like nothing else in this world mattered. Like teaching me whatever lesson this was had surpassed all other concerns in this world.

"Is this what you had in mind, huh?" he growled, punctuating it with another deliciously violent spank on my ass. "When you kissed me?" He twisted his lips into a smirk, but his eyes still held a glittering amusement that indicated he only partially meant the things he was saying. "Did you think I'd freeze up and leave you alone? You filthy fucking idiot. Didn't I teach you better than that?"

"Who knows, *Uncle* Thor," I teased, biting my bottom lip as I held his stare. "Maybe I wanted a good spanking. Ever think of that?"

That seemed to piss him off even more, and he hit me harder, my words goading him on. I cringed as my skin burned and my pussy throbbed, my muscles almost unable to tolerate any more.

"Of course." He laughed and tightened his grip in my hair so hard that I winced, chills shooting down my scalp and over my spine. "You always go for the jugular, don't you? Just like my fucking wildcat." I watched him in the mirror while he spanked me again, stinging my already sore flesh and staring at my ass like he'd seen a miracle. "I wonder if I could make you purr like a kitten."

He'd said it so low that I could barely hear it, but I did. My nerves had been lit on fire and the burn of imminent release rushed through my veins.

Fuck, am I about to come?

My muscles clenched, and I moaned as Thor speared his fingers over my cunt again, finding my clit and massaging it while I arched my hips up to meet him, spreading my knees wider to give him more access.

God, this was so wrong in so many ways. He shouldn't touch me like this. I was a grown woman. I didn't need anyone to spank me back into obedience, but I suspected he had let his emotions get the best of him just as I had. Now, my hormones were taking over. I should have wrestled him off me. I could have easily outmaneuvered him, but I didn't, and the thought of that sent me skyrocketing into my climax.

He worked me through my orgasm, slipping his rough, callused fingers under my shorts to apply the perfect amount of pressure right to my panties as my entire body erupted with euphoria. It had been such a long time since anyone had made me come, and the fact he had with a few minutes of impact play and some mesmerizing touches should have made me scared that he'd ruin me for anyone else.

But fuck it...I'd been well past that point for years.

I collapsed into a limp pile of mush in front of him, my lungs unable to get enough oxygen into my blood fast enough and my heart beating so hard it echoed in my head. The whole fucking thing had been mind-blowing, and I secretly hoped he'd pull down my under-wear and stuff himself inside me. The erection pressing up against my leg told me how much he wanted it, too...until I glanced up at Thor.

He raised his hands in the air, staring down at me with his mouth hanging open and shock in his wide gray eyes.

"Fuck," he growled before backing away to storm out of the room, slamming the door shut behind him.

I woke up on a gasp, struggling for air, sweat beading down my forehead. It was one of those fucking nightmares again, the ones that haunted me, reminding me I was a monster and always had been.

My mother's screams still echoed in my ears, the smell of singed flesh choking me as my father burned alive, the struggling form of Aunt Edie trying to get out of the SUV etched into my retinas. Of course, I hadn't been there when my parents died, but in many ways, my imagination made it worse. Did they die as soon as the bomb went off? Or did they suffer for an agonizing period of time until their bodies gave out?

Not that it mattered either way. I'd gotten my revenge for their deaths years ago.

Shaking off the chill from the November air seeping in through my windows, I got out of bed and headed to my bathroom to get ready for work, wincing as my ass protested my movements. Then, I remembered what happened last night and my cheeks burned. The look in Thor's eyes right before he left troubled me the most...like he'd realized how much he'd overstepped and how badly he wanted to do so much more.

I had a brief moment of wondering how in the fuck I was going to face him today, but *he'd* been the one who slammed me down on the vanity and turned my ass various shades of violet and rose. I figured we'd both go on ignoring that the way we had everything else. So I hopped in the shower to get ready for a busy weekend after Thanksgiving spent at one of the only reputable garages in Madison County.

Even though Bear had asked me to swing by Leo's holding cell to see how he was doing, I didn't end up making it over there before work. By the time I got to Rose Garage, Thor had already barricaded himself in his office while my cousin bitched about the amount of orders we'd taken in for the week.

"He knew KC was going to be doing the Beacon thing." Bear ran his hands back through his hair and down his neck, clearly stressed to be the only mechanic working until Hollywood got in. "Why the fuck would he take on this many orders?"

I shrugged and went back to my smutty romance.

Visions of the night before swam through my mind every time I shifted in my seat, my ass bruised and sore from how much Thor had taken out on me. Every time he walked past the front desk to go to the mechanic's bay, the memory of his strong hands holding me down echoed across my mind and my legs clenched together on their own to alleviate the longing.

He left me afterward, I reminded myself. *He hasn't looked at me since.*

He obviously regretted it. Aunt Gemma would be appalled and my parents outraged. What little morals I had left screamed at me for kissing him. Yeah, he'd turned my ass red, but I'd crossed the boundary first, and not even because I wanted to, though I did. I'd done it so he'd stop asking me questions. What a fucked-up thing to do to a person I cared about.

After we closed, I went home to shower and change before going to the Beacon for the grand reopening. When I got there, I had to complete a membership check and a thorough security pat down before I walked through the thick wooden doors and entered into the main area. Gleaming black floors greeted me, complementing the dark countertops and matching leather furniture in the foyer. Booths lined the walls on either side, some open to the public, some covered with a dark curtain for privacy. I marveled at how much it looked like an entirely new place. Not that I'd spent much time here when it was a strip club, but Ru had completely outdone herself now with turning it around.

A main stage jutted out perpendicular to the bar, where a man dressed in black vinyl wrapped a length of thick black rope around a much smaller man with blond hair. He trembled against a wooden X, his arms spread overhead, his legs shoulder width apart. The larger man loomed over the smaller one, whispering something in his ear that made the blond nod and huff out a desperate laugh.

I found Hollywood and Lore across the room, sitting with a few other SRMC members around our age, and I walked to their table, purposely ignoring the gunmetal gaze that tracked me from a spot near the bar as soon as I arrived.

"You made it!" Hollywood put his arms around me, pulling me into a hug. "You missed an awesome needle-play scene that I *know* woulda got your motor purring."

"Jesus Christ," Lore said, rubbing a finger over his eyebrow. "I should have known you'd be into all that shit. Me, I'm fucking traumatized for life."

I glanced behind the bar, thinking I'd see Saint back there slinging beers, but they'd hired a whole new crew. People I didn't recognize ran the shift, and when I glanced at the far end, Thor stood with Slip and Doc. He cut his steel gaze to mine almost as if he sensed me looking at him and froze, seemingly debating what to do.

The memory of his palm coming down on my ass went through my molecules again, the taste of his tongue in my mouth surging down to my pussy. My skin burned, and I squirmed in my seat, refusing to wince when the pain on my rear flared up again. Perhaps he could see my discomfort anyway because the fucker curled his lips into a pleased smile and sipped at his beer, returning his attention to his brothers.

"Alba and KC are upstairs signing autographs and taking pictures," Lore said, catching my attention.

"Did you know they sold a hundred tickets alone?" Pollux added, pulling up a seat next to Hollywood. He whistled and shook his head. "The life and times of a cam power couple, huh?"

Something revolted inside of my gut at the thought of my twin brother and his wife doing meet and greets with fans who paid to watch them fuck on a daily basis. But I'd come all over our widower uncle's hand last night, so who was I to judge when my life was already so fucked up?

"Can you believe this?" Lore shook his head, scratching at his eyepatch. "Ru did an amazing job!" The same night that Nikki attacked us, the Caputis had delivered a severely injured Lore to our doorstep. The bastards had torn out his eye and left him to die. Luckily, I'd been able to sew him up before he bled out.

"It's much classier than I expected." I fingered the waist-high countertop, recalling how she'd found a bunch of old propellers in one of the abandoned hangars in the airfield out back and paid someone to turn them into high tops. The black floors contrasted with the chrome accents and gave the place a grunge that still identified it as a property belonging to the Steel Roses.

The dominant on stage finished his scene and unhooked the submissive, who dropped to the floor on his knees to kiss the larger man's boots. This went on for a few seconds before the dominant helped the submissive up, and they walked toward the back of the room.

Wheels sat down on the other side of Lore, handing me one of the beers he'd gotten at the bar. "Hey ya, Sel. I didn't know what everyone wanted, so I just grabbed a bunch." He flashed us all a smile, his mahogany eyes shimmering against his dark skin. "Are you excited for the next performance?"

"Who do you think Mistress Mayhem is?" Hollywood cut in, picking up the schedule from the middle of the table.

I snorted, anticipating how hilarious Hollywood's reaction was going to be when he realized the truth. Before I could say anything snarky, the blue lights on the stage came on, and Ru walked out, wearing a top hat and a sparkly tuxedo top with a red corseted bodysuit on underneath. Her dragon tattoo twisted down her leg under fishnet tights and black boots that went up to her knees. She twirled a long black stick around as she walked, marking her as the master of ceremonies for this dungeon circus.

"Whew," she said. "Let's get another hand for Master Pablo and his submissive, the gorgeous January." Everyone clapped, and Hollywood hooted, making sure the performers knew their show was well received. "The time has come, my dear friends. The moment you've all been waiting for. Some of you drove hundreds of miles to be here for this." Shouts from the crowd around me cut her off, some people already clapping, already knowing what would be coming next. "Some of you started emailing about tickets the minute she posted that she would be here." More cries of excitement came from around me, and I grinned at the sparkle in Ru's eyes. This was exactly what she'd wanted. This had been her dream since she came home from college. I couldn't be more proud of her. "Here she is, my lovelies...The powerful Mistress Mayyyhemm."

The lights went dark while a hush fell over the crowd. Whispers died down and drumming echoed over the loudspeaker, the start of a popular heavy metal song about fucking the object of a person's affection like you hated them, which was a poignant choice for what greeted us when the red spotlight came back on.

A woman in ten-inch platforms stood center stage, the boots lacing up to her mid thighs. She wore a black bodysuit similar to Ru's but made of leather instead of sequins, and her long black hair had been pulled back into a tight ponytail high on her head. A matching black mask twisted around the top part of her face to hide her features, but those bright violet eyes caught my attention.

No one else had eyes like that.

V whipped the cat-o'-nine-tails with one hand, teasing the long strips across the floor, and flipped a wooden paddle around in the other, hearts cut out in the space that did the most damage.

My jaw dropped. She looked amazing...powerful and strong and sexy as hell. When she turned to the woman strapped to a spanking table behind her, the excitement inside my gut twisted into unyielding admiration. The submissive wore a mask, too, but I recognized her as Candy, one of the dancers that had worked at the Beacon before the renovation.

Verona was my cousin, and watching her flog somebody wasn't really my kink, but when she brought the cat-o'-nine-tails down on Candy's ass for the first time, I'd admit, the sight was beautiful to behold. She had complete trust in Mistress Mayhem, who paused to check in every few minutes, running her lips over Candy's flushed skin, whispering sweet nothings in her ear that made her squirm and pull at the straps holding her down. Then, she began again, alternating the whipping with the paddling on Candy's ass, thighs, upper back, anywhere Verona could safely hit her.

I thought of last night, of how hard Thor had slapped me and how bright those marks had been this morning. I had always bruised easily, so the sight didn't concern me, but Thor's continued distance marked such a stark contrast to the attentive way V interacted with her submissive.

Of course, I wasn't Thor's anything, and he certainly wasn't my dominant, not like this. I flicked my attention to him again, expecting him to have left and found somewhere else to lurk, but he stood in the same spot with those hunter eyes still trained on me. I pretended like that had no effect on my body temperature, like I didn't love the thrill of being stalked by him, chased by him, caught by him.

Once Candy's flesh was sufficiently pink, Mistress Mayhem picked up a shiny metal crop with a tiny hand on the end of it, bringing it down on the back of Candy's thighs with a solid *swoosh*. She hissed in a breath and arched her back, making V take a step back to admire her work. A bright handprint radiated on the submissive's flesh, strikingly bold on her alabaster skin.

I went to take a sip of my beer, but my focus caught on Hollywood, who had become transfixed by the scene on the stage. His jaw hung open and he white-knuckled the drink on the table in front of him so hard I thought he might crack it. I flicked the back of his hand, making him jump and glare at me.

"Are you okay?" I mouthed, not wanting to draw anyone else's attention.

He looked like he was about to be sick. His face paled, his eyes widened, and he stood up so fast that the table rattled and his chair flew out from behind him.

"I...uh..." He shook his head as he reached into his pocket and slapped a twenty on the table before barreling toward the exit like his ass was on fire. I furrowed my eyebrows and glanced at his retreating form, debating whether I should go after him when a flash of long blond hair whisked behind him.

I twisted my head to the side so I could look around the person blocking my path, but I only caught the back of a leather jacket with an SRMC logo on it. We didn't allow cuts in the Beacon, so who the fuck was that and how did they get in wearing it? Curiosity piqued, I stood and went after them, the hairs on the back of my neck raising.

Something wasn't right, and my gut twisted with the need to keep going, to figure out who that was. I knew that shade of blond. I knew those legs. I knew that cut.

No...It couldn't be...could it?

Just as I walked outside, my knees locked into place and I froze.

There she was...the woman I'd spent eight weeks investigating. Right there. Right in front of me.

Nikki climbed onto the back of a bike, wrapping her arms around a big, burly man as she curled her lips into a smirk and gave me a little wave before they took off.

I blinked, woefully unprepared to face her, and I had a moment to wonder what the fuck she was doing showing her face around here before a hard force knocked me forward, heat enveloping the entire back of my body.

5

THOR

Selene moved toward the exit and I narrowed my gaze on the person a few paces ahead of her. Was she following Hollywood? No, I saw blond hair and cutoff jeans. I debated with myself, knowing that going this long without talking to Selene after what I'd done last night wasn't a great look. We needed to clear the air, and what better place to do that than a BDSM club neither one of us wanted to be in.

Just as I moved toward the exit, a blast of heat hit me in the face, a surge of pure power knocking me back. I collided with something hard, likely the wall, banging my head on the plaster before sliding down to my knees.

Pain erupted through my skull, blurring my vision. My jaw snapped shut, and I tasted metal. Screams punctuated the explosion, people running to hide as bits of the building crumbled around us, and I curled myself into a ball to protect my head as a spotlight fell from the ceiling and nearly crushed me.

The chaos couldn't have lasted more than thirty seconds, a minute tops, but waiting for it to stop so I could look for Selene dragged on for an eternity. As soon as the rumbling ended, I shoved to my feet, ignoring the telltale signs of a concussion as I stumbled over obstacles. My legs weren't coordinated with my arms, and I blinked to try to see straight, but my vision wouldn't focus so I tripped over my own feet and toppled into a barstool.

"Sel!" I tried to yell for her, but my throat burned and I coughed up dust and more copper. The ringing aftermath of destruction pounded painfully in time with my pulse, resonating through my brain. Gore and body parts splattered everywhere. Some people were capable of walking, but they looked like zombies—shell-shocked and groaning to themselves.

It reminded me of war. It reminded me of Afghanistan.

No, no, no, I shouted at myself, refusing to open that box of horrors tonight. *Focus, Erickson.*

It must have been a bomb. That was the only thing that could have caused this much destruction so quickly. Sirens sounded in the distance, indicating fire and rescue on their way. But I only had one goal, one primary focus: find my girl.

"Sel!" I tried again, but I still couldn't be sure my vocal cords were working.

Panic sliced down the center of my chest, coating my stomach with rancid fear. *What if she died? What if she's buried under the rubble? What if I never get to tell her how badly I want her, how badly I need her? What if...what if...what if...*

I shoved that voice into the dark part of my mind, refusing to accommodate its freak-out. I didn't have time for that; I needed to get to her. Just when I cleared the exit, coughing and choking out into the night air, I found her kneeling over a person with a giant metal pipe sticking out of their stomach.

"Don't fucking move, okay?" she said, grabbing another person's hand to put it over the wound. "You, hold this steady. Don't pull it out." The witness shook violently and tried to nod but only clenched their eyes shut as tears streamed down their cheeks. "Hey!" Selene grabbed their chin and forced their attention to her with confident reassurance pouring out of her expression. "Look at me. You can do this. I know you can."

She struggled to her feet and turned around, meeting my gaze as her shoulders sagged with relief. Fuck, it was so good to see her upright, even if she had a bloody gash on her head that had leaked down the side of her face. I walked toward her, wrapping my arms around her shoulders to pull her in for a hug, not caring who saw or what they thought.

Gods, the thought of losing her had terrified me, and even though I faced this possibility every single time she'd run off, this felt different. I'd just lost my best friend last year, my brother by choice. I couldn't lose her, too. I didn't know if it was because of the line I'd crossed last night or the fact that all the reasons I'd said I couldn't have her suddenly seemed so fucking insignificant, but holding her in that moment meant more to me than it ever had. My entire body trembled, full of adrenaline and gratitude.

When she pulled back, I brushed her hair away from her face so I could examine the gash near her hairline.

"This is deep," I said, pleased my voice had returned. "You need stitches."

She nodded and touched a spot near my eyebrow that made me wince. "So do you."

I stared down at her mouth, willing the courage to kiss her, to tell her how scared I'd been for the few moments when I thought she was gone, how I never wanted to face that possibility for real. But before I could do that, a voice floated out of the Beacon that demanded our attention.

"Sel!" Castor yelled, carrying an unconscious and barely recognizable Pollux. A gaping wound marred the younger man's chest as he hung over his twin's bruised form. "Help me. Please!" V and Candy crawled out behind him, battered and busted, but otherwise okay, followed by KC and a limping Alba.

"Fuck," Selene said, racing to get to her cousin so she could assess the damage. They laid his broken body on the ground, and the doctor in Sel came out, all the emotions from moments ago retreating deep inside her. She rushed to grab my belt from my waist, ripping it off me so she could wrap it around his mangled leg to stem the squirting, bloody flow. "Put pressure on the chest wound." Castor followed her order, blinking back tears while his twin bled out in front of him. Selene ran her fingers over Pollux's neck. "He's alive, but barely."

The first responders arrived in time to take over for Selene, an EMT pulling her away from her cousin so she could be treated herself.

"No, I'm a doctor. Let me go. I need to save him," she said, struggling to get away. "I can't let him die."

"Listen to me," the EMT said, grabbing her shoulders. "You're all fucked up and not in your right mind. Even if you have trauma experience, you have a head injury and probably a concussion."

"It's okay, Montgomery," I cut in, letting my own EMT poke and prod at my wound. "You did what you could. Let them handle it from here."

She steeled her jaw and stared with fire in her eyes, the ice from moments ago having thawed and given way to her fury. She wanted to fight me, but just as quickly, she blinked that away and returned to her usual self.

Of course, she had every right to be angry. I was, too. This had been a targeted attack. Despite not allowing colors in the Beacon, everyone knew it was a Rose establishment. Whoever had done this wanted to hurt a lot of us at once. My mind immediately went to the Caputis. They had the means and the motive. But we'd been so careful about security.

What the fuck had gone wrong?

"How did they get in?" Crow asked, running his hands through his long dark hair, blinking back unshed tears for his son. We'd been sitting in the hospital waiting room all night, hoping for word about Pollux, but so far, no one could give us an update. "How did we let this happen?"

Aris shook his head and sighed. "Switch is looking into the Beacon's camera feed right now. We should know more soon."

"I've had all of our houses swept," Slip said, glancing at me before continuing. As sergeant at arms, that should have been my job, and I appreciated Slip stepping in. "They're clean. They only hit the Beacon."

"You think it was the Caputis?" KC asked, his swollen eyes hinting at the amount we'd all cried for our fallen family. It wasn't *just* Pollux that had gotten hurt. Ten people had died in the blast, including three prospects, and twenty more civilians were in critical condition.

"It has to be," Aris added. "It's *my* club. They went after Ru and Saint three months ago, and when they didn't get the job done, they tried again."

There's something there, the soldier in me said, tripping an alarm that put me on even higher alert. I struggled to think straight, the concussion mixing with exhaustion to cause a massive headache and brain fog. It wasn't the Caputis that had failed to finish the job in August. It was—

"We got so damned lucky tonight," Alba cut in, breaking my train of thought. "Pollux is going to pull through. I know he is."

KC pressed his lips to his wife's temple, pulling her closer when she trembled and let out a quiet sob.

Despite the boot on her broken leg, she had a point. Most of us had made it without much more than superficial scratches. KC had second-degree burns on his back from crouching over Alba to protect her during the worst of it, but with some time and ointment, he'd be okay. Wheels and Lore were banged up, but nothing a few weeks of R&R couldn't fix. Pollux had the dumb fucking luck to be right in the middle of the destruction when it went off, and he had a hole in his chest and a decimated leg to show for it. He'd been in the ICU since they brought him in, and the prognosis wasn't good.

Selene had been released about an hour ago, only to sit silently next to Crow and Bear with their hands in hers. The alarm blared in the back of my mind again, telling me to pay attention, reminding me of my training and forcing me to focus through my injuries. A twinge sliced through my chest, and I brought my hand up to soothe it away.

What the fuck am I missing?

This didn't smell like Gabriella, too sloppy and uncoordinated, but it also couldn't have been Leo. Was there another player on the chessboard? Did we have another snitch within our own ranks?

"Randall Montgomery?" came a voice from the doorway. I looked up to see Detective Jordan, standing with her hands on her hips and a pleading look of sympathy in her eyes. Anytime something bad happened to the SRMC, the Fed sent her in to investigate. She'd been up our ass since the shootout last year, but so far, she hadn't gotten enough dirt to be anything more than annoying.

"No," Crow said, shaking his head. "I'm not dealing with your shit tonight."

She held up her hands and took a step closer, putting me on edge enough to have me shoving to my feet.

"I wanted to extend my sympathies. I heard your son was injured in the blast." At five three, she barely came up to my chest, but her height had nothing to do with how tough she was. She stared us in the eyes and never backed down. I'd heard her say things to Crow that I wouldn't even dream of whispering within earshot.

Crow swallowed but didn't dignify that with a response. Everyone in the waiting room, all of the SRMC in attendance, had gone on high alert as soon as the cop walked in. Now, they stared at her with vengeance, like a pack of wolves that had just discovered a hyena moseying onto its hunting grounds, daring her to make this worse.

If she made one wrong move...if she said one wrong word...

"Tonight's not a good night," I said. "I know you need your statements or whatever—"

"I'll want statements from everyone," she said, nodding before glancing at Crow again. "But...I understand."

"Like I said, some other time." I wouldn't stand down on this. We needed a night, just one fucking night, to get our shit together before the pigs tried to eat us alive.

"Pollux Montgomery's family?" A nurse stood with her hands in her pockets, waiting for Crow and his family to stand. "Please come with me." He stood, wrapping an arm around Castor's shoulders while Bear hugged Verona close, but paused when he passed Detective Jordan.

"Thank you for..." Crow shook his head and turned away, unable to finish that thought.

Despite having a history of being an enormous pain in my ass, Detective Jordan didn't hang around to press the issue. She hadn't even brought her dickbag partner. No, perhaps she *had* only come to give her sympathies. She nodded at Crow and turned to head down the hospital hallway.

After she left, Selene scooted closer to her brother, grabbing his hand when he leaned in to whisper something to her. I went back to my spot in the corner, trying not to think about what would happen next. Once we learned which of the Caputi fucks was responsible for this, the brothers would demand justice. We wouldn't be able to wait it out any more; we'd have to act. We'd have to do something with Leo, even if he wouldn't talk, and we'd have to make a show of bringing down Gabriella. I wanted to urge patience, that acting out of revenge would only lead to more bloodshed, but even I had to admit, this was a low blow.

They hit us in a blind spot, on our territory, in our own backyard. This was the third time they'd come after our women instead of hitting us directly, and didn't that just speak volumes about the cowardly pieces of shit running that family?

I ached to pull Selene into my arms, to feel her against my body and know, deep down inside, that she was still alive and not bleeding out on an OR floor. I wanted to tuck her in close and keep her safe so that I'd never have to walk in on another motherfucker assaulting her or abducting her in the middle of the night or bombing her friend's bar.

She caught me staring, and for one brief instant, rage churned in her eyes again. The frozen exterior that she put up as a front to everyone had melted, and underneath that thin ice, Selene had built up a lifetime of furious retribution.

I understood, Gods knew. After Gavin, my parents, Gemma, and Trojan, my losses had piled up. I'd wanted blood for a long time, just the same as her, but I didn't trust she'd be as patient about revenge as

I was. Just like she did earlier in the parking lot, she blinked and hid all that fire under a deluge of winter calm.

Crow eventually came out to tell us there was nothing more we could do and they wouldn't let any of us back there to see him so we might as well go home. Aris dropped Selene and me off at the house, Verona having stayed behind with her family, and I followed her inside, pausing at the door to the basement.

Exhaustion seeped into every one of my joints, and in all my years on this earth, I'd never felt as almost forty as I did in that moment. Selene stayed stoic and stone-faced, her bright blue eyes now a darker, stormier shade of navy. I'd only ever seen her look like this a few times before, and it usually led to one or both of us cleaning up a body.

"You did good out there," I said, hoping to break through the frozen veneer. I'd settle for any reaction, something to tell me Selene was actually processing this, not letting it simmer on a back burner until it boiled over. I'd known her a long time, and she'd yet to deal with what happened to her parents, much less all the fucked-up shit since.

"Thanks," she said, forcing a smile before walking through the kitchen and down the hallway. "I'm tired. I think I'll sleep for a while."

I cleared my throat, that churning suspicion flaring in my sternum again, dripping into my gut. Whatever she'd been up to, last night had escalated her timeline. She was planning something stupid...like taking off on a revenge mission stupid, and while I might have trained her like a soldier, like a weapon, I didn't teach her to be a hothead. That was one hundred percent Montgomery.

"Sel," I said. She stiffened and turned around to face me, but I didn't know what I planned to follow that up with, just that I couldn't bear the thought of losing her again. I dreaded going into the freezing cavernous basement while she fought her demons up here alone. "Do you want me to stay with you?"

The question sounded ridiculous, even to me, especially because we hadn't talked about how I'd made her come and walked out like it was an everyday occurrence. I'd meant to say something today at the shop, but...where the fuck would I even begin?

Sorry, I lost control and took it out on your beautiful, precious ass? I so rarely let that brutal side of me out of his cage, so when the beast saw an opportunity, he took it. And once she started enjoying it, well, I wasn't going to stop.

Indecision warred with something more desperate behind her eyes, and when she gave me a small nod, a weight lifted off my shoulders. I swore I wouldn't touch her, not like I had last night. I'd keep my fucking hands to myself like a good person or some shit. I just wanted to be near her, to breathe her in and know she was there... that she was alive and breathing, too.

Filthy and reeking like smoke and hospital, we collapsed into her bed, where she closed her eyes and sank into a deep sleep. I watched her drift unconscious, debating about snooping, but unconsciousness ultimately took hold and I fell asleep before I could think anything else about it.

6

SELENE

Words couldn't describe the fire boiling in my blood. Anything I tried to say failed to do it justice. There had been moments in the hospital when I'd almost told them the truth, that I'd seen Nikki right before it happened, and instead of grabbing her, I'd stood there like a fucking idiot.

What the fuck, Montgomery?

Even in my sleep, I berated myself. Since finding out where Nikki had been hiding, I'd bided my time and waited for the right moment, ignoring the twist in my gut that told me something terrible was about to happen. In twenty-nine years, that instinct had never failed me, and I'd picked this time to fucking ignore it.

If I had gone after her as soon as Marissa called me, Pollux wouldn't be in the ICU. If I had gone after her weeks ago, Ru's club wouldn't have gotten blown up and Alba's leg wouldn't be broken. Ten people died, dozens more were injured, and for what? Because Nikki had failed to kill Ru and Saint three months ago, and now she had to prove she still could? Did she cut another deal with the Caputis?

The EMT had been right earlier; I hadn't been thinking straight. But now, I was. Now, I saw clearly what I had to do. I'd waited too long, and I couldn't afford a moment longer. Somewhere in the depths of my mental library, an old book with long forgotten memories shook with fury, trying to get my attention. I pretended not to hear it.

I knew what I planned to do in the morning, Pollux's critical condition aside. Marissa had reached out again, letting me know Nikki was back in town. She and her cohort must have ridden all night to get back to Buffalo by the next morning.

It smelled like a trap, but I didn't care. I could do it without anyone knowing. Get in. Stabby stab stab. Get out. I'd done it before.

During my last shift as a trauma surgical resident in the emergency department at Thomas Washington Hospital, a group of victims from a nearby mob-related shootout were brought in. I went to work as usual—assessing my patient's injuries, prioritizing next steps, deciding on the best course of action. But then, the nurse announced the name of the bruised, bloody man on my gurney and my heart stopped.

"Giuseppe Caputi."

Benito had been the Caputi boss at the time, but Giuseppe was his younger brother, Leo's father. He'd claimed responsibility for physically planting the bomb that killed my parents, and there he was, bleeding out in front of me. I had to fix him. I couldn't stop in front of all my colleagues. Nearly twenty minutes later, Giuseppe was stable and on his way to the surgical floor.

Then, I threw up. Twice. Fresh out of med school, I'd taken my stupid oath seriously, telling myself it was a new beginning. What else could I have done? Giuseppe Caputi hadn't deserved the air he breathed. He'd killed dozens of people over the course of his life in the DC mafia, and those were just the ones I knew of.

I couldn't stand the thought of how many more he would go on to kill. I'd wanted to be a doctor to make up for my parents, but that was a child's point of view on the world. There *was* no making up for the shitty things that happened in life.

As for Giuseppe Caputi, I'd saved his life, so I figured I could end it. I'd bribed Doc for one of his concoctions of fast-acting oleander that was undetectable in a modern lab analysis before sneaking into Giuseppe's penthouse apartment. There, I'd stabbed him in the neck with a needle the size of my hand and sat on his chest to watch the life drain out of his eyes. After I'd watched Billy die, I had cried for three days. When I left Giuseppe there to rot, I'd felt surprisingly cold. Numb.

I decided then—fuck the oath. Words were nothing but air, and air changes...fades away. Some vows were meant to be broken, and I never went back to the hospital.

Thor had been right to be suspicious of me recently. I *had* been sneaking around in Doc's pantry, and now that I had what I needed, I wouldn't waste another damn second.

Nikki knew my parents had died because of a car bomb. She knew Jer and I had severe issues related to it. Instead of coming in with an assault rifle and shooting the place to hell, which arguably would have been easier, she'd tried to kill us the way the Caputis had once done to our mom and dad. And that...well, that stoked the fire of my retribution all damned night, even while unconscious.

I let myself have an hour and a half of shut-eye, just to give Thor enough time to make a discreet exit and fall asleep in his own bed. Under no circumstances had I expected him to stay, so when I opened my eyes and his enormous arm was wrapped over my waist, his hand on my back and my face tucked firmly into his chest, I didn't know what to do. We'd certainly slept side by side before, but I'd never woken up wrapped together like this. Never so close. Never for so long.

I focused on the soft expression in his features, and my heart gave a sharp tug that almost had me forgoing my plan altogether. He seemed completely relaxed like this, the perpetual indent between his eyebrows gone. It took ten years off his face, making him resemble the man I'd first met...not that I didn't appreciate the present version.

Taking a deep breath, I extracted myself from his embrace, careful not to wake him, and tiptoed to the bathroom, cleaning myself up as best I could before silently getting dressed. Thor wasn't usually a heavy sleeper, not after all those years in the military, but his deep inhales and soft exhales indicated he was still unconscious. I grabbed my book bag, already packed with all the essentials, and put on my leather jacket, the one I'd inherited from my mother after she passed. If I closed my eyes hard enough, I could still smell her jasmine perfume deep in the fabric.

Once I had everything I planned to take, I stood at the side of my bed and stared at my uncle...my mentor...finally letting myself take a moment to reflect on what he would think when he woke up. Yesterday had shaken us both in different ways. After the explosion, there had been a moment where I'd worried about his safety, but when people started piling out of the destruction with severe injuries, I had to put those complicated feelings for him on hold. He'd obviously faced my disappearance with fear and panic, which had landed him next to me in bed.

Nothing scandalous happened, but that wasn't the point. There existed intimacy in sharing sleep after a horrifying ordeal, a kind not found in even the best one-night stand. Some couples struggled for years to have what we had, and we hadn't even fucked.

I was about to ruin everything.

You don't have to, whispered a small voice from that shaking book in the back of my mental library. *You can stay. You can ask for help. You're not on your own.*

The thought had crossed my mind. He knew the worst parts of me, all the terrible things I'd done, and he still stood by me. But I knew how that conversation would go, the same as it always had. He'd tell me to mind my own business, and after the attack, I couldn't do that anymore.

My muscles ached from the fall and my head throbbed where I had stitches, but I had to soldier on. I turned on my heels and quietly closed the door behind me as I left.

7

—————

THOR

For half a second after I woke, I knew what true happiness could be. I was in my room...er, Selene's room, her flowery scent seeping into every part of my soul. She enveloped me, and for that one moment, I let myself believe our problems were solved, that we could have this private heaven, that there was nothing fucked up about me sleeping so soundly next to her.

Then reality sank in. The other side of the bed was empty and cold. She hadn't occupied it in a while. It was 8 a.m., and *fuck*, I'd overslept. I was supposed to meet Aris at the clubhouse to figure out what to do next.

"Sel?" I ran my hands over my face and brushed them back through my hair as I climbed out of bed and went to the bathroom, finding it empty. With another burst of panic shooting through my veins, I walked out of the bedroom and down the hallway, only to find the rest of the house silent. I scrambled for my phone to call her, my anxiety amplifying when it went straight to voicemail.

Fuck.

Rage had bubbled just below the surface in her eyes yesterday, and I knew her well enough to start formulating scenarios in my mind. Maybe she'd gone after Leo. Maybe she'd finally gone after

Nikki. Maybe she blamed them for what happened. Taking a deep breath, I told myself to stay calm. I didn't know anything yet, even if I suspected she'd done something stupid. When I called the prospect in charge of watching Leo Caputi next, he told me our houseguest was still alive, alone, and silent.

I narrowed down my options and headed to Rose Garage, sighing with relief at her Jeep parked in its normal spot.

Thank fuck.

But that pulse in the center of my chest wouldn't go away until I put eyes on her. Walking inside, I prepared myself for the confrontation we'd likely have, but she wasn't in the office when I swung the door open, nor was she in the mechanic's bay.

"Montgomery?" I called, my pulse pounding harder when no response came. "Sel?"

My attention caught on the black rectangle sitting on the counter next to the keyboard, and dread replaced the panic in my chest. Her phone lay next to her credit cards, wallet, and a note that read, *"Be back in a few days. Don't come after me. - S"*

"Fuck." I looked up to the key rack behind the desk, one prominent hook desperately empty.

No.

Scalding fury pulsed in my veins when I glanced out the back window and found my pride and joy missing—my 1968 Chevy Impala.

No, no, no.

I ran outside, thinking my brain must be playing tricks on me. She wouldn't do that, would she? But when I got to the empty spot where I kept it, I swallowed down the rising tide of rage, putting it some place in my mind where I could assess and use it at a later time. Right now, I needed to focus on tracking her down before she made a huge mistake and got herself killed.

I thought about calling her brother and maybe looping in Ru, but my thumb hovered over the lock screen without swiping it open. If I told them, they'd panic, especially after last night. When it came to the women in KC's life, he'd been known to fly off the handle and see red on a rampage, all brawn, no brains. Ru would want to tear off after her, and she needed to focus on Pollux and the Beacon.

No, I had to handle this myself—find her and bring her back before anyone knew she was missing.

This, of course, put me in a difficult position. I was the sergeant at arms of the SRMC. It was my responsibility to keep everyone in line, to make sure the club kept order. My place was with my brothers at a time like this. But fuck, Sel was headed down a dangerous road, and she had no idea what threats lay at the end of it. I'd sworn to protect her, to keep her safe...even if it meant from herself.

What could have happened? What could she know that had set her off so suddenly after her family suffered such a devastating blow?

I closed my eyes, remembering Selene walk toward the front door of the Beacon like she was chasing after someone. She must have seen something...something she'd kept to herself. Whatever it was, I'd get proof on the security footage. I needed to head to the clubhouse.

"Hey, you're early," Switch said from his spot in front of his computer monitors. "Aris's in the back but Crow's still at the hospital. Pollux made it through the night, so he might be okay."

As our resident tech guru, Switch had been in top-secret IT security before joining the Roses. Sometimes, when he got drunk enough, he'd tell us stories about the things he'd seen in the NSA, and between him and Castor, there was nothing in the world of computers the Roses didn't have access to. But he wasn't the average nerd stereotype. Switch worked out more than anyone else I knew, making the hang-arounds flock to him like birds to the bread lady at the park.

"Pull up the footage from the Beacon last night," I said, gesturing to his screens with a snarl on my face. I didn't stop to talk to anyone on my way into the clubhouse, just stormed in and went straight for the guy looking for the culprit.

"Good to see you, too, brother." He balked and took a swig of his coffee, mumbling to himself as he turned around. "We're still combing through it. The feed cuts out a few seconds before the bomb goes off, but there's a lot to review."

"Try all views of the entrance," I said. "Back it up to ten minutes before it goes off."

Switch furrowed his brows. "I already went through it. I've got facial recognition running on everyone who came in or out of that place for the two days before. It's going slow."

"Trust me on this." I couldn't help that my voice came out as a growl. Every minute I wasted was another mile between me and my girl. Maybe this was a wild goose chase, but my gut told me otherwise. She'd been keeping something to herself, and whatever happened last night, whatever pulled her outside moments before the bomb went off, was connected.

What did she see?

"There! There! Stop." I pointed to the monitor in the upper left-hand corner, squinting as I tried to make out the image. Hollywood's face came into view as he walked outside, and then a blond woman wearing a cut appeared behind him, farther down the hallway, but unmistakable.

"Son of a bitch. Is that—" Switch zoomed in on her. "How did I miss that?"

"Fuck." I ran my fingers back through my hair and sighed, trying to calm my runaway thoughts. Selene had seen Nikki at the club and chased after her. As we deliberated all night about who could have attacked us, she knew but said nothing while she slept next to me and plotted her attack. The puzzle pieces fell together in my mind. "I need you to find Nikki and then find my Impala."

"What?" Switch looked at me and raised a dark eyebrow. "What the fuck for? We need to tell Aris about this. We need—"

"I'm going to talk to him right now." I took a step toward the door. "Just find out where Nikki is, okay?"

"Oh, that's easy," he said, tapping more buttons on his keyboard. "She's still in Buffalo." He moved his mouse around, bringing up more pictures, more information. "I don't understand. She's been there all night. How..."

"She knows we're tracking her," I concluded, recalling the thought I'd had yesterday. It hadn't been the Caputis that tried and failed to killed Ru and Saint. It had been *Nikki*. She came after us because that was the deal she'd made to save her own ass. Perhaps they hadn't tossed her out. Perhaps she hadn't run. Maybe this was an elaborate play to get back into their good graces.

Fuck, Selene could be walking right into a trap.

Trying to keep a lid on the part of me desperate not to lose her, I went to find Aris in the back. He sat at the head of the table, preparing to lead the group when they got here since Crow obviously had his plate full. This had the potential to be a difficult conversation. Everybody knew Nikki was a liability we needed to take care of, and given the reputation the Montgomerys had for being hotheads, it might not surprise him that Selene took off after her. But I suspected Aris might want to send some prospects after her instead of me, given the fact Crow would be down for a few more weeks and I was an officer.

They needed me more now than they ever had.

"Hey, Thor," he said, his gravelly voice indicating how rough the night had been for everyone. "Any updates for me?"

"Nikki blew up the Beacon," I said. "Selene went after her."

His features dropped, and he snapped up straight. "God fucking damn it. How do you know?"

I explained everything to him, including what I planned to do next. "Let me go after her. I can bring her back."

Aris pursed his lips and leaned back in his seat, his eyes bloodshot from the rough night, his gray hair sticking out at odd angles like he'd been running his hands through it for hours. I could only imagine how I looked.

"I can't lose our sergeant right now." He shook his head, leaning forward. "Let me send—"

"No, it has to be me," I cut in, holding firm. "I know Selene. I'm the only one she'll listen to."

For as long as I'd been in the Roses, I'd never spoken about my feelings for Selene or the reason I'd married Gemma. I'd never explained why I hadn't moved out of the house or why she and I hid in dark corners with secret smiles that never went anywhere further. But anyone who spent any time around us could tell we were close.

"It could be a trap," I continued.

"Hence the reason I need to send more than one person." Aris was short for Aristotle, a nickname he'd gotten for being a jack-of-all-trades—a modern-day polymath. Mechanic, business owner, contractor, there was nothing Aris didn't know something about. But in the subject of Selene Montgomery, I had a PhD.

"That's what they want," I said. "They want to lure us out, to make us mad enough to react." The more I talked, the more sense it made. If it was just me, I could grab her and turn home without them even knowing we were there. "I'm not saying we shouldn't do something, but we need to be more strategic than taking off like a pack of angry dogs with no plan."

Aris narrowed his eyes, apparently considering my plan. He'd been the one to authorize Saint taking Leo Caputi hostage instead of killing him on sight. If anyone was going to be open to this, I was glad it was him.

"Okay, go," he finally said. "But listen to me, brother. If you don't check in every day, if you turn off the tracker app on your phone, I'll send the fucking cavalry for you, understand?" He paused to let that sink in, piercing me with his icy stare. "And no heroic shit, okay? You get Selene, you bring her back. If you happen to shoot a hole in Nikki's head along the way, I won't be upset about it. If it is a trap, I need you both safe."

Relief flooding through my chest, I nodded before turning for the door. The truth was, I understood why Selene wanted her blood. I did, too. The Roses had waited too long to do something about her, and not that Selene's idea was a good one, but I could get behind the intention.

Nikki had surpassed the typical lifespan of a snitch, and it was time someone rectified that, but it didn't have to be Selene. I'd sworn an oath to protect her, and I wouldn't let her own impulsiveness interfere with that.

"I'm heading north," I said to Switch on my way out. "Call me when you find my car."

I swung by the house to pack a few things for the road, determined not to spend too much time lingering around Madison County. She couldn't be too far ahead of me, maybe a few hours, and she'd have to stop to sleep sometime. If I kept driving, I could hit Buffalo shortly after she did. Maybe I could find Nikki first and wait for Selene to catch up.

After I was packed, I headed out, trying to keep my temper under control while I drove. I'd been in her shoes, once upon a time, and all vengeance ever brought me was more pain and heartache. I'd gone into the Navy fresh out of high school, right around the time George Dubya decided to send everyone to Afghanistan. Having been raised in the forests of Vermont, I already knew my way around a rifle, and once the military found out I could shoot, I got into the SEAL program—Special Ops.

I started doing missions before I could drink in the States and shot my first man the day after my twenty-first birthday. I'd been proud at the time. Me and my buddies celebrated the fresh kill by getting shit-faced and admiring our bravery in the face of terrorism—ya know, all that propagandist bullshit the government fed us in the wake of 9/11. Like a lot of my fellow countrymen, I'd been angry, and I'd wanted blood.

Despite all the training I'd been given in how to kill people, no one ever prepared me for how to *deal* with killing people, where to draw the line and when to say no. Eventually, they sent me into the heart of the fucking desert, looking for some extremist's shithole so I could wipe him out discreetly. When I found it, he was there with his entire family—his three wives, their ten children, and his elderly parents. I'd been given orders to take out whoever stood in my way, but I couldn't wrap my conscience around killing in front of kids.

It turned out to be a trap. We were ambushed, and the attackers decapitated my best friend and spotter, Gavin, in front of me. I'd been fighting off my own assailant, unable to help him, unable to save him. My stomach still churned when I remembered his screams. After I got free, I lost it. I stalked across that property like a monster in an old-time movie, drilling bullets into anyone that wasn't on my side.

At the end of my death gauntlet stood one of the extremists with a woman and a child in front of him, guns aimed at their heads while he shouted at us in Pashto. The woman on his right looked to be in her early twenties, her arm protectively wrapped around the younger one. Mother and child, probably, or maybe siblings. But the way the younger one looked at me sent a chill down my spine—chin up, eyes stern, shoulders straight. My ma would've said she had fire in her eyes, a fight that nothing and no one could extinguish.

"Drop our guns or he'll kill them," said the translator, but I was seeing red at that point. I'd just witnessed one of this guy's companions murder my best friend in the most brutal way possible. I'd been given orders—*no matter what stood in my way*. In between heartbeats, I raised my weapon and shot between his eyes. He jerked in reflex, and so did the people in front of him. The little girl had managed to dodge out of the way, but the woman...

The child fell to her knees next to the body, wailing and sobbing as the woman bled out in front of us. Shouts came from my right, the other family members having witnessed the whole thing, helpless to do anything about it. When the little girl looked back up at me, she burned with rage. At her young age, I was shocked to see it painted so vividly in her expression—the scowl between her eyebrows, the grimace on her lips, the inferno in her gaze.

It mirrored my own.

She shouldn't know this feeling. She shouldn't know men like me or see what she'd seen. I'd stolen a life from her while she was at her most powerless. How many more mothers, siblings, friends had I taken from other children? How many futures had I robbed from them?

"Goddamn, Erickson," my colleague said, clapping me on the shoulder. "Nice shot."

He didn't comment on the dying woman. No one did. But I stood there and watched the little girl hug her mother until the body turned cold and it was time to return to base. A person from my squadron came through and pulled the child from the corpse, kicking and screaming and biting. When she finally gave up, she glared at me while they carried her away, tears streaking down her flushed cheeks. I never forgot that look in her eyes...those big brown eyes that had stared right through my helmet and night goggles to see what I'd so desperately tried to keep hidden—this depraved fucking beast that lived inside me. Perhaps in that moment, I'd seen hers, too.

For my bravery and quick thinking in the heat of battle, the United States government gave me a Navy Cross. The president himself put it on my uniform.

"Thank you for your service," he said. "You should be proud."

After that, mine became a story as old as war itself. I'd been rewarded for the worst thing I'd ever done, and because of that, I couldn't do it anymore. Not for them. Not for this. Every target reminded me of that little girl and her big eyes, and my trigger finger wouldn't squeeze.

That was the night my beast grew relentless, and he wouldn't stop riding me until I washed out, came to Virginia, and found the Roses. Here, I became part of a family built out of true loyalty. I'd found a reason to get out of bed every day, to shove my inner feral thing into a cage and simply carry on.

Maybe that little girl had me sitting in a fucking Silverado, tracking down my dead wife's niece. Perhaps it was that little girl that made me marry Gemma in the first fucking place. For the life I'd robbed from her, I'd make sure to give one to Selene.

Just as I passed from Maryland into Pennsylvania, I made another promise to that little girl, wherever she was—I'd find Selene, and I'd protect her from the beast I'd created in both of us. I'd make sure she didn't make the same fucked-up mistakes I did in the name of vengeance.

8

SELENE

I pulled up to the bar where I was supposed to meet Marissa and parked in the back so no one could spot the Impala from the road. Then I sat in the driver's seat and waited, listening to the soft tinkle of flurries on the windshield and the occasional swipe of the wipers across the glass. I'd known her damn near all my life, and even though she was a few years older, she'd always been kind to me and the younger MC princesses. She'd been the daughter of the former SRMC vice president, and when Trojan arrived with his little brother, Hollywood, in tow, Marissa fell in love at first sight...or so she used to say.

It broke her spirit when Trojan died. No one was surprised when she left.

I watched the time change on the dash. Nine fifteen. By now, Thor would know I was missing. My brother, Ru, all of them would be trying to call me, only for it to go straight to voicemail. Perhaps it was stupid to have left the night after my cousin nearly died—as if they needed anything else to worry about—but there was nothing I wouldn't do to protect them. This bitch had to go, and if no one else was going to take care of it, then I'd be the one who fell on this sword.

Perhaps being a woman would make it easier for me to get in and out undetected. Perhaps it would make it easier for the Kings of Carnage to forgive any slight once it was over. Did they know what she'd done? Did they help her? One of their brothers had driven her off, so I had to assume they'd been involved.

Of course, a kill was a kill, no matter the slaughterer. Even if Thor had been the one to beat my abusive ex-boyfriend's face in, I'd sat idly by and let it happen. There had been no doubt in my mind that he deserved it, but that didn't negate my shock and grief, and as I cried my way through digging a grave for his body with Thor by my side, I reminded myself of what my dad used to say...some people just needed killing. He was right, of course. Billy had turned out to be like an old country song from the early millennia—a missing person no one cared was missing. I hated myself for it all the same.

"You live with monsters, Selene," Thor told me as we shoved Billy's corpse into the hole. *"Don't be surprised if you turn out to be one."*

The passenger door opened and Marissa slipped in, quietly shutting it behind her. I sat up, regarding her worn features and messy hair held back by a flimsy headband. She looked rough, so much worse than the last time I'd seen her.

"Hey," she said, her dark brown eyes hinting at the grief hidden behind them.

I gaped, unable to form words now that she sat in front of me. Before she was Trojan's wife, she'd been Aunt Gemma's friend, and that meant she'd been at the house ever since I was a child. We didn't just lose Trojan when he died; we'd lost her, too, and her abrupt departure had hurt more than I'd let myself believe. The book containing all the memories we had together rumbled on my mental shelves, forcing itself to the forefront so I had to face how hard it had been since she'd left.

"Hey?" I asked, shock pouring out of me in thick, heavy waves. "It's been fifteen months, Marissa. You don't call, you don't write... unless it's about a psycho rat bitch that needs poisoning."

"Yeah, the love of my life died. Sorry, not sorry I had a mental breakdown." She blinked back tears and finally met my eyes. "It's good to see you, Sel. I'm sorry to hear about Pollux."

Now, I was the one trying not to cry. I couldn't think about my cousin. I had to put my anger and grief into his pages and slam the cover shut. I wouldn't be able to do this with the sight of his broken body riding me the entire time.

"You're lucky I texted *you* at all," she continued.

"Why did you?"

Marissa shrugged and looked out the window. "I know you want her blood, and you can do it without getting caught."

That made me curious. "And just how do you know that?"

She rolled her big brown eyes and smiled, a faint blush blooming on her dark cheeks. "I know about Billy and the others."

I snapped my attention to her so fast, my neck damn near broke. "What?"

It hadn't ended with Billy and Giuseppe. Once I'd come home, I'd started going on runs with Thor, serving as his backup if needed. I was one of the only people he trusted with a rifle, and by now, I'd killed so many for the Roses I'd lost count. Perhaps that was why it chapped my ass so much that they didn't consider me a member of the club. I'd bled men dry for them, time and time before.

"Trojan told me," Marissa said. "He and Thor were drinking one night, and it came out. I haven't told anyone. I don't plan to. Obviously, I didn't call you up here to air out the skeletons in your closet."

"Marissa." I shook my head and stared back out the windshield, trying to keep my voice calm. I didn't blame her for what had happened at the Beacon, but I still had to ask. "Why didn't you take care of this yourself? She's been here, what? Three months? That's ample time to poison her beer or stab her in the neck or..." I drifted off when my demons reminded me it was my fault Nikki was still alive; I was the one that should have acted as soon as I found out.

"I'm not a killer, Selene." She took a deep breath, a twinge of regret in her eyes when I looked back at her.

You live with monsters. Don't be surprised if you turn out to be one.

"But I need her dead." Tears rolled down her cheeks while she struggled to contain herself. "I can't stand to look at her. And after Pollux..."

I understood that. Nikki's betrayal had directly led to Trojan's death, and she hadn't stopped there. "Why do you think she hasn't recognized you?"

Marissa shrugged. "Maybe she has and can't risk whatever game she's playing with the Kings of Carnage. She's going by the name Nadine Montgomery."

That fucking bitch.

"I thought you'd like that." Marissa smiled, her gaze amused by what must be hatred echoing out of mine. "She's got fake IDs, everything. She's been staying at a cabin twenty minutes outside of town. I don't know where she got it or if she's squatting." Marissa pulled more paperwork out of her purse and handed it to me. "I've emailed you the rest. If you're going to do it discreetly, I would suggest breaking in when she's alone."

"Where's her baby?"

Again, Marissa shrugged. "I haven't seen a baby. It's just been her, partying like she's dying."

I chuckled at Marissa's turn of phrase. "Appropriate."

"Look, I left this life behind." She sighed and wiped at her tear-stained cheeks. "I'm just a bartender these days. MCs exist everywhere, but I wanted to start over. I don't know why she's here, and frankly, I don't care. I just want someone to handle it, and I know you will."

I nodded, giving her a genuine grin as the praise warmed my heart. "Thank you, Marissa."

She returned the smile and reached across the car to grab my hand, giving it a firm squeeze. "I miss you, Sel."

"I miss you, too."

She sat back in her seat, like she had planned to leave, but now had something else to say. "You deserve better than that life. You all do."

I shook my head. "That's where you're wrong. There *is* no other life, not for someone like me. I tried to get out, but I'm too fucked up to make it in the real world. I need my family, and my family needs me."

"Uh-huh." She eyed me with a knowing look, one I'd seen on her face far too many times.

"Don't start." I didn't want to think about Thor or what he might be doing. It hurt to imagine how angry he must have been when he found my note, especially after waking up wrapped around him this morning, so I shoved those emotions into their proper pages as well.

"Are you two together yet?" She raised an eyebrow. "Is he here?"

"I ran."

"What?" She gasped and widened her eyes. "What do you mean you ran?"

"I didn't tell anyone about this. It's easier if I handle it alone." I swallowed down the rising tide of grief over my cousin. "They've got a lot on their plate right now."

She smiled, and it pleased me to see her grin, even if it was laced with innuendo. "You know the thing about those alpha assholes. You run, they'll chase."

I shifted in my seat and sighed, remembering when I'd said the same thing to Alba about my brother a year ago.

"He's a good man, Sel. I hate the way things went down with Trojan, but I've always believed that about Thor." Her voice croaked, and my heart sank into my gut at the sheer pain in her tone. I couldn't imagine her loss, and being out here by herself likely made it worse.

"Come home, Mars." I couldn't stand the separation anymore, so I reached across the seat and pulled her into my arms, sighing when she returned the hug.

"No," she said when she pulled away. "No, I'm done with that life." Marissa put her hands on my shoulders and stared at me, her expression turning stern before she continued. "You should try to get out again. There's nothing wrong with living softly."

She was probably right, and while she had the ability to be done with being hard, I never would. The MC was my family. They were the ones that had raised me, the ones I loved the most. I didn't pick it, but I couldn't change it.

We said our goodbyes, and Marissa promised to send me any updates, but I assured her I had it from here. I planned to stake out the bar until I saw "Nadine" and followed her back to wherever she crashed that night. As I watched Marissa walk away, I regretted that I didn't know if I'd ever see her again, and I prayed she stayed safe no matter what.

~

I sat in the back corner of a dive bar called the Stolen Swan, waiting for anyone resembling Nikki to show up. A group of rowdy bikers sporting Kings of Carnage cuts threw darts in the far corner, hollering and clinking their beers together every time someone got a good shot. Their old ladies brought them drinks and partied just as hard while a few hang-arounds sniffed the periphery, but none of them were my target.

Perhaps she wouldn't come out tonight. Perhaps she was already at home. I pulled up my map on my phone, putting in the location Marissa had given me. Nikki must have been squatting because I couldn't find any obvious connection between the house and her history.

Taking another drink of beer, I ran my fingers over my forehead and decided to blow this joint. It was almost closing time, and the bikers were shutting down their tabs to head home, so I figured I'd check out the cabin to see if she was there. Just as I stood to leave, my attention caught on a maroon truck pulling into the parking lot.

My legs locked, and my heart dropped into my stomach.

No.

It couldn't be...could it? I'd recognize the scratch on that fender anywhere because I was the one who'd made it. I reached into my pocket and tossed a twenty on the table before stuffing my things into my book bag like my ass was on fire. I grabbed Mom's leather jacket, stood, and walked to the entrance, ducking out while the red truck pulled around the corner of the building on the opposite side.

Fuck.

I'd parked the Impala back there. If it was him, he'd see it and know I was here. My pulse pounded as I took a deep breath, letting it out to the count of four while I pulled the brim of my hat over my head to keep my face down. When I got to the car, the truck hadn't come around yet, so I hopped in, started it up, and backed out of the space.

Stay relaxed. It's okay.

Making it out of the parking lot without being seen did nothing to settle my unease.

How had he already found me?

I didn't understand. Buffalo was a moderately big city. He would have had to spend hours driving around. I tightened my fist on the steering wheel.

That's exactly what he did.

Which meant both of us would be exhausted for my stakeout at Nikki's. While I'd learned to function on no sleep from my time at the hospital, Thor had military training beaten into him. He, too, could go for days on only a few hours of shut-eye. I sighed and ran my hands over my face.

This is going to be a long fucking night.

About twenty minutes later, I pulled up outside the address Marissa had given me, where Nikki was supposedly hiding. Calling it a "cabin" was too generous. The one-story, 600-square-foot A-frame had a small loft at the top and a kitchenette/living room combo on the lower floor. The entire front of the house was made of glass so I could see the dark interior, and judging by the Ford Ranger sitting in the driveway, Nikki must have already passed out inside.

The impulse to pull up, sneak in, and stab her in the fucking heart nearly bolted me into action. But hadn't Thor always taught me patience?

Let the prey come to you.

No, I'd have to wait this one out. Take my time. Strike when the time was right. I didn't know if Nikki was in there or how many people she might live with. It could be an ambush.

I would hide in the woods where I could wait and watch. There was nowhere that I could park without Nikki seeing me from the house when she woke up, so I stashed the Impala about a mile down the road, doing my best to hide it in the forest despite there not being much foliage to spare. I grabbed my book bag and my rifle, walking the mile back to the cabin in the cool midnight air. After double-checking that the safety was on and my gun was loaded but uncocked, I found a spot about two hundred yards away from the house where I could watch without being seen myself.

You prepared for this, the cold, logical voice inside my head said. I had. I'd packed everything I'd need to spend a week in the woods if I had to. I laid out my sleeping bag and started my rechargeable heater, gearing up for the long haul.

Once I was settled there, the silence of the woods crept in around me. This far from the city, the light pollution died away, and now that the storm clouds had cleared out, the sky lit up like a painting. Stars twinkled in the distance, the moon bright and full in its mockery of my poor life choices, illuminating all the reasons why this might end up being the stupidest thing I'd ever done. The sleeping bag grew warmer with my body heat, lulling me into the first peace I'd found in ages.

As I listened to the sounds of the cool autumn night, I thought about my brother, who by now was probably freaking the fuck out. I thought about Alba, Ru, and Verona, the other MC princesses that looked up to me the way I'd once looked up to Marissa. Would I become like her one day? Would my rage and anger at everything I'd lost drive me to hang up my MC hat and start a new life somewhere?

Hadn't I already tried that?

There was no other life for me. Only this. Only vengeance and bloodshed...

A snapping twig forced my eyes open, and I cursed myself for having fallen asleep. How long had I been out? I checked my watch, and dread lined my veins when it showed two hours had gone by. It was now three in the morning. More heavy rustling stole my atten-tion, and I sat up, tilting my head to the side so I could listen for anything else. Something big took another step, crunching through the undergrowth and leaves about thirty yards behind me. I turned and pushed to the balls of my feet, grabbing my gun as I made out the form of a human man, about six two or six three.

No.

My pulse sped up because I recognized his silhouette. His gray eyes peered out at me from the darkness, practically glowing in the moonlight. Long dark blond hair hung over his shoulders, turning him into the brute from my dreams, the predatory beast that had stalked me for years, waiting to sink his teeth into my soft fleshy bits.

I debated my options. I could give up and roll over to let him attack or I could run. If I ran, he would chase. The look on his face said he was furious with me, and the minute he caught me, he planned to let me know it.

He took another step, twisting his lips into a cruel smile that even I could see from this far away. With one last move, I made up my mind. Dropping my rifle, I took off, my legs pumping and my arms swinging. I tried to put as much distance between him and me as I could, knowing my chances of getting away were embarrassingly low. But I'd never been one to go down without a fight, and I wouldn't start now.

9

THOR

I'd be lying if I said I wasn't thrilled when she took off. I would've been disappointed if she hadn't. No, my little wildcat loved the chase. She'd put up a struggle until I successfully claimed her, and once I did, may the Gods help her poor sweet ass.

Blood pumped through my body like a freight train, fueling me into action. The freezing wind bit my cheeks and nose, my eyes watering against the frigid air, but I didn't stop. I followed that mane of wild, dark hair through the forest.

"Go away, Thor," she hissed over her shoulder. "I told you not to come after me."

I didn't answer her, only snarled and sprinted faster, finally getting close enough to wrap my arms around her waist and tug her down to the ground. I took the brunt of the fall, rolling on impact so that she was pinned under me, her back to my chest, her face buried in the leaves.

Gods, I was so fucking pissed, I could have throttled her. But the minute I had her in my arms again, my temper cooled. She was safe. She was *here.* I could protect her.

I didn't lose her.

"Get the fuck off me," she growled, thrashing in my hold.

I let out a sick laugh and gathered her wrists in one hand, holding them tight above her head. Using the other, I fidgeted with my belt buckle, loosening it so I could whip the leather through the loops and wrap it around her upper arms, making it easier to keep her contained.

She bucked under me, but that only urged me on. I shoved my free hand into her hair and grabbed, yanking her head up so I could press my mouth against her ear.

"Tell me one thing, Montgomery," I said, "and don't you dare fucking lie to me." Her scent assaulted me, roses and gardenia and cool dew at midnight—feral, untamable girl. "After years of chasing your ass across Virginia, did you honestly think I would let you go this one time?"

She panted, her heartbeat fluttering against my chest so hard that I could feel it despite my own pounding pulse. A white-hot flush shot down my spine, tuning out the side of me that warned against touching her like this. Her ass pressed right up against my groin, firm and round and delicious, and I grunted, adjusting my knees so I could hold myself off her.

When she didn't answer, I fisted her hair harder, causing her to wince. "Did you?"

"If I say no," she said, rolling her hips so she made contact with my dick again, sending a rush right to my head, "would you hold it against me?"

My fury reached a tipping point at her flippant response, and I leaned over her to snarl in her ear. "This isn't a fucking game."

"No." The sudden rage in her tone surprised me, and I reared back in case she headbutted me. "This is life or death, and no one is doing anything about it except me."

"It's not for you to handle," I growled, my teeth clenched. "Do you know the wrench you've thrown into this whole thing? You can't just walk onto another MC's territory and start killing people."

"Wrench?" She laughed, tossing her body around to try to get loose, but I'd wrapped that belt tight enough to hold her until I was done with her. "Nikki killed twenty people; she almost killed Pollux. She broke Alba's leg. She won't stop until she's done."

"She knew we were tracking her," I explained. "She knew we would come after her. This is a trap."

Selene had gotten restless, and now she fought in earnest, yanking her arms, using the weight in her legs to attempt to throw me off balance so she could get free. I'd trained her well, but that meant I knew all her tricks. I held myself firmer, keeping my stance so her efforts remained fruitless.

"I don't care," Selene said, whisper shouting it into the night. "I can get in, do it, and get out before anyone knows I'm there. You know I can." Her growl grew angrier, more pronounced in her fury. "You've never benched me before."

"Helping me with a Rose job is a helluva lot different from running off on your own like a fucking idiot, especially right after Pollux got hurt. Jesus Christ, Sel." I let her go, sitting back on my haunches while she freed herself from the leather and turned around to face me, scooting away on her hands and feet like a scared rabbit. "What would KC and Ru think if something happened to you, huh? What about your cousins and your uncle? Don't you think your family has bled enough for this war?"

Selene's features went stone cold and lifeless. She'd caged away whatever feral beast had been unleashed here, and her apathy made the beast inside me pace like a trapped dog. I liked when she burned ice fucking hot from within, when she fought me like her life depended on it. "They are the reason why I'm here."

"Yeah?" I raised an eyebrow and pointed to the cabin a few hundred yards behind us. "You think she just showed up here, out of the blue? She's *luring* you here."

Selene swallowed, a brief flicker in her eyes hinting at a moment of uncertainty.

"If you think *you* want blood," I said, pushing to my feet, "I can assure you, the Caputis are already on their way to see the spoils of her rabbit chase. If they find you..." I trailed off, unable to consider that option. "If they smell a *hint* of Rose in this town..."

She nodded and stood, brushing herself off before meeting my gaze. "If we don't kill her, she's going to keep coming for us."

"You're the president's niece, a Rose princess, a valuable bargaining chip. Your twin brother is the one that killed Benito Caputi." I paused, letting it sink in. "And if they push hard enough, they'll find out you're the one that killed Giuseppe. What happens then?"

"You don't think I've considered that?" Selene snapped, her eyes twinkling in the moonlight.

"Have you?" I held my arms up, gesturing around us. "We're in the woods in the middle of fucking nowhere, surrounded by Kings of Carnage and the Gods only know who else with no backup and whatever we thought to bring with us." I took a step toward her, willing all my fury to dissipate as I steeled myself against her indescribable, alluring scent. "This is piss-poor execution on your part, Montgomery. Sloppy as fucking hell." Another step forward made her back away, heightening the anticipation in my gut. My beast sat at attention, praying she'd run again, praying I got another opportunity to chase her and catch her and pin her down. "If you were smart, you would've ditched the Impala in Pennsylvania. Switch found you in twenty minutes, and I caught up to you four hours ago. I've been watching you since then."

She glared at me, clenching her jaw at the accusation, but before she could respond, the sound of a slamming door from the house caught my attention. I grabbed Selene, yanked her close, and ducked behind a tree, holding her back to my chest with one arm snaked over her waist. Together, we peered around the thick maple and held our collective breath as three figures rushed out of the A-frame, hushed voices carrying on the wind. I recognized one as Nikki, and Selene wriggled in my arms.

"Let me go," she whispered. "She's right there. I can shoot the three of them and end this."

"Shut the fuck up," I hissed. They got in the Ranger, started it up, and barreled down the tiny gravel road.

"C'mon," Selene whined. "We can go after them."

"You're being impulsive." I held her firmer. "Why did they leave, huh?"

No way they saw us all the way out here, not unless they had cameras hidden in the trees, and I doubted that. No, they must have gotten a tip-off from someone else. Sure enough, not even two minutes after Nikki's truck disappeared, a black Range Rover pulled up. Two men dressed in suits got out of either side of the vehicle, the one closest to us straightening his cuffs before reaching into his jacket for a gun.

"This is the place, right?" said Cuffs.

"This is it," the other one answered, walking up the porch to the sliding glass door. "Looks empty."

They both disappeared inside for a few moments, reholstering their guns once they realized they were alone. My heart hammered as my worst fears were realized. I knew the Caputis were already in town, and here we fucking were, hiding the woods from the worst pieces of shit in the world.

"Caputis," Selene murmured, all her fight now evaporated.

The men turned the house over, destroying the furniture, flipping the television on its side. They were trying to make it look like a break-in, possibly to cover up whatever they intended to do to Nikki once they caught her. Ten minutes later, they walked back outside and stood on the porch, Cuffs talking on his phone to someone.

"She's not here, boss," he said, taking a deep inhale on a cigarette. "Looks like she left in a hurry. She couldn't have gone far." He stayed silent for a few moments, listening to the person on the other end. "No signs of a bouquet."

Selene froze in my arms, tensing when she apparently understood I had been right. They were expecting Roses to come for Nikki. Fire raged through my blood, the beast inside demanding I go kill both of them for the audacity. But I held still, knowing if we attacked now, we'd give away the only advantage we had left—surprise.

"We'll head out now." He hung up, flicked the cigarette into the woods, and walked to their SUV. We waited until they'd been gone a good two minutes before we moved, remaining silent until we got to my truck and I brought it to life.

"We have to go after Nikki," Selene said. "We have to get to her before they do."

I sighed and rubbed my fingers over my eyes, the exhaustion of the last few days seeping through the adrenaline now that I'd found her. Had the bombing only happened two days ago?

"Look, I'm sorry, okay?" She pressed her palms into her face, a sign that she was just as tired of this as I was. "I'm sorry I took off. I'm sorry I didn't grab Nikki when I saw her at the club."

"I don't blame you for that." Some of the pieces came together in my mind, and I understood why she'd taken off like she had. Despite her rational, logical brain, Selene internalized her emotions. She believed she was responsible for the death of her parents, and now, she'd taken on that role for Nikki's attack on the Beacon. "You shouldn't blame yourself, either."

"She was right there. I could have done anything, but I didn't." Tears brimmed at the corners of her eyes before she cleared her throat and glanced at the ground between us to blink them back. "I have to do this. I should have done it weeks ago."

I wiped my hand over my mouth, knowing I had no business entertaining this idea. Every protective instinct I had told me to shut it down, shut *her* down, and take her home. I would send a tow truck for my Impala. But Aris's last words rang through my mind, and the hole in my chest where Trojan used to be throbbed painfully. Nikki's betrayal had led to more than the losses two days ago, and I too believed she would keep coming after us until one side put an end to her.

Selene had a point. The Roses had waited too long to do anything about this, and between the two of us, we could do it quickly and quietly—maybe even take out a few Caputis while we were at it. More importantly than all that was one resounding truth...I knew Selene. She would continue to run from me, to pursue her goal, until she'd gotten what she wanted. In addition to their temper, Montgomerys were also known to be stubborn hardheads that refused to change course once they'd set their minds to something.

"Please, Thor," she said.

I pinched the bridge of my nose and sighed. She'd never once asked me for anything—not to kill Billy or to train her every day afterward, not for me to teach her everything I knew, not for me to breathe down her neck like a fucking obsessive drill sergeant. I'd done it because protecting her and teaching her to protect herself was an instinct I never could suppress.

So when her perfect pouty lips formed those syllables, I folded like a cheap suit.

"We do this my way," I said, meeting her hopeful gaze with a stern one of my own. "I'm serious. I say jump, you say how high. I say run, you sprint until I tell you stop. Are we clear?"

Her grin damn near blinded me, and she threw her arms around my neck, pulling me into a tight hug and assaulting me with her flowery scent. I instantly went back to that night she'd kissed me, when I'd lost control. We hadn't talked about that, and I wasn't sure if we should. Perhaps it was better left in the past, better put in a tiny compartment never to be examined again.

"Thank you," she muttered. "Thank you. Thank you. Thank you."

"You're welcome." I cleared my throat and leaned away, putting room for proper morals and our legal relationship between us. "C'mon. Let's find a place to sleep and regroup for a few hours."

10

THOR

The closest motel was a run-down, one-level building on the outskirts of town. I pursed my lips when we stepped inside the room. The orange carpet had been dusted with a brown patina that must have taken years to build, and one queen-size bed sat in the far corner across from a small two-drawer dresser with an old TV on top. A circular table was to the left, just inside the door, a chair on either side of it.

"Homey," Selene said, scrunching her nose as she walked inside and twirled to face me.

"They were out of two queens," I said, pretending like I wouldn't have chosen this anyway.

Selene narrowed her baby blues but didn't respond, just set about pulling folders from her backpack and putting them out in front of her before retrieving her laptop. I watched her, focusing on the way she ran her fingers back through her long, thick hair.

Last night wasn't the first time the two of us had slept next to each other, but it was the only time we'd sought comfort in each other's arms. I wouldn't deny my physical attraction to her, though I tried, but her presence calmed my beast, and the fact I'd slept better

knowing she was there had me thinking things about the future I had
no business imagining. Despite this, the adrenaline that had been
fueling me these last few hours subsided, and now, my mind
wandered down those dark, perilous roads, conjuring up dark,
perilous thoughts. Like the way she'd moaned when I sank my fingers
in between her legs...or how every primal instinct in my molecules
told me to claim her now that I'd caught her.

I'd almost lost her. I'd almost lost the opportunity to ever do it.

It should have made me ashamed to call myself a Rose. She was
legally my niece, for fuck's sake. Fifteen years of denying it had built
up inside me like a geyser, and now that I'd lost control of it once, I
needed to put a cap on it before it devastated us both.

"What?" she asked, bringing my attention back to where I stood
in the motel room, eye-fucking her like a Gods damned creep.

"Nothing." I cleared my throat, dropped my bag next to the table,
and headed toward the bathroom at the back. "I'm getting in the
shower."

It was as gross as the rest of the place, but I didn't mind. I'd bathe
in a fucking mud pit if it was available. At least this place had clean
water. While I stood under the tepid spray, I filed away this fucked-up
thing with Selene, putting its memory in a box in the pit of my heart
and promising myself I wouldn't touch her again.

The beast inside me reared its head back and howled its frustration, wanting nothing more than to yank Selene under him and rut
inside her until fifteen years felt like nothing but a blip. He didn't see
the reason in waiting, in putting off the inevitable. At this point, I
knew Selene wanted me, I wanted her; what was the fucking holdup?

I would have agreed with that argument if not for the gaping pit
in my stomach that reminded me to keep her at arm's length. She was
my dead wife's niece. She was my mentee, my soldier, stronger and
smarter than even me. Claiming her, making her mine, it would fuck
everything up more than it already was.

I'd lost everyone who'd ever gotten close to me: my parents,
Gavin, Trojan, Gemma. If I lost Selene, I'd never recover. KC might as

well take me out back and point a shotgun between my eyes like a rabid dog, because I'd be fucking useless to the world. And I hadn't even fucked her yet. I couldn't imagine how it would be if I let myself have her the way I wanted. Better that it stay like this between us... better to keep the boundary.

So I rubbed one out in that disgusting shower, telling myself the gardenia scent and the moans coasting through my mind had nothing to do with her. Yet when I came out of the bathroom with a towel wrapped around my waist, I knew I'd break every single one of those guardrails I'd just set for myself.

Selene snapped her eyes to me from where she sat on the bed, dragging a brush through the muzzle of her rifle. She raked her gaze over my long hair spilling over my naked chest, both dripping with water, and the heat in her stare sizzled down to my knees and back up again. My heart fucking skipped a beat, and I curled my lips into a smile.

"See something you like, kitten?"

Fuck.

Using that nickname was a mistake. It meant things that couldn't happen, that I wouldn't allow to happen. We'd already toed a line; crossing over it would damn us both.

"Why?" She chuckled and raised an eyebrow, leaning back on her hands as she eyed me playfully. "Are you gonna bend me over the nearest piece of furniture and turn my ass even more shades of purple?"

"How bruised are you?" It shouldn't turn me on that I'd left marks. It shouldn't send a pleased jolt of lust right down to my balls, but fuck me, I wanted to see the fruits of my labor. I was a weak man.

She bit her bottom lip, looking like an adorable mix of temptress and vixen.

"Never mind. Don't answer that." I shook my head and walked to my bag to grab my spare jeans. "You're gonna be the death of me."

Selene hummed a noise of approval and went back to cleaning her rifle while I slid my boxers and pants on under the towel, forgoing a shirt until my hair dried. She'd learned everything about that weapon from me, and in true Navy fashion, I'd made it an extension of her hand. She knew her gun like her own mind and maintained both with meticulous consideration.

Once satisfied it was in working condition, she returned to her notes on Nikki. I came to the edge of the bed and stared down at the photo closest to me, a picture of the traitorous bitch and Leo in the Caribbean earlier this year. We still hadn't gotten anywhere with that motherfucker, and after these useless months of taking care of him for nothing, most of us had gotten antsy. I'd wanted to kill him as soon as we caught him, but Saint and Aris had urged patience and I couldn't fault them for wanting to find a different way. Still, the picture of them together made me wonder how Leo felt about Nikki these days, after they'd spent so much time together before she bailed.

"I have to tell you something," Selene said. "And don't freak out."

Uh-oh. I already didn't like where this was headed.

"Marissa's the one who told me where Nikki is. She lives here. This is where she came to start over." Selene straightened her shoulders and tilted her chin, clearly daring me to react.

Ice dumped down my spine, numbing the tension brewing between me and my kitten. When I'd joined the Roses, Trojan had been the first friend I made. We both had a military background, both did shit we regretted. Then, he'd met Marissa, and it had been love at first sight. After he died, she'd taken off, and the only person who knew where she'd gone had been Crow, who told us to drop it and leave her alone. The loss hit us hard, especially Selene, who had looked up to Marissa like an older sister all her life.

"You saw her?" My voice nearly cracked, and I had to clear my throat to speak again. "She met with you?"

Selene nodded, and a flaming stab of regret sliced through me. Marissa should have called me. She should have laid this mission at my feet, not hers.

"She looks rough. She's trying to move on, but it's difficult."

"That's because she's all the way the fuck up here by herself. She needs her family. She needs us." My temper flared in my chest, vicious and angry, reminding me Marissa was also mine to protect. I'd promised as much to Trojan on his deathbed. Before we left this dismal fucking town, I'd have to at least try to talk to her.

"She wants out," Selene continued. "She doesn't want our life anymore. Can you blame her?"

No, I couldn't. Some days, I still questioned my sanity over the fact that I continued to stick it out, that I still played this stupid game with Selene, ignoring my most basic instinct of all.

"If this is a trap, I don't know why she's running from the Caputis," Selene said, bringing us back on topic. "But Nikki wouldn't leave town, not while she's got the protection of the local MC."

I took a deep breath and ran the length of Selene's map again. The Kings of Carnage controlled things this far north, and even being in their territory this long without announcing myself would cause problems if we got caught. If I were Nikki, I'd go to a safe house, maybe their clubhouse, somewhere the Caputis wouldn't feel comfortable raiding until they had backup. If this was a trap for the Roses, she shouldn't be running from anyone...unless perhaps she saw *us* in the woods and tried to lure us out by running.

What the fuck is this girl doing?

Frustrated about what to do next, I shot a text off to Aris to let him know what had happened. I sent him what I could remember about the vehicles and prayed Switch could find more information. Aris had told me to get Selene and come home, and if I could take Nikki out at the same time, great. But I wasn't sure how he'd feel about me wiping out a gang of Caputis. It could escalate things with Gabriella or it could go south, and we'd have fallen right into the trap they laid for us.

"I say we scope out the boyfriend's place." Selene reached into her bag for a bottle of whiskey, unscrewing the cap so she could take a deep swig. That same bottle had gotten us into trouble the last time she'd been sucking from it, so I grabbed it out of her hands, took a giant gulp myself, and put it on the table by the window. "Hey!"

"We're working," I told her. "You can have it when we're done."

She scowled but didn't disagree, just returned her attention to the map and list of known addresses she'd compiled.

"We'll rest for a few hours and then head out to find her," I said. "I agree. She won't leave if she's got people here to protect her."

"What if we told the Kings who she is and what she's done? They might hand her over." Selene chewed on her bottom lip again, making me wish I could dig my teeth into that delectable skin myself. *Stop that, Erickson.* "We'd do the same for them, wouldn't we?"

I shrugged. "Depends." For another Rose chapter, perhaps this wouldn't have even been an issue. But I didn't know these guys, and they didn't know us. Just because we rode bikes didn't mean we were automatically allies. My eyelids suddenly hung like anvils, and after the shower, I needed to rest.

"Enough for one night." I grabbed the paperwork out of her hand and put it back in the folder, causing her bright eyes to glare up at me. "Take a shower. Get some sleep. We'll head out in a few hours."

The urge to fight back flickered behind her gaze, and my nerves burned in anticipation that she might. Nothing delighted me more than slamming her ass down while she tried desperately to get away from me. The beast inside sat up at attention, and despite my earlier promise that I wouldn't touch her again, my resolve had started chipping away like cheap paint.

Her haughty look said she'd give me no reprieve. Now that I'd caught her, I'd have to tame her. Despite her normal calm, cool exterior, deep down, Selene was even more wild than me. Only I knew about that side of her. Only I had ever seen it.

My wildcat.

Mine.

She pushed to her feet, forcing me to take a step back so she had room to move, and I stared at her, my fingers itching for our next battle. A challenge in my eyes, I waited until she grinned and stepped around me before letting my guard down.

Perhaps that was part of the appeal between us. I'd taught her everything I knew, but Selene had always been too smart for her own good. That brilliant brain hadn't stopped churning since I'd hunted her down in the woods. She was still trying to outplay me, maybe even take off again, and I had to be prepared for whatever she might come up with.

11

SELENE

It's what she does, the monster inside of me snarled. *Blend into a new family. Find a new husband to dupe into protecting her.*

All Nikki had ever known were bikers and outlaws. It didn't surprise me she'd gotten in good with a new crowd. She'd have them waist deep in a war they had no idea they were fighting before anyone could stop it. I had to get to her quick.

I rinsed the rest of the shitty conditioner out of my thick hair and turned the water off, toweling myself off and yanking my white tank top over my head before slipping on a clean pair of undies. I didn't bring any other sleeping shorts, and I probably could have put my jeans back on, but he'd run his hands through my cunt a few days ago, so I thought little of walking out in nothing more than that. Still, I bit back a grin when Thor glanced up from his spot at the table by the window and ran the length of me. He cleared his throat, shifted his hips in his seat, and took a sip of whiskey.

Well, if we're done working...

I walked closer and grabbed the bottle to take a long pull straight from the neck, and went back to the bed. I sat down with one leg bent under the other and held back a wince when my ass protested the movement.

"Does everyone know where I am? What I'm doing?"

Thor shook his head. "Aris does, but he's keeping it under wraps until I bring you home. After Pollux, everyone has enough to worry about."

I took another drink of liquor, swallowing down the burn. "Does he know you're helping me?"

He didn't answer that, just sipped at his tumbler and looked out the window again. A small fire lit deep inside of me at his nonresponse. That was the unbreakable promise of committing yourself to a club like the Steel Roses—nothing came above the MC. Nothing. Yet Thor had left the vice president out of this very important part of the plot. Knowing Aris, he would have insisted Thor find me and bring me home, but here we were, on yet another hunt together.

My cold, dead heart gave half a heartbeat that he might have put *me* before the club, the way a member does for his old lady, but I smothered that down. He was my uncle. I was his niece. We might have had one relatively PG-13 mistake after a night of drinking and regret, but that changed nothing. I should have been more ashamed of myself, but I was too fucked up, too much a monster to care.

Might as well revel in the grime, whispered that depraved little shit. I quickly hushed her and returned to the present.

"Are you going to lurk at the table all night?" I scooted closer to the far side, peeling the sheets back so I could slip under them. "Or does getting some rest include you, too?"

My cheeks burned as I remembered the way I'd felt when I woken up this morning, burrowed deep into his embrace. Warm. Safe. Protected. Like nothing would ever be able to hurt me again.

I expected Thor to ignore me, but he swigged back the last of his drink before standing and walking closer. He had on dark jeans, zipped but not buttoned, and nothing else, so when he walked, they hung low, revealing the V of his hips and a line of dark hair leading down under the denim.

I licked my lips and wondered what he tasted like. What sounds would he make when I ran my tongue along the length of him?

Would he like it if I pulled his hair for a change? How would his beard feel on the inside of my thighs?

Stop that, Montgomery. I shook my head and ran through my list of reasons why finding out would be so very wrong.

"You lost the right to look at me like that when you took off and scared the shit out of me." He raised an eyebrow and twisted his lips into a devilish smirk, the one that told me he had a punishment brewing behind his eyes. He got that same look whenever I missed my mark or couldn't land a kick.

"You found me, didn't you?" I cleared my throat, clenching my thighs against the heat between them as he lifted the sheets and scooted under, sitting back against the headboard instead of lying down. He flicked off the light on the bedside table, bathing us in the soft tangerine glow of the lone fluorescent in the parking lot. Mixed with the moonlight, it created a safe haven there in that room, just me and him and the secrets we kept between us.

The silence stretched on, but the heat from his body soaked through the sheets, making my skin come alive. I felt him everywhere, and my heart pounded against my ribs so hard, no amount of focused breathing calmed it down. I was aware of every move he made—the dip in the bed when he shifted and finally lay down beside me, the scent of soap and pine and *him* as it swirled down my throat, the mix of trepidation and loosening in his muscles as he sighed and relaxed.

Forcing my lungs to suck in more oxygen, I exhaled to the count of four and closed my eyes, swallowing against a dry mouth and telling myself it was nothing—the kiss, the spanking, the amazing orgasm, all of it—nothing. I'd done it as a distraction. I'd wanted him looking left so I could sneak to the right.

Neither of us said anything, and after a few moments of eternity, I somehow managed to fall asleep. But rest did not come easily. My dreams terrified me. I ran through the woods with an unknowable monster chasing after me, my legs shaking as I sprinted across the freezing undergrowth, my arms pumping, my lungs gasping for air. I tripped on a root and fell to my hands and knees, anxiety crackling through my muscles at the thought that I'd given my attacker precious time to catch up. After pushing upright, I barreled forward again, but it was too late. They were there. They'd caught me.

Arms wrapped around my midsection like a vise, dragging me to the ground, where I landed on my side and all the oxygen pushed out of my lungs.

"*Stop it!*" I screamed. "*Get off me!*"

"*No,*" the monster snarled, holding my arms down above my head with its slimy claws, the weight of its torso on my hips, keeping my lower half in place. "*Look at me, Selene. Look at me.*"

I clenched my eyes shut, tossing my head back and forth, refusing to meet the creature's dreadful gaze. Once I did, it would consume me.

"Selene," came a deep, soothing voice. I ignored it.

"*Open your eyes,*" the creature hissed. "*Look at me. Open your eyes.*"

"Open your eyes," the voice echoed, this time louder and deeper. "It's a dream."

Forcing myself awake, I sobbed and sat up, running my hands over my face as I came back to the real world. The nightmare had been coming for years now, so long I didn't remember where it started. I never looked at the monster, not once. I didn't want to see its gleaming teeth or its bloodred eyes. If I peeked, I gave it permission to devour me, and I was too horrified to do that. Not yet.

"Are you okay?" Thor asked, pushing himself up to lean against the headboard. He'd taken off his jeans, now lying next to me only in his boxers, and I let the sight distract me. His body had been built for battle, honed and carved from marble into a warrior's form. I'd never asked him why he left the Navy, but I had a feeling he wouldn't tell me even if I did.

I climbed out of bed and walked across the room to my book bag, retrieving a pack of joints I'd rolled before I left. I didn't like the taste of cigarettes, but cannabis always took the edge off whatever angst tumbled around in my gut at three in the morning. When I sat down at the card table to light it and take a deep puff, Thor stood and walked to me, lifting a long leg over the other chair before lowering his body into it.

"I think Giuseppe Caputi is haunting me." I smirked and took another puff on the joint before handing it to Thor. He raised an eyebrow, clearly deciding whether to deny me, before he reached out to take it.

"What makes you say that?" Thor inhaled, coughed lightly, and handed it back.

"He chases me in my dreams." I shook my head, feeling stripped raw after my nightmare. Thor and I had done terrible things together, but I'd never been more exposed, more naked, than I was sitting at that table with him. "Do the ghosts of the people you've killed ever come back to you?"

He took the joint from me, drew in a breath, and let it out in a cloud of smoke. "Not as much as the people I've let live."

"So you understand, then? Why I have to do this...with Nikki?"

"I understand, but that doesn't mean this was the right way to do it." He handed it back to me and ran a hand through his long golden hair, brushing the strands back away from his face. "If you're going to do it anyway, I might as well make sure you stay safe."

I swallowed down my rotten pride, damn near choking on it as I muttered a quiet, "Thank you."

He raised his eyebrows and snapped his gaze to me, seemingly surprised by my gratitude, before putting his elbows on the table so he could lean in closer. "I need you to do me a favor, since I'm being so nice in helping you."

"I knew it." I rolled my eyes so hard, they almost hit the back of my head. Of course he had an ulterior motive.

"Don't ever, and I do mean *ever*, try to use sex with me as a distraction again." His stormy gray eyes met mine, daring me to refuse as he leaned in and dropped his voice lower. "What we have... It's deeper than that. It's more important. And you know it."

It was the first time either of us had mentioned it directly since it happened, and certainly the only time we'd ever talked about what existed between us. Didn't we have the rules of society telling us it couldn't be as close as he described? Didn't we have the boundaries of matrimony and a relationship forged in trauma keeping us apart?

Despite this, flames licked against my skin, tempting me toward an inferno I had no business touching. After the chilling effect of my nightmare, the heat soothed that deep nervous ache, and my tank top grew a thousand times tighter, damn near baring me completely to him. My nipples pebbled in the cool night air, tender as they rubbed against the cotton, making me shiver. Thor's eyes traveled the length of me, missing none of it, cataloging my tells the way a feral thing does so it can use them later to its advantage.

I knew that look. I'd seen it in the eyes of every man who'd ever looked at me since I grew a set of hips. He hungered, and I longed, and together, we made a fucking mess.

Shut this down, Montgomery, whispered the cold voice of logic.

No, hissed the monster. *Fight back.*

She shouted louder.

"Did I hurt your feelings when you woke up alone?" I stuck out my lower lip in a condescending pout. "Poor Uncle Thor." Another reminder that I skated on thin ice. Neither of us was tipsy this time, and cannabis had never lowered my inhibitions enough for me to make terrible decisions. If we did this, we did it because we wanted it. There could be no other reason.

For a moment, the words hovered between us. My inner animal teased the surface, and when he flicked his gaze up to mine, I saw his lurking just beyond those silvery depths. A heartbeat passed...then another...

He snapped his hand out and pinched my lower lip between his index finger and thumb, squeezing so hard it hurt. I whined, but the agony sizzled down my spine and ended in a throb between my legs. I wanted him to do it harder. His eyes twinkled at the squeak, or perhaps he could read my mind, because the predator had finally decided to play with his meal.

"Don't do that," he said. "Don't pretend like this is nothing or brush it under the rug." Thor tsked and shook his head. "You can't hide from me. You never could."

12

———

SELENE

"We can't," I said, whipping my head away from him. My pulse thundered through my body, my thigh muscles shaking uncontrollably, but despite my protests, I didn't dare move. If I gave chase, he'd hunt me down. Some part of me screamed for that to happen, for him to make my wildest fantasies come true.

"We want to." The words fell from his lips in a soft murmur, but they roared through my blood all the same.

I swallowed, and he narrowed his hunter's gaze on the movement. I could almost see the thoughts flitting through his head, like how badly he'd like to have his fingers wrapped around my neck when I did that again, or maybe how much he'd like to be slotted down my throat instead.

"We shouldn't want to." The words sounded weak even if I knew they were true.

"Are you saying no?"

"No." The word rushed out of me in a panic, as if the thought of tonight not ending in sex was devastating now that we'd brought it there. Suddenly, all my reasons, all my morals, none of it seemed strong enough to withstand my worst impulses. "No," I said again, more calmly. "Are you?"

He snickered, low and deep, before pushing to his feet so he could circle around the table and come to stand behind me. "No, kitten."

There was that pet name again. The first time he'd said it, I wanted to snarl and lash out with my claws to show him just how much damage this *kitten* could do. Now, it held an undertone that I hadn't picked up on before, one that sent heat licking through my body. The more he said it, the wetter I got and the more my panties stuck to me.

The weight of my chair shifted as he placed his hands on the back and leaned down to press his lips to my ear. His hot breath spilled down the side of my neck and into my shirt as he whispered, "Are you saying yes?"

"Yes." I sighed, the butterflies in my stomach swarming out of control. I clamped my fingers down on the arms of the chair to keep from burying them between my legs.

He moved quicker than I anticipated, circling my throat with one hand, and shoving the other into my hair, yanking a fistful back. I winced against the sharp slice in my skull, but that too sent shivers racing down my spine.

"I want to tease you," he murmured, loosening the fist in my hair so he could trail his fingertips down my shoulder and over my chest, his caress so light compared to how hard he held my neck. "I want to rile you up, handcuff you to the bed, and leave you there to go kill Nikki myself."

The picture he painted had me reeling, and the urge to lash out at him sparked in my gut. My monster didn't like the suggestion, and if he did that, I'd break every oath I'd ever sworn just to prove a point. Besides, the cuffs wouldn't hold me. I had double-jointed thumbs and I'd just slip right out of them.

"That's what you deserve."

"Fuck off," I snarled.

"Oh, there she is. My wildcat, my *kitten*." He continued his exploration down the front of my tank top, grabbing my breast with shocking possession, like he owned me, like I was nothing more than his toy. The thought shouldn't turn me on as much as it did. I was an intelligent, independent woman. I'd gone to fucking medical school. But the way I wanted *his* rough hands on me, tearing and scratching the way only he could, rattled me down to my core.

He pinched my tender nipple between his callused mechanic's fingers, the agony sparking down my stomach and the back of my legs to my toes.

"Fuck," I whined against the wince, gripping the chair harder. I could get out of this if I wanted to, but the heavens might rain down upon us and I wouldn't move. I yearned to see this play out.

"You like that, huh?" he hissed, gripping my windpipe harder, pulling my head back against his chest. He went to the other nipple and gave it the same abuse, tugging and squeezing until I crossed one leg over the other in a desperate plea for release. He laughed and reached down to part my knees, smacking the inside of my thigh so hard, my skin immediately shined with finger marks. "I've had so much time to imagine the horrible things I'd do to you if I ever got you alone like this. Years and years."

My heart beat faster, the tension in my stomach twisting into a blinding ache. I needed him to drag those fingers higher, to make good on these terrible threats. He dug his nails into my slapped flesh instead, causing me to whimper a frustrated groan. It was agonizing and euphoric and...*how did he know?* How could he know I loved the pain as much as the pleasure, that I'd thrived on both as long as I'd lived?

"Tonight, I'm gonna take you the way I want." He released my throat so he could slide that hand along my shoulders to the back of my neck where he palmed my spine like a wolf with a rabbit in its mouth. "If it's too much, say red and I'll stop."

No. Don't stop.

"But I don't think you're gonna need that, are you?" He trailed the hand on my thigh higher, my attention glued to the way his big fingers dwarfed my thighs. I'd never been model skinny like Ru, and I didn't hit puberty like a rocket and grow a whole foot overnight like

Verona. I'd always been sturdy, midsized, and muscular. Because of my height and thick build, I'd never fit in anything under a size ten, but Thor was so big that he made me feel petite. When he swept his fingers in between my legs and over my wet lace panties, I arched off the chair, the touch so sensual and vulgar, I couldn't stand it.

"Thor, please," I begged, the logical part of me so deeply hidden inside my subconscious, I'd given my whole self over to the monster. I'd become literal ancient instinct and raw emotion.

"Please, what?" He chuckled at my misery, and I struggled to stay still as he dragged one of my tank top straps to the side, allowing the fabric to slide down my upper arm. He moved the hand between my legs higher, teasing the elastic band around my underwear with his fingertips. "Does it hurt? Poor Selene."

Now, he mocked me, and that amplified the intoxicating pull in my gut. I clenched my fists, poised to launch out of my seat, but he shoved under the fabric and cupped me, sliding his fingers along my sensitive skin. Sparks of ecstasy collided with over a decade of sexual frustration inside my nerve endings, and I sagged into the chair, spreading my legs farther apart to make room for him, pushing my head back on his chest.

"There's my good kitten." He ran the back of his knuckle down the side of my cheek, a touch incredibly too tender for the deliciously vile things he did between my legs. I gasped as he pushed one finger inside me, curling to hit just the right spot while he rubbed at my clit with his palm. I rocked against his hand, desperate for more, praying this never ended.

A sharp yank at the back of my head had me clenching my eyes shut, and the pinch of teeth on the side of my neck sent contrasting shock waves down my body and back up. He'd grabbed a fistful of hair, forced me to one side, and sank his teeth into the meat where my neck met my shoulder.

"Don't stop," I said under a heavy pant. "Please, don't stop."

"Your mouth is so pretty when you beg," he murmured, biting my earlobe hard enough to hurt but not deep enough to mark. I groaned and melted into the chair as he finger-fucked me deeper, working my body like he'd been doing it for years, like he knew every single part of me, inside and out. "Go on. Beg again."

So close. So close.

"Please. Please, please." I repeated it as my body tightened, my muscles clamping down on his penetration, the wave of ecstasy threatening to take me under. Our passion had become so torrid and heavy, I wanted it to crash down on me and fucking whisk me away. Just as I was reaching for it, Thor yanked his fingers out of my cunt and grabbed my knees, holding them open so I couldn't use my thighs to finish the job.

"This is what you get," he growled, his mouth right next to my ear as he leaned over me to grip my knees, keeping my thighs apart. I writhed against his hold, nerves sparking through my legs like a downed power line. My ruined orgasm devastated me, and I wanted to hate him for it, but oh, how I loved it at the same time. "This is your punishment for leaving me like that. How could you do that to me?" He sank his nails into my skin, there'd be imprints for days, but God, I loved that, too. I wanted it harder. Rougher. Meaner. "Me? Of all fucking people on this planet, *I'm* the one you tell this shit to. *I'm* the one who helps you do this. It's always been me."

The chasm in my chest split wide open at the realization. I thought he'd been angry that I'd put myself in danger, that I'd ignored him to do as I pleased just as I always had. But it was more complicated than that. He was also upset that I'd left him out, that of all the times we'd hunted down the bad guy together, I'd chosen now to abandon him. It broke my heart. In my haste to protect him, I'd fractured the most precious thing about us—*we killed together.*

"Do you understand?" He grabbed the back of the chair, tilting it and spinning me around like the combined weight was nothing for him. When we faced each other, he put one hand on my shoulder and leaned down until he came face level with me, his irises the color of a storm cloud in a hurricane, the bits of black swirling to indicate his devastation. He held my gaze, forcing me to watch as he stuck the fingers that had been inside of me between his lips, sucking my taste off his skin.

I heard what he didn't say, what he meant by handling me so roughly, by swallowing down my taste and sinking his teeth so deep into my neck it would probably ache for days.

I was his.

He was mine.

We might not have stepped over this indecent line until tonight, but that much had been true since he walked in on Billy beating the hell out of me. The Commonwealth of Virginia made us family, but this thorny tether between us had twisted into something far more ethereal and precarious in the time since. I could not exist without him. This was him telling me the same.

"Say you understand," he said, cupping my chin so I had to look at him.

"I understand," I said.

"Good." He straightened, nodding at the ground between us while he tucked his thumbs into the waistband of his boxers. "On your knees, Montgomery."

Lips twisting into a smile, I debated putting up a fight. I wouldn't use his safe word, but edging me was a vicious thing to do, even if he'd always liked putting me in my place. However, it was early in the morning and I had been dying to do this for years. So, I dropped to that disgusting carpet and stared up at him with nothing but bad life choices ricocheting through my mind.

Luckily for me, he must have read them and sympathized because he traced a thumb over my bottom lip and took a step closer.

"Open wide."

13

THOR

Hands shaking and trying like hell to hide it, I pushed the tip of my cock in between her lips, watching as her big eyes peered up at me with that perfect mix of admiration and rebellion. Her warm mouth enveloped me, dousing my nerves in fire like I couldn't get enough of her. As I eased myself farther in, she smiled and burst my fucking restraint wide open.

One of my favorite things about Selene was how savage she was deep down inside. It took fucking balls to track Nikki halfway across the Gods damned country, even more to do it suspecting I would come after her. Watching her come out of the bathroom wearing practically nothing had tested my patience, but when she teased me with that adorable pout? I'd lost it. All the reasons we shouldn't do this disappeared, and I figured...fuck it, ya know? We were far away from anyone who would give a shit, and between her and me, this was long overdue.

The way she ran her tongue along the length of my dick hinted at the wicked thoughts in her mind. I never really knew what she'd do next, and after some of the shit I'd seen from her, that scared me. I'd fought in wars. I'd killed countless people. But when Selene Montgomery gave me that devilish grin, I had to brace myself. Her creativity was matched only by her ruthlessness.

She sucked me deep into her mouth, grabbing my hips to tug them forward so she could get more. She didn't ease into it. No. Once she had her mouth on me, she fucked me with her face and hands like she could earn a medal doing it.

"Gods, kitten," I groaned, grabbing her hair to try to slow her down. Admitting how long I'd imagined her like this would make me question what little morality I had left, so I ignored it and refocused on the present. "Touch yourself."

She didn't waste a second. One hand went between her legs, and as soon as she touched her clit, she moaned around me, sending vibrations through my soul. Gods, that fucking felt amazing.

"Do it again," I told her. "If you get yourself off while you're sucking my dick, I'll give you a reward." She worked in earnest then, spit sliding down her chin and neck while she increased her speed, fisting me with one hand and moving the other between her thighs.

The scent of her wet cunt filled the space between us, flowers and female and sex, amplifying the lewd slurping sounds of her mouth. Groans and mumbled expletives radiated out of me, escalating in time with her rapid flicks over her cunt, and fuck...I didn't think *I* was gonna last to see her come.

When she did, she squealed and squeezed her legs together, letting my cock fall out of her mouth while she relished in her own pleasure. Fuck, it snapped that last bit of control holding my beast at bay. He'd waited too long for this, and now he wanted everything he'd ever dreamed of. A growl ripped out of my chest as I snatched her off the ground, tossing her on the mattress so hard she bounced.

Her gorgeous grin told me she didn't mind, but as long as she wasn't shouting red, the barbaric thing inside me didn't give a fuck what she wanted. It needed to get her off. It needed to roll around in her mouthwatering scent until every single note had been etched into my skin. And then, it would sink teeth marks into her most delicate bits so that anyone who came for her would *know* she was my territory.

Mine.

She pushed to her knees and bit her bottom lip between her teeth, red-rimmed eyes sparkling with abuse and anticipation. She looked fucking fierce—her hair matted and tangled around her head, her tank top half hanging off her shoulder, her lace panties barely covering that beautiful pussy. The light trickling in through the window cast her in a pale glow that almost made her iridescent, like she was the personified version of her namesake. My moon goddess, right here in front of me.

"You're a fucking brute," she said, taking measured breaths like she did in a sparring session, like she was already planning her response to my next move.

"Yeah?" I stalked closer, my pulse pounding so hard, I felt it in my fingertips. "You think that was brutal?" In one quick movement, I grabbed the back of her thighs and flipped her onto her spine, moving so that her knees were over my shoulders. She gasped and squealed as she flopped on the mattress, but I held her down by the throat as I ripped her lace panties clean off her body in one sharp yank, revealing her completely to me. Gods, she was so fucking beautiful.

"Thor, please," she whimpered.

"That's enough," I snarled, putting my hand over her mouth. "If you want me to stop, say the word. Otherwise, shut the fuck up and enjoy this."

She stared up at me with wide eyes, but she smiled behind my palm and nodded.

Good. No more talking. I had other things I wanted to do with my mouth. Gripping one knee, I spread her farther open to me and bit the inside of her other thigh, marking my territory there, too. She hissed in a breath, and I did it again, this time lower, closer to the place I wanted to mark the most.

I did it to the other leg, taking my time, drawing it out as much as I could, licking and kissing each bite after I made it. I loved the way her skin gave under my teeth, and when I scratched down the inside of her calf, she trembled and shook, her breathy moans rumbling against my hand. The bruises on her ass and thighs from a few nights ago shined a bright violet, and some part of me should have felt guilty for making them, but in that moment, I loved the sight. It pleased me to know anyone who dared to peek at that private flesh would see the evidence *I* left behind.

Mine.

Only when I had her squirming and writhing in that desperate way of a woman on the edge did I finally spear my tongue through her warm, wet pussy, ignoring the pulse in my balls when she curled in on herself and sank into the mattress. I did it again, swallowing down the taste of her. It fucking riled me up. I wanted more.

Desperate for it, I sucked on her clit, licking and twirling her around in my mouth like maybe this would be the only time I'd get a chance to. Which was bullshit. I'd caught her. I'd tamed her. I'd marked her.

She twisted her fingers into my hair, fisting handfuls as her thighs pressed against my shoulders, trying to close around me. I wouldn't let her. I fucked her with my lips and surged two fingers inside her, rubbing at the spot I'd found earlier, the spot that sent her into a frenzy. She bucked off the bed, rolling against my face.

Fuck yeah.

She was close again, the muscles in her pussy clamping down on my fingers so tight, I couldn't wait to push my cock inside her. I kept going until she moaned behind my hand, dug her fingers into my scalp, and curled into a tight ball of tension. She came hard, so fucking hard, pushing and shoving at my forehead to get me off her. But I wouldn't stop. No, I kept on her until she rode it out completely, until I was satisfied no one else had ever done that to her before. Only then did I detach myself and prowl up her body, taking one knee with me under my arm so it was the perfect position to slip my cock inside her—one fluid motion, all the way to the hilt.

Fuck, she was so warm and wet, well fucking abused and ready for me. She gasped and arched, turning her head to the side to give me a perfect view of my bite mark. It stood out, angry and red against her pale midnight skin, but fuck, primordial instinct snaked up my spine. I leaned down and licked it, and she sucked in air through her teeth. The sound urged me on, so I did it again, pulling my cock out only to surge it in harder and deeper.

She tasted like sweat and Selene, and the combination unleashed the years of pent-up frustration between us, all the times I'd wished I could have done this and hadn't. Now that I had her right where I wanted her, I couldn't take my time anymore. I rutted into her like she was made of steel, like there was nothing that could break her, like I didn't outweigh her by at least a hundred pounds of muscle.

"More," she pleaded, her voice cracking as she said it. "More, please." She dug her nails into the back of my legs, tugging me forward, and I held on to the flimsy headboard, trying to use it as leverage to get farther inside her. We slammed together like two colliding moons, loud and explosive, punctuated by the bed banging onto the wall.

"I'm almost there," she said, her breathy whispers cracked and hoarse. "Don't stop. Please, don't stop."

When her eyes met mine, everything crashed into me—all the time we'd lived around each other, all the secrets we carried between us, how right this was despite all the reasons we'd stayed apart. I didn't care about Gemma. I didn't care about Crow or KC. I didn't care what anyone else thought, and perhaps I never had. This connection had become irreversible, and I'd stopped fighting it.

Finally.

Defeat had never tasted so sweet.

Fingernails sliced up my back as she crested a third time, and I couldn't hold myself back. I exploded inside of her with three hard pumps and a deep guttural groan that came from my soul. Perhaps I was hallucinating from sleep deprivation and the fact I'd come harder than Christ himself, but I'd swear the bond between us shifted. What once had been reluctant hesitation to accept the inappropriateness of our adoration for each other had now become open, rebellious intimacy and unbridled, wanton acceptance.

I had never been as flayed open as I was lying on top of her, and I'd never seen her so completely vulnerable. We were truly spent, and

I couldn't find it in me to roll off her or care. But I'd roughed her up pretty bad, and the least I could do was make sure she was okay.

"Let me see." I nudged her head to the side so I could look at the bite mark, running my fingers over it. She gave me a lazy smile and kissed me again, sweet and gentle.

"It's okay, Erickson," she said, nudging her nose against mine. "I think I can sleep now."

Then we did.

14

THOR

I should've known better than to trust her after only one night. When I woke up the next morning, the bed was cold and lonely. Again.

"Sel," I called out, shocked by how dry and hoarse my voice was. I lifted my head and looked around to find nothing but a dark room and the bright glow of sunlight creeping in through the blinds. "Fuck." I launched myself out of bed and over to the door, ripping it open and preparing myself for the worst.

The parking spot where I'd left my Silverado sat horrifyingly empty.

"Gods damn it, Montgomery." Stalking across the room, I grabbed my phone to call her when the sound of a truck engine pulled up out front. I paused and walked back to the door, freezing when she slowed into the parking space. Taking a deep breath, I let it out on a relaxing sigh and crossed my arms over my chest while she hopped out.

Selene smiled and held two medium coffees as she walked closer.

"Good morning," she said. "I woke up before you, and the coffee here is piss."

I ignored the skip in my heart at the simple relief that she was okay, that she hadn't run off again after promising me not to last night. She scooted past me into the hotel room, and I took my drink from her, taking a long-drawn sip.

"Thank you," I grumbled and closed the door.

"We should hit the road soon." She stuck her hand in her back pocket as she sat her coffee down on the table. "I want to find Nikki before she takes off again."

Taking a small gulp of my own, I agreed, letting the caffeine flow through my veins. "The best place to start is her boyfriend's house." Selene grabbed her pack to pull out the folder Marissa had given her, flipping through the pages until she found the one she was looking for. She held up a photo of a tall white guy with a bald head and covered in tattoos. "Steven Day, nickname: Cheesecake." Selene laughed and rolled her eyes. "She has a type, huh? First Pie, now Cheesecake? They even look the same."

"Well, if he's taken her in after only two months, he's probably a fucking idiot, too." I ran my knuckles down the side of her face, brushing back a stray piece of hair. She leaned into the movement, tilting her face toward my wrist so she could press a tender kiss to my palm. It opened her neck to me, revealing my teeth marks in an angry bruise near her pulse point.

I winced. "Shit. Let me get some bruise cream or antiseptic to put on—"

"No," she said, covering it with her free hand and taking a step back. She eyed me with a defiant stare, her jaw clenched as she prepared to fight me. "Don't you dare."

I was confused at first until I remembered that Selene *liked* her bruises. After a good sparring session or a fight she'd won, she wore them proudly, almost like badges of honor. She must have felt the same way about these marks. I straightened my shoulders as a sting of pride shot down my chest, the scratches on my own back pulling as I moved.

Fuck, we matched in all the right ways. Not only did I love the sight of my marks on her skin, but the ache of hers on mine also made me proud. Like a true warrior, she didn't give easily, and if someone was going to break through that tough outer shell to even try, they'd have to give as good as they got. Some fucking idiots could never know how to handle a woman like Selene. Being brutal didn't always mean being violent, and lucky for her, I understood that nuance better than fucking anyone.

"Did you like that?" I grinned like a wild thing having spotted wounded prey, and took another step closer to her. "How are the ones on your legs?" I glanced down to the jeans covering her delectable thighs and bit my bottom lip, remembering how they'd tasted liked honey when I had my way with them not three hours ago.

"Fine." She held my gaze while I crowded her and ran my hands over her waist to her ass, pretending my fingers didn't itch to rip her jeans off so I could see for myself. I was too fucking greedy now that I'd gotten a bite, and I wanted to gobble her right the fuck up again. A sharp alarm screamed at the back of my mind, reminding me why I hadn't crossed this line before. I'd been borderline obsessed with her for years, and now that we'd removed the last thing keeping us at arm's length, I worried I'd lose myself in this...in her. I worried that wasn't such a bad thing anymore.

"Let me see." I nudged her nose with mine. "Take your pants off."

She giggled and shoved me away. "C'mon. Get dressed. We have to go."

The beast inside me reared up at her insolence, threatening to bend her over the table and force her pants down to her ankles regardless of her protests. I reined it in because she was right. We needed to find this bitch and plan the next steps in our execution. After I dressed and packed the few things I'd brought, we loaded into the truck and headed out.

Selene had been right; Nikki didn't run. She was at the very first place we checked, her boyfriend's house in the woods. Unlike Nikki, Cheesecake had some money. This place was on twenty acres of land, way up in the mountains. We parked the truck a few miles away, grabbed our shit, and hiked back through the woods. He'd installed security cameras in the hundred yards leading up to the place, which we spotted before we trespassed.

Even from this far out, I could make out the two-story log cabin and the smoke billowing out of the chimney. I pulled my binoculars out of my pack and pressed them to my eyes, scowling at Nikki inside the house, sitting on her new boyfriend's lap while they watched television. They weren't alone. There were five other dudes in cuts standing next to ten men in suits. A few women mingled about, kissing whichever guys they were with and giggling with each other. We were vastly outnumbered, and any hope of sneaking in to kill her and getting out without being seen quickly deflated.

"Let me see," Selene whispered, taking the binoculars from me. "That fucking bitch. We were right. Look at her, just lounging with the Caputis like she didn't spend her life hating them."

"Wouldn't you? If you had nowhere else to run?"

"I wouldn't have betrayed the only family I had." Selene shook her head and handed the spectacles back to me before shrugging off her pack and settling in for the long haul. In order to get close to her without tipping off the Caputis, we'd have to find the right moment. We'd have to wait until she was alone, or at least, less well protected.

Now, we settled in to watch. Selene read for the first hour or two, likely something smutty, judging by the blush on her cheeks every so often. I made a mental note to check her library later for inspiration. The scene must have been filthy as fuck to turn my kitten that shade of rosy pink, and I couldn't wait to check it out.

I refocused on the house and thought about this morning. I'd been rough with her, and she hadn't stopped me. She knew what to do to get me to back off, and she hadn't pulled that trigger. Did she like it? Did she want more of it?

Of course, I'd been a fucking slut in my teenage years, before and during my time in the Navy. After I got out, I fucked around here and there. I certainly hadn't kept my dick in my pants once I married Gemma. We both carried on living our lives like nothing had changed. But lately, I didn't have that urge anymore. When Selene caught me with that hang-around on Thanksgiving, it hadn't been what it looked like. Yeah, she'd cornered me and gave it a shot, but I wasn't interested.

Things were more than physical with Selene. For fifteen years, she'd been a safe haven for me...a home. There was a reason I slept so well by her side. There was a reason I could find her no matter where she went. She matched me in both intellect and prowess, but she also softened me, reminding me what it was to have family.

Now, I had an itch and only one person could scratch it. I was a fucking waste for anyone else. Selene and I had created this untenable thing between us, instilled it in each other through a decade and a half of verbal and physical sparring. In retrospect, this could've been the only end between us.

"Where do you think her baby is?" Selene asked, breaking my train of thought.

I considered. "I bet the Caputis have it. They'd use it as leverage over her."

"And she ran." Selene rubbed a finger over her lips, narrowing her eyes as she contemplated this. "The fucking bitch."

Nikki was obviously scared and caught up in whatever this game was. A baby would only slow her down. She couldn't show up at this MC's doorstep with an infant in tow, hoping to score a man capable of helping her bomb another MC and keeping her safe afterward. She'd have to be free and unencumbered. She'd have to appear as openly available as she could.

The hours dragged agonizingly by. The sun hit mid sky and we ate the jerky and fruit she'd brought with her. Then we waited some more. Nikki occasionally paced, running her hands back through her long, blond hair. Cheesecake would throw his fists in the air, gesturing while he talked her down, joking with the Caputis. The others joined in, laughing or clapping him on the shoulder.

They presumably hadn't figured out we were here, and as long as we stayed this far beyond their cameras until we attacked, they never would.

I refocused on Selene and glanced down at her e-reader, my gaze catching on words like *rubbed her clit* and *thrust deep inside her, again and again.* This got my beast's attention, who sat up inside my mind and stretched, claws sharpened, teeth ready to sink into her tender ass. Whatever was on those pages, he wanted a piece of the action.

"What are you reading, kitten?" The words came out on a low intimidating growl, my feral side having blinked fully awake.

She turned the e-reader away from me so I couldn't see, which only provoked me further. Now I was curious she wanted to hide from me.

"Nothing," she said, her cheeks turning an even more vibrant shade of pink. "It's smut."

"Let me see it." I grinned and bit her earlobe, giving it a small yank that told her I was only partially fucking around. I'd get the damn thing one way or another. It would go whole a lot easier if she complied.

"No," she said, pushing me away with one shoulder, holding it out farther with the other hand.

"Why not?"

"Because..." She paused, seeming to consider this question before glancing back toward the house. Nikki and Cheesecake were still fucking off, and other than the people in the house, there was no one else around except for the birds and squirrels. "Because there's some fucked-up shit in here, and the contents of my library are between me and God."

I laughed and kissed my way down her neck, causing her to moan and tilt her head to the side so I had access to more skin.

"Read it to me."

She froze and pulled away. "What?"

I grinned, relishing in her reaction even more because of what I planned to do next. "Read it to me."

Selene swallowed and met my gaze with uncertain eyes, taking long, measured breaths. Realizing I needed to coax her, I ran a finger down her camouflaged chest, pausing at a nipple just enough to tease her before traveling farther south toward the button of her pants. "If you read it to me"—I plucked the metal through the fabric hole before rubbing the metal zipper between my finger and thumb—"I'll reward you, little wildcat."

15

SELENE

I stared at him while my heart pounded, waiting for him to pull the rug out from under me. For fifteen years, we'd gone on hunts together. We'd sat out in the woods for hours at a time. I'd read my little stories, and he'd fiddle with whatever project he'd brought with him or sit peacefully and stare out into the woods. We were supposed to be quiet. We were supposed to keep still, so we didn't scare the prey away.

Now, he wanted me to read my "full-page-of-trigger-warnings" smut to him? Out loud? What if someone heard? What if the Caputis were out in the woods, just waiting for the right time to pounce? Or worse, a mountain lion or a bear?

Still, I met his stormy stare and nodded, returning my focus to my e-reader while he slowly tugged down the zipper on my camo pants.

"And keep your voice down," he said. "We wouldn't want any of the other wild things to hear."

I cleared my dry throat and found my place, returning to the part where the masked villain, Dante, finally had his way with the heroine, Geri.

"I wasn't supposed to like this," I said, reciting the part where Geri admits her attraction to Dante, despite the fact he'd abducted her and kept her to himself this whole time. "He was out for my father's money. I was nothing but a pawn, a piece in his chess game. But it didn't matter to me. Sure, it was fucked up that I wanted this villain wearing the Ghostface mask to pound me hard against these jail bars, but secretly, I wanted to make my father even angrier. I hated him more than Dante ever could." Thor ducked his hand under my pants, brushing his fingers under my underwear so he could cup me. Knowing I was already wet from the buildup to this scene, I ignored his moan of approval and continued.

"Look at me," I read, "his perfect little girl, wanting to be spoiled by his enemy, the vigilante that had rampaged through his town." I sighed when Thor pushed his fingers inside me, curling to send sparks through my nerves. "He moved behind me, rubbing his hands up my arms to the cuffs at my wrists. I trembled when he unlocked them, detaching me from the bars so he could guide me to the bench at our side.

"'You are a sight for sore eyes,' Dante said, whispering in my ear." Thor palmed my clit, rubbing while he finger-fucked me, and mixed with the filth I was reading, I could barely keep my focus.

"Keep going," Thor said, kissing my neck, dragging his tongue down my collarbone as he moved over me, pulling his hand out to force my legs apart. He ducked his fingers under the waist of my pants and underwear, pulling them down to my ankles but not off my boots.

I tried to hide my shiver, pretending it was the cool autumn air that caused the quake in my muscles, but I knew the truth. Every time Thor looked at me like a full-course meal, my body responded with excited trembling. I wanted this. So. Fucking. Much.

But the cold, logical voice inside my head fought me, forcing me to remember we were on a stakeout. We were supposed to be watching Nikki and making sure she didn't take off again. I checked over my shoulder, reassured when the house remained quiet.

"Montgomery," Thor whispered, biting the inside of my thigh to draw my attention back.

I hissed in a breath at the sharp slice, focusing on the way his tongue soothed over the spot afterward, his lips caressing the marks he'd left earlier this morning.

"Keep reading." He rubbed his fingers over my pussy, spreading my skin while he stared in fascination, like he was memorizing everything about this most sacred part of me. I went back to my book.

"He pushed me down with a hand on the center of my back, forcing me to bend over the cool metal. I put my hands in front of me to hold myself up, and Dante kicked my feet farther apart with his boots." Thor flicked his tongue against my clit, and I surged upward, arching against the undergrowth. He put his massive shoulders over my thighs to hold me down, his heavy arms draped over my pelvis to keep me in place. "His hands slid up the back of my thighs, taking my sundress with them, until the fabric scrunched at my waist.

"'You're shaking,' Dante said, punctuating my humiliation with a laugh. 'Are you afraid?'

"'N-no,' I managed to say, but the tremble in my voice told another tale. I was terrified...of him, of this, of my sexual attraction to this entire scenario. I shouldn't be so turned on. But his body was hard and the power in his hands made me want to—" Thor hit a particularly sensitive area and I moaned, rolling my hips against his face, digging one hand into the leaves to hold myself upright.

"Don't stop, Montgomery," he said. "What does Dante do to that pretty pussy, huh?"

"'—made me want to fuck his fingers in the worst way.'" I moaned as Thor slid his fingers inside me. First one, and then the second, continuing to lap at my clit like he didn't intend to stop until he was satisfied he'd rung me dry. "'I'm waiting for you to do something that would scare me. So far, your performance has been lackluster.' I walked a thin line, and any second, Dante might snap and slit my throat. But if he was going to kill me, he would have already done it. So, I might as well have fun with him if he was going to annoy me by keeping me locked up here all this time.

"'Lackluster?' Dante sneered, twisting his hands in my hair to yank my head back. The slice that went through me made me wince, but fuck, I loved that, too—'" My euphoria rose and I couldn't concentrate on the book anymore. I didn't give a fuck about Dante and Geri. I only wanted this intimacy with Thor, this orgasm that I chased with reckless abandon. I put my e-reader to the side, meeting his gaze while he worked me over. He worshipped me like he'd been slowly dying at my altar for years, and only now did I offer him salvation.

"Thor, I'm—" I dug my fingers into his hair, fisting it the way I liked, the way I knew he liked. "Fuck, I'm about to come." Fireworks erupted behind my eyes, my skin now alight with the magic between us. We were untouchable, unbreakable. We were infinite.

I finally toppled over that edge, and Thor rode me through it, sucking and licking until I squirmed and writhed away. Then he laughed and grinned, crawling up my body so he covered me and leaned down to kiss me.

"You taste so fucking delicious," he said. "Like woman and strawberries."

I giggled as he kissed me again, wrestling his tongue between my lips to coax mine out to play. He wrapped one hand around my jaw, holding my head in place while he pulled back. "I love licking you." A shiver shot down my spine as he dragged his hot, velvety tongue across my bottom lip in a gentle lap. "Stick out your tongue."

I did as he said, struggling to contain the lust that blazed through me when he dragged the tip of his tongue over that, too. Fuck, the sensation rattled right down my spine to my clit. No one had ever done that to me before, and the evil little thing inside me melted into a pile of sexually frustrated goo.

Continuing to hold me down by the throat, he scooted up until he straddled my chest, his knees on either side of my ribs.

"Stick it out more," he demanded, and I did. He gripped me harder, shaking my head when he growled, "I said more." I stuck it out as far as it would go, something delectably rotten sparking in my blood when he pursed his lips and dribbled spit into my mouth. God, it shouldn't have turned me on so much. If anyone else had done that to me, I would have been revolted. But this was *Thor*, beautiful, magnificent Thor. I would crawl across broken glass to have him spit on me anywhere he liked.

"There ya go. Such a beautiful little wildcat, all eager and ready for me." He used his free hand to unbuckle his belt and unzip his pants, freeing his beautiful nine-inch cock. When he pushed it over my tongue and in between my lips, I moaned and greedily sucked it back the way he liked. "Fucking hell, Sel." I didn't waste any time. I licked the precum off his slit and rolled my tongue around the head, milking him for anything else he'd give me.

He wanted me fierce and ferocious, and well, that's what I gave him. Now that he'd had me the way he wanted, I needed retribution. I wanted him pleading and begging for release, knowing my throat was the only place he would find it. I wanted his fingers twisted in my hair, his hips thrusting uselessly against my face, his intimate growls filling the space between us.

"Fuck, your mouth is nirvana." One of his hands turned into a fist in my dark locks, and I reminded myself to breathe in through my nose while he shoved himself to the back of my mouth, all the way down. I swallowed, using my muscles to constrict around him. The way he used me should have been degrading and humiliating, if not for the adoration pouring out of his stare anytime he reared back and looked down at me.

On and on it went. My eyes watered, my nose clogged, and the more he fucked my face, the more I drooled down my chest. But, honestly, that was the part I loved the most. I loved that he took it rough on me and left marks. I loved that he knew I *loved* the bruises he made.

It would be easy for someone on the outside to look at the way we treated each other and think it was abusive. But I'd survived someone who'd tried to rape and kill me, and I could see the difference, plain as day. I consented to this from Thor and Thor alone because I trusted that he would stop if I wanted. He'd given me a word to use, he'd encouraged me to use it, and heaven fucking help me, it would take a lot more than a good skull-fucking to make me utter it.

The way I trusted Thor should have terrified me. The way I laid all of my control at his feet, knowing he would never use it against me, should have had me screaming at the skies about the injustice of him being married to my deceased aunt.

But fuck it...life suddenly seemed entirely too short to care.

He tightened his grip on my hair and mumbled something about being close moments before he froze and exploded deep down in my throat. I gagged and forced myself to swallow around his kicking cock, but fuck, it was so goddamn hot that nothing would have made me stop. Once he was sated, he let go of me and pulled out of my mouth, leaning down so he could devour my swollen, sensitive lips. He shoved his tongue between my teeth like he was desperate to lick the taste of him off me, and after a lifetime of that connection, he broke free to sit up straight and smile down at me.

Fuck, I'd never seen a more powerful man so utterly decimated by a blow job. His eyelids were heavy, his hair had leaves and twigs in it, and his chest heaved for oxygen like he was suffocating. I loved this most of all. I could turn him to putty. My mouth could make him say the most depraved shit.

"Why are you so giddy?" He swung his leg to the side so I could sit up and pull my pants back into place. Heat flooded my body, my heart pounding so hard that I felt it in my toes. I could live to be a thousand years old, and I would never get enough of him, enough of this.

"I love this side of you." I smiled when he groaned in response. "You turn into such a brute. It makes me so hot."

He hummed his approval and leaned in to kiss me again before stuffing his cock back into his pants. I looked back at the house, pleased when it appeared nothing had happened.

"Want me to wear a Ghostface mask next time?" He leaned down to kiss the bite mark on my neck. "I'll even tie you up."

I laughed and ignored the pulse that went through me at the visual. We'd have plenty of time to talk about the things I wanted him to do and the scenes I wanted him to recreate. But now, we needed to get back to business. Nikki and the Caputis could make a move any second, and we needed to be prepared.

Almost as if my thought had conjured the devils themselves, a black Range Rover pulled into the driveway and slammed into park. All four doors opened and Caputis flocked out of the SUV like a clown car at a circus, including the ones we'd seen at Nikki's place last night.

"They're here," one of them shouted as he rushed inside. "We found a Silverado a few miles away, packed full of guns and other shit."

"It's the Roses," said the guy in the back. "We towed it to the safe house so we can pull it apart."

My breath caught in my throat as I stood there and stared.

"Fuck," Thor said, pulling me back down to the ground. "This isn't good."

We were vastly outnumbered, and if they searched the property, there weren't many places we could hide. We had some of our weapons, but not all of them. We'd left the ones we couldn't carry in the truck, and now they were probably in filthy Caputi hands.

"We should run." I stuffed my things into my pack as fast as I could. "We need to get out of here. Go back to the Impala and regroup. We can't take on twenty of them with the little supplies we brought."

Thor hesitated for a moment, pulling his lips into a thin line as he deliberated. Finally, he grumbled, "Okay, you're right."

We pushed to our feet and retreated farther from the house, backing into the woods as the group continued to argue among themselves. I walked on the pads of my feet, trying to keep as quiet as possible despite the dried leaves and crunchy winter grass.

"Shit." Thor grabbed the map and ran his eyes over it. "The closest town is fifteen miles south of here."

"That's a six-hour hike."

"Guess we better get started."

I didn't like it, but I didn't argue. It was almost three in the afternoon. It would be close to ten or eleven by the time we made it there, assuming the terrain was easy going once the sun went down and we didn't take many breaks. If we started now, perhaps we could hide from the Caputis until things settled. Then who the hell knew? We could get a taxi and go back to the Impala to regroup. Maybe Aris could send reinforcements.

"Hey!" came the shout from our right. "Who the fuck are you?"

I whirled in that direction, surprised someone had snuck up on us, but Thor had already launched into action. He had a knife in his hand, slicing across the man's throat before I realized it was a Caputi.

Thor put his finger over his mouth, gesturing me to be quiet so we could listen for anyone else. This guy probably wasn't alone, but when the only sounds that came were from my own heartbeat, Thor searched the guy for anything we could use—two nine millimeters and a hunting knife. After slamming his phone on a nearby rock, we shoved some leaves over his corpse. It wouldn't take much for someone else to find him, but it would buy us some time.

Then we carried on.

As we walked in silence, making sure to keep our footsteps light so no one tracking us could hear us, I shamed myself for not taking care of Nikki when I had the chance. I should have gone straight into her place last night, consequences be damned. Who cared if I was outnumbered? Who cared if I didn't have a plan? I could have taken her out before her accomplices took me out, and then all of this would have been over.

I should have seen this coming. Nikki was a survivor first. Of course, she'd cut a deal with the Caputis. Of course, she'd figure out a way to weasel herself out of this one. When I found her, I swore to God I'd wring her fucking neck with my bare hands before I stabbed her with my special blend of forty herbs and spices.

16

THOR

"Goddamn it!" Selene held her phone up higher. "If I could get to the top of the mountain—"

"No." I pushed farther into the woods and hitched my pack higher on my shoulders. "We need to keep going."

I knew this was a trap from the beginning. They'd lured us up here, not caring which ones came, only that they had some leverage. They had my truck, which meant they knew who I was. It wouldn't take them long to sort through her shit and figure out who she was, too.

I'd left my satellite phone in my primary bug-out bag, choosing the lighter one to watch Nikki since I figured we'd make our way back to my truck by nightfall. Regret punched me in the gut as Selene struggled with hers.

She ran her hands back through her hair, clenching big fistfuls while she led the way in front of me. She'd suggested stopping before sunset to make camp, and I was starting to agree with her. Basic survival said that if you were lost in the woods and you wanted to be found, stay put. If you were running from someone or something, keep moving. But it was going to drop below freezing tonight, and for the end of November in Buffalo, we were lucky there wasn't already a foot of snow on the ground.

"We should look for firewood," she said again, "and a place to sleep while we still have some daylight."

I smirked and tried not to be insulted by my own words coming out of her mouth. I had trained her well.

"We'll have a better chance at hiding once the sun goes down." We only had another half hour or so before we could take advantage of cover. Even then, it was only a matter of time before our luck ran out. Aris had promised to send reinforcements if I missed a check-in, but the Caputis were violent, impulsive idiots. We might not make it that long.

Selene climbed over a fallen tree and waited for me to do the same before walking again.

"We should make for the river," she said, glancing down at her map again. "Follow that to hide our scent. Just in case they bring dogs."

"Wet socks in freezing temperatures means frostbite." We had our sleeping bags and the heater, but that would only get us so far. "Did you bring a change of clothes?"

"Hmm...We're two miles from the road." She shrugged. "We could head there and look for someone who lives local. Maybe we can steal a car to get us to town faster."

"The Caputis are going to be trolling those streets, searching for us." I shook my head. "It's too risky."

"So we're just gonna wander through the woods after dark?"

I laughed despite our desperate circumstances. "Are you scared?"

She shot a biting glance over her shoulder. "No."

"Then what's the problem?" I raised an eyebrow and watched her ass through the camo pants. I shouldn't have been eyeing her up like that, not when I was supposed to be focused on getting us out of this shitty situation, but fuck, her hips were Gods damned mesmerizing. "Weren't you the one hell bent on revenge, no matter what?"

"Getting shot in the head by the Caputis is different from getting mauled to death by a mountain lion."

"You'd be lucky if all they did was shoot you in the head." Truth be said, if we got caught, they'd do horrifying things to both of us. A few months ago, they had taken one of my brothers, Lore, as a hostage. They'd tortured him for weeks before carving out an eye and sending him back to us, clinging to life. We'd wish for death before it took us. "I'd take the mountain lion."

She smirked and stopped, nodding to a group of rocks to our right before looking down at the map. "That's supposed to be an old mine shaft. I bet there's a nice, cozy tunnel for us to crash in, just for a few hours."

I pursed my lips and took the map from her, glancing down again before ultimately relenting. Caves and mines were notoriously unstable, but I didn't have any better ideas and my cheeks had started to protest the rising cold in the air. We couldn't walk through the night, and we couldn't risk being exposed to the elements should a storm sweep through. Hypothermia was the silent killer. It lured you to sleep before choking the life from your lungs, and we'd come too far for this to end that way.

"Fine," I said, gesturing her ahead of me again.

She grinned in victory and hitched her pack higher on her shoulders as she walked in that direction. We'd brought our sleeping bags and a few rifles with us, but I lamented the food and other camping materials in the back seat of my truck. No way we'd get to them now, but still…the thought of what could sneak up on us in that mine shaft only made me slightly more unsettled than the Caputis cornering us at the end of it.

We rounded the edge of the cliff face and found a break in the rocks that led to a clearing ten feet tall and eight feet wide, just big enough to house two humans looking for a quiet place to hunker down. I grabbed my flashlight out of my pack and clicked it on, shining it down the path. Perhaps once it had gone farther back, but time or the local government had long since sealed it up with rocks. Graffiti decorated the mossy granite sides and old beer bottles lay in the far corners. We weren't the first ones to use this place as a hideaway from the world.

When I glanced back at Selene, she sat on the dirt and opened her pack to riffle through it for her sleeping bag and MREs.

"We'll have to zip our bags together," she said. "Conserve body heat."

I tried to hide my smile at the thought of curling up next to her all night. Once, the mere suggestion of it would have sent me into an existential crisis. I'd slept next to her before, definitely, but never so close. Never like this. As she zipped our flannel pouches together, I imagined cuddling her close, knowing anything that came for her would have to go through me first.

"What?" She'd caught me staring at her, and I shook my head, taking a deep breath as I retreated toward the entrance again.

"I'll find wood for a fire." I pulled my hair away from my face and ducked through the rocks.

"See if you can find a better dinner, too," she called after me.

I did. After I gathered enough wood and kindling to get us started, I found a group of wild turkeys and took one out with my knife through the eye. It wasn't huge, so it wouldn't last us more than tonight, but it was enough to sate us both.

While she built the fire and I dressed our supper, we talked about what we should do next. Assuming we made it to the morning without the Caputis or the Kings of Carnage tracking us, she still thought heading back to the Impala was the best idea.

"I left it hidden in the woods," she said, blowing on the small flame as she sparked her lighter in other places around the leaves in the center. "Even if Nikki knew we were behind her house, they wouldn't have known the Impala was ours."

"It's risky," I said, using my hunting knife to finish cleaning the turkey. Just a few more slices would make it ready for the fire once Selene got it hot enough. "I think we should hide out for another day or two and wait for reinforcements. Aris said he would send someone after us if we didn't check in. In an hour or two, the brothers will be on their way."

Her features dropped like I'd spoiled the end of her new favorite book. She evidently did not like that plan.

"We're vastly outnumbered, kitten," I said. "If there were ten of them, sure. You and I could probably knock that out...*probably*. But I counted twenty in that house, and more when the others arrived. They were expecting an army to come after them, not the two of us."

She gulped and went back to poking at her fire, adding more twigs to make the flames grow.

"We could hit them at night when they're asleep," she said, grasping at straws.

"I know you want her blood." I paused, glancing up at her while she rationalized continuing her hunt for Nikki. "Believe me, I do, too. So does the whole MC after what happened at the Beacon, but we need to be careful. I won't lose you at the expense of revenge."

She sat back on her haunches, sighing as she ran her gaze over me, scalding me where I sat.

"What? What are you thinking?" I asked once I couldn't stand it any longer.

"Remember when the Roses sent you after Joseph Parris?" She raised an eyebrow, bending one leg so she could rest her arm across it. "It was supposed to be just you, but there were too many and you called me in at the last minute."

I cleared my throat, recalling that raid. It had been me and her up against fifty Caputi cronies that reported to a boss named Parris. She couldn't have been more than twenty-one at the time. We had swept the place in under ten minutes, fucking precision in action.

"That was different," I said. "We had a plan, we were heavily armed, and we had backup on standby."

"I'm just saying"—she flashed me a trademark Montgomery grin —"we're a good team."

Yeah, we fucking were, and in the deepest part of my heart, I'd admit that was one of the things I loved about our relationship. If I had to disappear into the woods with only one person at my side, only one person to spend the rest of my life with, it would be her. No question. No contest.

"If we can get to the Impala, there's more guns in the trunk," she said. "We can regroup with whoever Aris sends our way and finish this."

"Let's just focus on dinner and getting some rest right now, okay?"

She nodded, but didn't have much to say after that. Once the fire roared to life, I fashioned a rotisserie over the flames big enough to hold the meat so it could cook.

"What happens with Dante and Geri?" I asked, gesturing to her pack where she'd stuffed her e-reader.

She chuckled and shook her head, piling some jerky into her mouth from the MRE bag in front of her. "Dante fucks her brains out, Geri gets pregnant, and they kill her father together."

I pursed my lips, considering this. "I can see why you're into that."

"Are you saying you're not?" Her eyes met mine across the fire, her cheeks blooming with that adorable blush.

"Kitten, I'm into whatever you're into."

Selene giggled, and the sound sparked a small flicker of joy in my gut. Sure, we were trapped in the Adirondacks with only what we had on our backs, but if I could make her smile, then life still had meaning. She pulled out her e-reader, turned it on, and sat back to whisper the next few chapters while I tended to our dinner.

Turned out, Dante and I had a lot in common—we were fucking obsessed with our women, and we'd go to amazing lengths to protect them.

I TOOK THE FIRST WATCH, slipping behind Selene in the sleeping bag to wrap her close to my chest, my arm around her body. I could have sworn she fell asleep in seconds, faster than any other time we'd camped like this. I tried not to let it get to my head.

If we made it out of this alive, there would be no going back to the way things were. I couldn't pretend anymore. Inhaling her flowery scent, I made us both a promise in that freezing, filthy cave. I wouldn't let our own stubbornness hold us back from happiness any longer.

I'd faced the possibility of losing her too many times in such a short period, and I couldn't do it again.

She completed me in ways that I'd never considered before. She softened where I was hard. She urged action where I might freeze from indecision. Separately, we were both lethal, but together, we were terrifying.

What if we have to face the entire Caputi army?

I clenched my eyes shut and tried to form a plan. If it came to it, we'd have to get uphill as fast as we could. We had two rifles between us and a few handguns. If we were precise, we had the ammo to take out nearly half of them before we'd have to fight hand to hand. After that, I just prayed they didn't send more than we could handle.

Every so often, I extracted myself from Selene's embrace to put another log on our tiny fire or check for predators near the opening. Owls hooted in the distance, providing the backdrop to other winter creatures making their way into hibernation. A wolf howled somewhere to the north, sending chills down my spine as a few others joined in, reminding me we were at home among the wild things.

"Everything okay?" Selene asked, pushing herself upright.

I nodded and blew hot air into my hands, lying down in the sleeping bag with her.

"Go back to sleep." I tucked her in close, her back to my chest, her ass perfectly snug against my pelvis. "We still have a few hours before dawn."

"What about you?" she said. "Don't you need to rest?"

"I'm all right, kitten." I kissed her temple, nudging her with my nose to encourage her to listen to me, but just like my stubborn wildcat, she fought back.

"If you're having trouble falling asleep," she murmured playfully, rolling over to face me and tucking her warm fingers up against the button on my jeans. "I could help you find some...release."

Gods help me, I wanted to give in. She peered up at me with those big blue eyes and that grin on her pouty lips, and I turned to mush. Our connection had felt so good...*too* good...and even though a distraction sounded fan-fucking-tastic right now, we needed to stay focused.

Another howl sounded outside the cave, this time closer, and I narrowed my eyes as a suspicious chill snaked down the center of my chest into my gut. My instincts went on high alert, the beast inside me rearing up for an entirely different reason.

That doesn't sound like a wolf.

No, that sounded like...

Selene kissed the side of my neck, sliding her hand down the front of my pants, and if I hadn't heard the noise again, I would have forgotten about it. But this time, the pitch was off and it didn't echo quite as deep or as long. Which meant it wasn't wolves...it was dogs.

"Shit," I said, yanking Selene's hand out of my pants and shoving to my feet. "Get up."

"What?" She wiped at her sleepy eyes.

"Do you hear that?"

"Hear what?" She squinted up at me, looking so adorable in the firelight. But panic had already seized my reflexes, and I had my rifle in one hand while I kicked out the fire with my boots.

The howling came again, this time louder and more intense. That got her attention, and she stood, quickly moving into action to repack her bag with the essentials. Shouts punctuated the growling animals this time, at least four or five distinct voices, and they weren't that far behind us.

Fuck, we need to move.

"Run," I told her, forgoing most of my supplies in favor of grabbing our guns. She took off next to me, leaping over a log as we raced through the undergrowth. "Go, go."

"The river is up there." Selene pointed toward her right, and we ran as fast as we could. Even though I was a lot taller than her, she had long legs that could open up into a massive stride if she tried. Heart pounding and scalp prickling, I pumped my arms, tightening my grip on my rifle as I went. The fuckers gained on us, the barking closer now, punctuated by shouting voices.

"This way," they said. "I see them. I hear them."

"Fuck." I paused to aim my gun at the closest person, taking a deep breath before firing. I nailed him in the shoulder, making him collapse to the ground. We'd gotten a moment's reprieve, a few more seconds' head start, but it wouldn't last for long. I'd given away our location; the others were heading our way now.

We sprinted, jumping over obstacles and dodging trees. Selene was a streak of brown hair in the distance ahead of me. If I stopped here to take as many of them out as I could, she would have a better chance at getting away.

"Keep going, Montgomery," I said, slowing my pace so I could duck behind a thick pine and take aim again. I angled for a tall fucker with two dogs in front of him. Careful not to hit the animals, I shot the man's face clean off his body. Then another. And another. When my rifle was out of bullets, I switched to my pistol, knowing I'd get the next six or seven of them before they caught up to me.

Selene slumped down to my left, raising her own rifle to take a shot.

"Montgomery, get the fuck out of here." I growled and fired, clipping one cocksucker in the arm before nearly getting hit in the head myself. I ducked out of the way at the last second. They were getting closer now, at least twenty of them with half as many dogs.

"Fuck off," she snarled, taking another two out in quick succession. "I'm not leaving you."

"That wasn't a request."

"I don't take orders from you."

Her presence frustrated me, but I couldn't focus on that. I'd managed to take out another Caputi when one of the hounds finally got close enough to strike. The German Shepherd whipped around the tree, teeth bared, barking and growling, seemingly waiting for the command to lock onto my arm. I didn't want to hurt it. I'd always been an animal person. So I took aim at the ground nearby, firing off a round or two, which sent it whimpering back to its owners. That was enough to make the other canines unsure, and they stopped barking to pull back.

The Caputis didn't care. They kept coming, some even letting the beasts go when they wouldn't lunge forward anymore. I fired until my clip was empty, and then I tossed that to the side, grabbing my hunting knife out of my boot. I wouldn't go down without a fight, and if I knew my kitten, she lived by the same creed.

We'd managed to knock them down to ten by the time they gained on us, but even on our best day, five to one with only our knives to play with were pretty miserable odds. Heart pounding and vision crisp, I let my inner beast out of its cage. It prepared for a rampage of epic levels, shoving whatever morality Thor the person had to the darkest parts of my heart.

Selene let out a war cry and jumped on the first guy who came near us, repeatedly stabbing his face with her knife. I sliced at the Caputi fuck with blond hair, ignoring the snapping dogs in the background as I slit his neck open, hot, sticky blood pouring from the gaping wound. He grabbed at it and backed away, falling to his knees while I went after the next guy. He held a gun to my head, but I could see his weak grip from here, so I transferred my knife to my left hand and waited until he was on his nondominant foot.

Then I snapped out and reversed the gun in his grip, forcing it into my own palm. I squeezed the trigger and his brains exploded out the back of his head. On autopilot, I shot the three guys closest to us. They dropped to the ground, and I stepped over their corpses to fire at the remaining assassins.

I turned and froze.

"Drop the gun," the Caputi fuck said. He had Selene in a headlock, a nine millimeter to her temple. Her busted lip oozed blood down her chin, and her crimson cheek would be bruised in a few hours. The pile of bodies around her told me she'd fought her hardest, only to be bested by someone that was as tall as me and weighed at least a hundred pounds more.

We'd almost made it.

Within milliseconds, I assessed my options. I could do as he asked and submit to whatever these sick fucks had planned for us. Or I could keep fighting.

The crazed look in Selene's eyes told me which one she'd prefer, and if she could get him to stop moving, I could hit him in the head.

"Don't be stupid," he said. "There's four guys behind me. Put it down."

I took a deep breath, memorizing the beat of my heart. *Inhale...Ba-da...Exhale...Da-dum...Inhale...*

I raised my gun and took a quick shot, hitting the guy right between the eyes. His gun went off, but Selene had jerked, moving just enough so the bullet went over her head. I grabbed her hand and turned to run, but I met eyes with a dark-haired Caputi, gun raised over his head.

Before I could react, he brought it down on my temple and the world went dark.

17

SELENE

Thor dropped and the control inside me snapped. No one hurt him. *No one.*

I threw my knife at the guy who'd pistol-whipped him, nailing him right in the eye. He stumbled backward as I picked up the gun Thor dropped, shooting before thinking, hitting three guys in the chest before one wrapped his arms around my torso like a vise, lifting me up in the air. I threw my head back, crunching my attacker in the nose to make them let me go, but it did no good. There were more of them waiting to attack me. It was like a scene from a movie where no matter how many bad guys I killed, they just kept coming. Nothing stopped them.

"Selene, give up," a familiar high-pitched voice said.

I whirled, the barrel of my pistol pointed right at Nikki's stupid face. In all the fighting, I'd forgotten she was a part of this. Now, she stood in front of me with the same shade of box-colored blond on her head and a revolver aimed back at my head. We were face-to-face, each one of us panting down the adrenaline-laced high of a chase at its conclusion.

"Can't you see this is pointless?" she said, furrowing her brows. "Can't you see we've won?"

The remaining dogs barked in the distance, still circling us and waiting for the word to attack, the others having run off to seek shelter once the bullets started popping. The shouts from more men echoed in the distance, but I didn't care. *Let them come.* I'd make a fucking mess in these woods. I'd paint the trees red and leave a feast for the scavengers.

"You're lucky they found you first," I said. "I would've fed you to those dogs by now."

Nikki laughed, shaking her head and rolling her eyes. "You're so stupid. This is a trap, Selene. This has been a trap the whole time."

I'd figured that much out for myself. Hell, Thor had told me that when he arrived, but I was tired of talking. At this point, I didn't care if she killed me in the process of me killing her—as long as she went down with me. All it would take was one pull of the trigger, one single shot, and this would be over.

"Enough," came another voice, this one deeper and more harsh. Men moved out of the shadows, seven of them circling me. Some had on suits, identifying them as Caputi. Two others had on Kings of Carnage cuts with nicknames that read *Cheesecake* and *Hooch.* "That's enough, Nikki. We promised we'd bring them in alive."

Hooch walked closer to me, a tall man with black hair and dark tanned skin, and held out a hand, approaching slowly like he would to a scared horse.

"Easy now," he said. "We're not going to hurt you."

I could shoot him. I could shoot him and then shoot Nikki, and it would be done. But the others would fill me with bullets so quick, I wouldn't live to see the ground. If only Thor wasn't there, if only the stupid fuck hadn't followed me, if only it had just been me. This would have been an easier choice.

Instead, I let him take the gun from me.

"There ya go." Cheesecake circled around me to pat me down, removing both of my hunting knives, my other pistol, and the small pigsticker I kept in my boot. He took my phone and smashed it to bits right there in the forest. My heart raced when his hand neared the bulge in my pants where I kept my dirty little secrets, but he kept going, either missing them or thinking they were part of the fabric. "Jesus, she's loaded down for a doctor."

These were my hunting clothes for a reason. My pants had a hidden pocket where I'd stuffed a few essentials, like the poison I planned to use to make Nikki suffer. If things got bad enough, I might have to use it on myself.

"Don't let her occupation fool you," the rat bitch said. "She's more deadly than the big guy."

This inspired Cheesecake, who turned his big, dopey brown eyes toward me. "Are you?" His grin taunted me to make a spectacle of myself, as if all the people me and Thor took out weren't proof enough. "What about that pesky little oath?"

I grinned and snapped my teeth at him, causing him to rear back with shocked, wide eyes.

"Don't fuck with her, Cheese," Hooch said, wrapping my arms behind my back so he could put the cuffs on me. I smiled, knowing these wouldn't hold me for long. I'd wait for the right time, when both Thor and I could escape safely, and then I'd attack. They gagged me with a sweaty, disgusting bandanna, and I nearly vomited, forcing myself to take a deep breath to calm my stomach.

Once they had the cuffs on me, I smirked and walked with them while four Caputis struggled to carry Thor's dead weight. Some of the dogs walked back to the car with us, letting out a snarl or a growl every so often, and when we got there, one of the guys mentioned rounding them all up.

Yeah, it was fucking ridiculous to be worried about dogs while me and my mentor were getting shackled and stuffed in the back of a Range Rover, but I was a sentimental shit. They pushed Thor in next to me, still unconscious. He slumped against the back seat, his breathing relatively even. That calmed my panic. I didn't know how hard they'd hit him, but if he was still out after all that jostling, he might have a concussion when he woke up.

Cheesecake slammed the hatch closed, locking the two of us in silence while they debated what to do next.

"Are you sure they're alone?" Hooch said, his voice muffled by the windows. "That's a lot of guys to take out for just the two of them."

"You saw the heat she was packing, and that wasn't even half of what we found in the Silverado," Cheesecake said, making me smile with a sick pride. "If she was loaded down like that, you can bet he was, too."

"The Roses don't fuck around," Nikki added. "They'll send people after them; you can be sure of it. You'll get what you want."

A few Caputis walked closer, crowding Nikki toward the SUV. I saw the back of her head from my spot on the ground, and I resisted the urge to buck out of these cuffs and stab her with the syringe in my pocket.

"You better be sure about that. The boss is on the way," one of the Caputis said, lighting a cigarette. "Where are you taking them?"

"We have a bunker a few miles from here," Cheesecake said. "It's underground. No one knows it's there."

"Perfect, let's go." Cigarette Caputi nodded toward the front of the Range Rover.

"Now, hold on a second, Jimmy," Hooch cut in. "This ain't *our* bunker. It belongs to the MC."

"How is this my problem?" Jimmy seemed annoyed by the question, taking another long drag on his cigarette.

"We can't show up unannounced with a Rose and their doctor in tow. Prez ain't gonna like that." Hooch rubbed the back of his head.

"Call your president." Jimmy shrugged, clearly growing more bored by the second. "Tell him about our deal."

"Wait." Cheesecake put up his hand and pulled Hooch to the side, curling an arm over his shoulder while he spoke in a hushed tone. I couldn't make out all of it, being inside the car, but I overheard, "...no one has to know."

The whole picture came together. Most of the guys who had come after us tonight were Caputis. Whatever deal Cheesecake and Hooch made with them, they evidently hadn't shared with everyone else in the MC. If they survived the rest of the night, they were looking at splitting the deal between the two of them instead of the entire club.

Jesus, what fucking idiots. *When* their Prez found out, not *if,* they would both have their heads on the chopping blocks. I'd be willing to bet Nikki would make it out of that alive, too, the fucking cockroach.

"Time's wasting, boys." Jimmy flicked the butt to the ground and turned to Nikki and her MC idiots.

"Let's do it," she said. "We can take them there for now. No one will know." She wrapped an arm over Hooch's shoulder. "Right, Hooch? It'll be our secret."

Her blatant manipulation disgusted me. I thought of how she used to do that to my brother, though I'd like to think a part of her had really cared for him. These two suckers were pawns, dispensable pieces in her game of survival. If they both died during the course of this, Nikki wouldn't bat an eye.

"Archie," Jimmy said, pointing to one of the other Caputi men. "Call a cleanup crew. Take our guys home. Dispose of the rest."

Hooch clearly didn't like that either, but he didn't argue. He nodded and circled around to the passenger seat while Jimmy hopped in the driver's side. Nikki, Cheesecake, and another Caputi got in the back before we took off.

Cheesecake glanced in the back occasionally, and each time he did, I made eye contact with him. He shifted uncomfortably and turned his gaze back to the front.

Hah! If I hadn't been gagged, I might have teased him with a sarcastic, *"First time abducting someone?"* Fucking newb.

I scooted my foot down closer to Thor's arms, tapping him twice on the elbow to try to get his attention. When he didn't respond, I took deep breaths to calm down my heart rate. Getting panicked wouldn't help us in this situation. I glanced out the back window, dismayed to find at least three other black SUVs following us. Even after that massacre in the woods, we were still completely outnumbered.

I closed my eyes and shoved all of my emotions into their proper place on the shelves in my mental sanctuary. I needed to hear that cold, logical voice, that one that had never steered me wrong. My pulse thumped, hard and steady, and the night air slid down the back of my throat with a refreshing coolness that brought me back to my senses.

A few minutes later, the SUVs behind us turned off, leaving just us as we continued higher into the mountains. Cheesecake and Hooch mentioned a bunker underground, and I was certain that once we were inside, we would have a helluva time getting out. I needed Thor to wake the fuck up so we could attack the second they opened this door. He had been doing check-ins with Aris, and as soon as he missed one, the calvary would descend. But from what Hooch said, it sounded like the rest of the Kings of Carnage didn't know this was happening.

"Right up here," Hooch said, and I waited for the SUV to slow down, preparing to push my thumb out of place so I could slip the cuffs off.

I hesitated when I looked at Thor again, and he'd blinked his eyes open. I widened mine, hopefully telling him I was going to spring as soon as I could, but then I hesitated. If he had a concussion, he needed some time to regroup. He'd been out this whole time. He had no idea what was happening. If we were to have a fighting chance, I needed him in working order.

"Whoa," Jimmy said. "This place is like Fort Knox."

My heart dropped, dread lining my stomach as we slowed so he could punch in a code to open the security gates, and when they squeaked apart, I cringed. They called it a bunker for a reason. It would be incredibly hard to overtake anyone in this place, and knowing that, I braced myself for the worst.

18

SELENE

They blindfolded me when they took me out of the back, a guy on each arm leading me through this supposed bunker. It smelled dank inside, like wet grass and decaying moss. Hooch had said we were underground, but I guessed a cave system, especially given the squishy earth under my boots.

Eventually, that gave way to concrete, and judging by the echo on the walls, I suspected we were in a more developed area. My heart raced as I tried to figure out what to do. Thor's boots kept step behind me as we walked, reminding me I wasn't alone. I wanted to get this blindfold off so I could assess him and make sure he was okay.

When they did finally remove the bandanna around my eyes and the disgusting one between my lips, I blinked against bright fluorescent lights hanging in the middle of the room. Thick metal bars surrounded me, my six-by-six cell immediately setting off the part of my monster that hated being confined. By the door, four men stood with their guns pointed at me, daring me to make a move—Jimmy, Cheesecake, Hooch, and another Caputi.

Thor groaned from the space next to me, his own band of assholes making sure he stayed still while they handcuffed him to the bench in the corner of his cell. I'd been attached to mine by a thick length of chain. Given the state of things, the cuffs remained on for the time being.

"You know who we are?" Jimmy said.

"Of course," I replied, stretching my jaw. "You know who we are?"

Jimmy smirked and shook his head, the gel in his hair catching on the light coming from above the table just outside our cells. "You got a smart mouth; real nice and pretty, too."

I scoffed. *Original.* Glancing at Hooch and Cheesecake, I repeated my question. "Do *you* know who we are?"

"I don't give a shit," Cheesecake said. "Just some Rose slut."

That made me laugh, considering who the hell he was sleeping with these days. "I'm going to get out of here." I shook my head at these idiots. "And when I do, I'm going to take my hunting knife"—I eyed it on his belt—"and I'm going to stab your fucking eyes out with it."

He looked at Jimmy and Hooch before closing the distance between us and smacking me so hard that my head whipped to the side and my ears rang. Agony ricocheted down that side of my body, but I couldn't let him have the satisfaction. I'd bitten my lip and blood dripped down my chin as I turned back to him and smiled.

"Leave her be," Jimmy said. "At least until the boss gets here."

That had to be Gabriella. With Leo still locked up, there was no other Caputi boss to come.

"You two, watch them." Jimmy pointed at the MC brothers. "Make sure they don't talk to each other, got it?"

Hooch rubbed at the back of his neck, clearly uncomfortable with our presence here. Jimmy gestured to his other Caputi guys and walked through the door, leaving the four of us alone. Hooch turned on his buddy and glared at him.

"This is fucking stupid, Cheese, even for us." Hooch ran his hands over his face.

"Listen, brother." He put his palms on Hooch's shoulders and met his eyes. "They're paying us two hundred grand each. With that kind of cash, we can skip town, never see the Kings again."

"Prez would never let us go." Hooch shook his head, and I glanced at Thor, who now sat at the opposite end of his cell, facing me. He looked more focused, like he'd finally gotten his bearings back, and the expression dancing behind his eyes told me he was thinking the same thing I was. Of the two, Hooch was clearly the weaker link.

"Prez won't be able to find us." Cheese gave his buddy a shake. "Get your head in the game, brother."

If the Kings were anything like the Roses, once the president found out they'd gone behind his back, made a deal with an outside group, and bombed another MC to do it, he'd fucking kill them. But that was assuming I didn't get the opportunity first.

I looked around for security systems, a window, anything anyone could use to find us. Three cameras sat in either corner, one behind me, one behind Thor, and one diagonally from my cell. Red lights blinked on either side of the lenses, but that didn't mean they worked.

Thor cleared his throat while Cheese and Hooch talked in hushed tones, and I glanced up at him. He blinked at me three times in long, slow succession, followed by a longer one, a quick one, and another longer one.

Fuck. Morse code.

He'd made me memorize it when I was younger, but it had been a while since I'd brushed up on it and I didn't know if I still knew the alphabet. When I winced, he tried again, taking his time. I was pretty sure the first letter was an O, and the second was...J? No, K.

He was asking me if I was ok. I nodded and gestured back to him. He nodded and blinked out the letters for *H-E-A-D*. He had a headache. That figured; he'd been hit pretty hard.

I tried my best to blink back *O-U-T,* but he shook his head, either telling me there was no way out or he didn't understand what I'd meant.

W-A-I-T, he said.

Wait? For what?

I could break out of these cuffs, lure Hooch over, knock him out, and steal the keys. End of story. Except...I didn't know how far the Caputis had gone. If I broke out of this room only to be detained again once I got into the other parts of the bunker, it would all be for nothing. They would secure me harder next time, and I would have wasted my advantage.

A-R-I-S, he blinked.

He was banking on the Roses finding us. Sure, that might have been a good plan if we'd been able to stay in the woods. Now we were at a secondary location. The Roses would find the Impala and maybe the things in our cave, but after that, they'd be unable to tell where we'd gone. Even if they brought dogs, the trail would lead to wherever they'd put us in the SUV, and after that, poof. Nothing. Nada. Dust in the wind.

When I'd been researching Nikki, I hadn't come across any bunker. It would take Crow or Aris reaching out to the Kings of Carnage for help, and that was assuming they would even give it.

No, we were on our own. We had to get out of here as soon as we could.

"He said his boss will be here tomorrow morning," Cheesecake said, bringing my attention back to their conversation. "You only have to hold out for the night. Come on, let's go find something to eat." Cheesecake nodded toward the entry.

"They said not to leave them alone." Hooch looked at us before glancing back to his friend.

"It'll be fine. C'mon." Cheesecake headed out, clearly not afraid of the Caputis should he break their commands. My heart nearly skipped when I thought Hooch might stay. I figured I could talk sense into him, maybe try to reason with whatever had made him join a motorcycle club. We weren't so different, after all. We were the same species, just with different stripes. He couldn't side with the fucking mafia over us. But I didn't get a chance. With one last look full of regret, Hooch left me and Thor alone to follow his friend through the doorway.

I pulled as close as I could to the bars between me and Thor, jolted to a stop two feet from the bench when the chain snapped taut.

"We have to get out of here," I murmured.

"I'm dizzy." He clenched his eyes shut and shook his head.

"It's probably mild. It should go away soon." Even I had to admit, from this far away, I couldn't be certain.

"Gabriella's the boss," he said, his tone softer now, like he was trying to comfort me. "She's not as ruthless as Leo and Benito."

I sighed, pacing back to the bench so I could sit and run a finger over my forehead. "I'm not so sure about that."

"She's more strategic," he went on. "She's been trying to cut us off at the knees, making deals with the Canadians and the IRA. We're more valuable to her alive."

"Ru once said something that's always stuck with me."

He raised an eyebrow, gesturing for me to go on.

"She's a woman fighting a blood feud in a man's world. Whatever she's done to get the Caputis' respect should terrify you."

Thor straightened and shifted his shoulders, like he was only now coming to this realization. What it must be like to be a cis-het man in a society designed around oneself?

"She's dangerous. She promised us retribution," I continued. "And when Nikki tells her who I am, who I *really* am, she won't think twice about wrapping my guts around my throat."

Last year, Jer had killed Benito Caputi by stabbing him in the neck. I'd helped from the sidelines, taking out at least six of those cocksuckers on my own. In return, Gabriella had promised us her wrath.

"You know what happens next," Thor said, bringing me back to reality.

Yeah, I knew. If Gabriella didn't immediately kill us, she'd sic her cronies to torture us. They'd use us against each other by hurting me in front of him and saying it would stop if he cracked or vice versa. As far as I knew, Thor wouldn't break. Not for me. Not for himself. Not for anyone. He'd taken a vow when he joined the MC, and he'd never betray it.

As for me, well, there was nothing these fuckers could do to me that I hadn't already imagined. I'd destroy my mental library if I had to. I'd burn it all down before talking. I clutched the syringes in the hidden pocket of my pants, deciding not to tell Thor about them until

I absolutely had to. We could use them to kill ourselves if things got too bad. But, until that time, it was better if I was the only one who knew they were there.

Hours passed like millennia. Cheese brought us microwavable dinners after the sun went down, but didn't say anything about our conversation if he'd overheard us. They were supposed to be keeping watch, but they'd done a piss-poor job thus far. If I wanted to get out of the cell, I could have already done it. But I didn't know what waited for me on the other side of that door, and until I had Thor as backup, there was no need to do anything rash.

"Well, well, well," Nikki cooed, walking into the room with her arms crossed. "How the tables have turned."

She'd cleaned herself up after the massacre in the woods, and I envied her fresh, clean skin. I still had the blood of multiple other people under my fingernails, itching and flaking off my hands and wrists. I probably had more than I'd like to know in my hair. She walked to my cell door, leaning toward it so she could rest her forearms on the horizontal bar at chest height.

I didn't acknowledge her presence, just continued to stare at Thor across the jail.

"You thought you could track me down?" She laughed. "You know me better than that, Sel. Give me *some* credit."

Yep, I knew her. Just like I knew she'd inevitably come here to gloat. She'd taken out the Beacon in some obnoxious display of violence. It had been about more than hurting the MC. It was personal. She'd purposely lured me out, and now that she thought she had the upper hand, she wouldn't miss the opportunity to show off.

Do it. Right now, the cold voice said. *Draw her closer. Stab her in the neck like Giuseppe Caputi.*

Again, I clutched the hidden syringes at the waistband of my pants, but said nothing.

"Yeah, you always could do that, huh? Lock it down. Turn it all off." Nikki sighed and tsked like we were children. "Look at you. You don't even seem scared."

"I'm not." I didn't say it because she goaded me, though she had. I said it because I wanted her to remember, *really* remember, who I was.

She started dating my brother when we were fifteen. She'd been around the house when Thor and I had disappeared for weekends at a time, only to return with a ten-point buck and a winter's worth of venison for the club. She'd watched me date Billy, had been around when he mysteriously disappeared and I refused to talk about it. Certainly, the only people who knew were Thor and me, but everyone else talked. They suspected. Nikki had stood by Jer's side when he sent me off to college and medical school, tears in his eyes at the thought of having to be without his twin sister for even a day, let alone months on end. Hadn't she said it earlier? I was more deadly than the big guy.

She was right.

"You should be." Nikki straightened and looked at Thor. "You both should be. Gabriella..." She shook her head, almost like she couldn't bear the thought of continuing her sentence. "She's a vicious, terrible woman." Her eyes glazed over and her cheeks flushed as she touched her lips and cleared her throat. Clearly, whatever she was thinking about wasn't happy.

"Why are you doing this, Nik?" I used her nickname, the one Jer called her, hoping it might stoke whatever familial bond still existed inside her rotten, despicable heart. "Didn't we mean anything to you?"

"Sure, and then Crow threatened to rip out my tongue and feed it to the pigs."

I chuckled, remembering my uncle telling her that in the waiting room in the hospital after Benito Caputi had abducted Alba and Ru last year. Trojan was in intensive care, while five others needed patching up in the emergency department.

"I did what I had to do," she hissed through a tearful grimace.

"Whatever you have to tell yourself at night," I said.

"Enough," Thor cut in, staring me down. "She's not worth your breath."

He was right, but his interruption had gotten Nikki's attention. She turned to him, that obnoxious smirk coming back to her lips. "Is that what you think? Then why am I out here and you're trapped in a cage?" She let out a giggle that sounded more like a cackle. "This is where you belong, you know? Yeah, I heard the stories. I know why they called you Thor." She walked closer to him, her boots echoing on the concrete. "You beat the former sarge's head in with a sledgehammer."

He had. He'd beat Billy's head in with one, too. They had both deserved it. The sickening crunch of metal on bone still haunted my nightmares.

"You're a monster. You all are," she went on.

I'd had enough. Like Thor said, she wasn't worth my breath, but I wouldn't sit here and listen to her vitriol, either. "Where's your baby, huh?"

She stiffened and turned to face me, rage replacing the fear in her eyes. Now she was the one with nothing to say.

"Did the Caputis keep it?" I shrugged, furrowing my brows in mock confusion. "Did you lose it? Give it up?" I laughed. She wasn't the only one who knew things that could hurt. "Leave it at a gas station? Didn't your mother do that to you once?"

She slammed her hands against the bars to get me to stop speaking, but I grinned, knowing I'd hit my mark. Those eyes brimmed with tears again, her teeth clenched so hard, the muscles in her jaw twitched. Something about her baby triggered her, and whatever it was, it flipped a switch in her expression. Before, she'd been arrogant and impudent. Now, she looked broken...maybe horrified.

"Don't talk about my child again," she hissed. "Or it'll be me cutting out your tongue."

She turned and walked away while I analyzed her reaction. I had expected hostility. What mother would want a known assassin asking questions about her child? But that horror in her eyes? Whatever flicked through her mind in the seconds before she spoke had rattled her so much that she couldn't continue with whatever she'd come to do in the first place. I looked at Thor, who took a deep breath and let it out on a sigh.

God, what a fucking mess she'd made. I wished I had heard from Marissa sooner. I wished I'd gone after her the first time she betrayed us. All of this could have been prevented, and maybe that baby would have still had a chance.

19

THOR

The longer that went by without them beating one of us, or at least threatening to do so, the more itchy I got. They were waiting for Gabriella to get here, but if the reverse had happened, they would not have been afforded the same courtesy. What were they planning? And why was it taking so long for Queen Bee to arrive? She was the richest woman in DC. She could have taken a personal jet and been here in an hour, two at the most.

Of course, like Selene had implied, these idiots weren't particularly threatening. I could use the metal on my belt to undo these cuffs and be out of these bars in a heartbeat. But I hadn't because I knew they were packing heat beyond that door, likely more if and when Gabriella got here.

"Before things get really bad, I wanted to say I'm sorry you got dragged into this," Selene said after hours of silence and darkness, drawing my attention back to her. "You shouldn't have followed me."

"You *wanted* me to." I raised an eyebrow at her. "Otherwise, you would have stolen a car instead of taking the Impala."

She gasped, blinking a few times at me like she hadn't considered the possibility. Then she hummed a soft approval and leaned her head back against the bars. "Maybe part of me did. The other part just wanted it to be over with. Nikki. The war. All of it."

"Is that why you didn't tell me what you were doing?" I didn't realize how much that had bothered me until we were sitting in a cell with the end likely to come in the morning. This might be the last time I get to have a heart-to-heart with her, so why not cut right to the chase? "Why you took off without telling anyone? Because you wanted it all to be over with?"

She didn't answer, which confirmed my suspicions.

"You didn't even say goodbye to your brother." If I were KC, I'd be pissed as fuck.

"That's not the point," she said. "This is about protecting them; it always has been."

"Bullshit," I said, anger starting to flare up in me for real now, heating my chest and my words as I continued. "This is about you thinking you have to fix what happened to your parents." She cleared her throat and shifted, widening her eyes, but I continued because I wanted her to hear me. Maybe, for the last time in her fucking life, she might actually listen. "You can't solve all the world's problems."

She shook her head. "I'm not trying to solve *all* the world's problems, just this one."

Gods, she loved the fight, and if my trepidation about what would happen next wasn't filling my stomach like concrete, I'd lean into the tease. But any second, Gabriella would barrel through that door and our easy stay at Chez Dungeon would be over.

"The best way you could've protected your family would have been to stay with them." An aching chasm opened in my chest at the thought that I'd come so close to losing her. If I hadn't been here, she would have already gone out in a blaze of glory. Nikki would be dead, but so would Selene.

The thought fucking terrified me. I could not exist in a world without her.

Up until two days ago, I would have admitted to loving her the way any family member loved another. Hell, perhaps even then, it was more than it should have been. But staring at her from across that cell, trapped in yet another trench with this woman by my side, I yearned with longing so desperate and all-consuming, it vibrated through my marrow like electricity—the deep down sort of shit. We might die tomorrow, and I regretted all the years I'd spent letting her think she didn't mean as much to me as she did.

"My family has each other." Even from this far away, I could see her blink back tears. "No one else was going to do this except for me. What else matters?"

That hurt even more. Why did she consider herself so dispensable? More importantly, why did she consider herself so dispensable *to me*? I'd never been selfish about anything in my life. When I swore myself to the MC, I did whatever they asked of me, even when it meant I'd lose some of my own autonomy and freedom. But her? She was the one person in this whole fucking world I'd ever considered mine. There was nothing more important to me, and I couldn't even fucking hold her while I told her.

"What about me?" I asked.

She raised her eyebrows and sucked in a breath, rustling her feet on the concrete to try to hide it. "You?"

"Do you think you don't matter to me? Do you think my day doesn't rise and end with you? Getting up extra early to spar so your skills don't get rusty. Going to the shop early to turn up the AC so it isn't so fucking hot when you get there. Shoring up extra medical shipments from the Canadians so your stocks are always full—"

"That's for the club," she cut in.

"I wouldn't do it if you didn't ask me to." It was true. Doc never demanded a thing from me. He had his own connections, and however he got his meds was his own business. But she needed the shit we got from Canada in order to keep the club in first-responder order.

"What are you trying to say, Thor?" She huffed a sad sigh and looked to the ground, avoiding my gaze. "That you're in love with your dead wife's niece?"

"Yes," I immediately said. She snapped those beautiful blue eyes up to me, her jaw falling open. "And you're in love with me, too. You have been for a long time."

She swallowed, a look passing behind her eyes like she might argue, but she didn't, just leaned her head back against the metal bars and stared at me with eyes the color of moonlight.

"Tell me I'm wrong." It sounded more like a threat than a declaration of love, but those went hand in hand for the two of us. "Tell me."

Selene didn't say anything and glanced down at the ground again, clearing her throat.

"That's what I thought."

"I can't believe I'm fucking chained to a bench the first time you say that to me. How dare you," she murmured. "I could kill you for that."

"I'd like to see you try." I smiled, and she returned one of her own with mischief in her eyes.

"When did you realize it?" she murmured, almost too softly for me to hear her.

I laughed. "I don't know, Sel. It's been so damned long, I don't even know when it started."

"Ugh," she groaned and threw her head back. "You should have told me when you had me pinned to the bed."

I smiled, a warmth radiating up my neck despite the fact we were being held prisoner in a freezing, dark cell. "Yeah, I owe you for this one."

She fell silent, and the sound of my own pounding heart blocked out the rest of the errant noises in the room. Time passed differently down there. There were no windows, and they'd taken my watch when I was knocked out, so we had no way to tell how long had actually gone by. We existed in our own separate bubble, as if the outside world had fallen away for these few moments. I wasn't her uncle, she wasn't my niece, we didn't belong to the Roses. We were simply two humans that had known each other for ages.

"I've loved you for years," she said. "Probably since you killed Billy. I've wanted you since I can remember wanting anyone."

Her words sent a sharp slice down my spine and into my gut, and

I lamented that we were resigned to separate cells. I needed to hold her. My fingers itched to run through her beautiful, soft hair and pull her to my lips.

"Enough now," I said. "Get some rest. The fun starts when Gabriella arrives."

She hummed before scooting farther down on the bench and turning on her side, facing me. She closed her eyes, but it was a while before she actually slipped unconscious. I kept watch over her, even though there was nothing I could if anything jumped out of the shadows to attack her.

I thought about my brothers and what would happen if we did find a way out of this. Gemma had been legally declared dead years ago. I *could* marry Selene if I wanted. Imagining her in a white dress, walking down the aisle to me in some church, made me chuckle. She'd hate that, and she wouldn't want some big party like KC and Alba. She'd want it to be us, and with some perverse joy, I agreed with her. Me and my beast, we'd want her all to ourselves. I'd have my way with her over and over until I couldn't fucking stand anymore, and then I'd nuzzle into her neck for the rest of the night.

When she'd hooked up with that fucker from her high school a few months ago, I'd wanted to track him down and rip off his hands for touching her. Even if it had only been a one-night stand, I loathed the thought of anyone else sleeping in her bed. I had tolerated it because of all the reasons keeping us apart, but no longer.

I didn't care if people judged us for what it was between us. We were monsters, filthy, depraved creatures that had found a likeness in each other. I wasn't about to give that up, no matter what anyone else thought.

～

WHITE LIGHT STARTLED ME, forcing me to snap my eyes open. I was still seated on the bench with my head leaning back against the bars. I must have fallen asleep some time ago, but now Selene stood in her cell with her arms cuffed in front of her, staring at the door.

I jumped to my feet when I realized who she was staring at.

Gabriella Caputi stood in front of us in a smart black suit with her graying hair up in a polished twist at the back of her head. Even though she was Alba's grandmother through her maternal side, I didn't see any resemblance to the woman I called family. Alba radiated sunshine everywhere she went, truly an embodiment of KC's nickname for her. Gabriella carried an extra layer of guarded coldness, like her soul had died a long time ago and her body now rotted from the inside out. Maybe that wasn't too far from the truth.

"Good morning," she said, stepping closer toward us. Behind her stood five men in equally formal attire, black suits with their jackets parted so I could see the holsters carrying their pistols under each arm. I recognized one of them as the guy who'd brought us here; Selene had referred to him as Jimmy. Cheesecake and Hooch hovered in the corner near her cell, Nikki standing behind them with her arms crossed over her chest, biting nervously at her bottom lip.

"I take it you know who I am, yes?" She raised her eyebrows, tilting her head to the side like an adult talking to a child.

I nodded.

"Good, and I know who you are." She turned back to her guards, her heels clicking on the concrete in an ominous backdrop to her stiff posture. "So you understand why we're meeting under such...*strenuous*...circumstances."

Selene snorted out an indignant laugh, but Gabriella ignored her, turning to Cheesecake and Hooch.

"Everyone who knows about this from your silly little club is here, correct?"

Hooch nodded eagerly, taking a step forward. "Yeah. We kept our word like you asked. We didn't tell anyone. Just us."

"Good." Gabriella smiled and my stomach dropped, my instincts going on alert. I knew what would happen next. I could've called it. Gabriella turned to her henchmen and gave Jimmy a nod. He grabbed his pistol and faced the bikers, firing off two shots into each head before they could blink. Nikki screamed, covering her face as blood and brain drenched her hair, dripping down to her face and neck. When Jimmy raised his pistol to her, Gabriella put a hand on his wrist to stop him.

"We take her back," she said. "Someone needs to care for that weed she sprouted."

Despite the fact I had no feelings for Nikki, relief flooded my chest at the mention of her child. The babe was innocent in all this.

"No!" Nikki cried. "No, please. Just kill me. Kill me."

"Shut up." Jimmy grabbed her by the bicep, ready to haul her through the door, but Gabriella held up a hand to that, too.

"She stays," the boss said. "She gets to watch the mess she made."

Nikki sobbed, her face twisted in horror as she melted against Jimmy's hold, tears streaking down her face. Gabriella turned back to us, glancing at me and then Selene. "Start with her. Find out where my nephew is."

"Leo Caputi?" I raised an eyebrow. "Haven't you heard? He's dead, lady. Burned his fuck pad down myself."

Gabriella seemed intrigued by that, narrowing her eyes at me. "Is that so?"

"Why would I lie? Killing him was one of the highlights of my life." I smiled, watching as tears replaced the suspicion in her eyes. She blinked them back, refusing to let them fall, so I continued. "If that's all you wanted, I could've told you that hours ago. His body lines the same field as your fucking rat, Pie, and your nephew, Julian." I eyed Nikki while I said it, hoping to twist the knife deeper.

Gabriella blinked, returning my grin with a smirk of her own. "Leo is not dead." Tilting her head back, she stared down at me like I was dog shit on her Louboutins. "I know this. And when I find him, you had better pray he is unharmed. He is not yours to kill."

After KC killed Benito Caputi, two major players had emerged to take his place: his widow, Gabriella, and his eldest nephew, Leo. These two hated each other. Gabriella had always been the calmer of the two, the more level set. She thought strategically, and that was evident in the way she'd tried to lay siege to our arms supply. Now I saw something else in her, something that lit a spark of fear in my gut.

Desperation.

She had once said the Roses would come to know what she could do, but the idea of that same grieving human lashing out because she had been backed into a corner escalated the despicable things she might be capable of. Like Selene said, what had she done to get the respect of those five men behind her? What had they seen that made them act on her command alone?

Now I understood why Gabriella wanted to find her nephew. She had to be the one to take him out. Otherwise, the people who supported him wouldn't back her, and however she did it needed to be epic. He couldn't die by Rose hands. No. Otherwise, he would be made a martyr and his allies would rise up in his honor. They'd suspect Gabriella either way, but a show of strength would scare them into allegiance. It was how she had gotten this far.

Having made her point, she turned and gave one final nod at Jimmy before leaving the room.

"When you're done, send their heads to Crow. I want him to see who he's playing against now. I want him to know that killing my beloved Benito was the worst thing he could ever have done." Gabriella gave Selene and me one last disgusted look, her lips twisted with rage. "By the time they get there, I'll already have my final move in place."

I assumed more henchmen waited out in the hallway for her because none of the five followed. The moment I'd been dreading since we'd been captured had finally come. My stomach churned as a huge man with a bald head walked to Selene's door and twisted a key in the lock to swing it open. Steeling my muscles, I refused to tremble, knowing whatever was about to happen would change both of us.

They'd beat the hell of her. They'd bend her over that table, hold her down, and rape her right in front of me, knowing it would break me, knowing it would send me into a frenzy. I made eye contact with her, preparing the compartments in my mind and doubling down on the leash that held my beast at bay. I couldn't react to this. If I did, they would make it worse. But I caught the sparkle in her moonlight eyes. She had a plan.

She'd long ago told me her thumbs were double-jointed and handcuffs never worked on her. She could make her hand the size of her wrist, easily sliding them off. The reason that she didn't do it yet had been because I'd urged patience. We'd been outnumbered since we got here, and even if we got out, I'd need a weapon to backtrack my way out of this bunker. We'd need one of their guns.

Now that they were willingly letting her out of the cage, she wasn't going to let them have at her without a fight. They closed the door and, for a moment, while all of them were standing in the room together, they stared at each other. Tension and anticipation filled the space, suffocating us. I clenched my hands into fists, begging my internal alarms to calm the fuck down so I could focus. Taking a deep breath, I let it out to the count of four.

"Well?" Selene said, breaking the tension and looking between the huge men dwarfing her. "What'll be? Fisticuffs? A good ole-fash-ioned gang rape?"

I shifted my shoulders and cracked my neck, my unease growing when they grinned at her blatant flippancy. Baldy grabbed her arm and tugged her closer to the table, circling around to where Jimmy held Nikki. Selene went willingly until they got within a foot of the blond traitor.

Then, my heart stopped as she attacked.

20

SELENE

Oleander syringes hidden in my hands, I launched myself at Nikki and Jimmy, using everyone's surprise to my benefit. I stabbed both in the chest, my aim surprisingly great despite being in handcuffs, and depressed the plungers as fast as I could. It must've burned like a son of a bitch, but I needed her dead. I didn't care what came after that.

The bald Caputi pulled me back from my targets, his brutal grip sinking deeper into my biceps. But the hard part was over. Nikki clutched at the needle, her wide eyes going red as the poison entered her bloodstream.

I felt it before I heard it, the slice of pure agony ricocheting through my jaw as Baldy backhanded me. He outweighed me by over a hundred pounds, so I collapsed to the ground like a wet noodle, barely managing to catch myself as I fell. I'd taken harder hits from Billy when I was a teenager, so I blinked back the pain, pushed to my feet, and refocused on the present, only to be greeted with another fist, this one clocking me right in the cheek. I stumbled back, absorbing the hit before deciding I'd had enough.

"I thought you checked her for weapons?" a guy with a dark beard asked the bald dude.

"I did," Baldy said. "She was clean."

Beard yanked me to my feet and threw me across the table, and I had just enough time to pop my thumb out of place and yank the cuff over my hand before he went for my throat to pin me down. I'd been fighting Thor all my life. I knew how to handle men that outweighed me. I grabbed his wrist with one hand and snapped his elbow with the other, kicking him in the guts when he hauled back and groaned. Baldy came for me, swinging like a battering ram, and the two other guys closed in on my right side, both reaching for my arms, trying to grab me.

"Stupid Rose bitch," he growled, pistol-whipping me across the cheek. I went down hard, wincing as the pain exploded through my body. It came again, and I fell to my hands, but it was already too late. "Stay down."

It's like they don't know me at all.

Using the free cuff as a weapon, I whirled it out and smacked Beard across the face as hard as I could. He wilted to the side, but Baldy attacked from the right, and I dodged out of the way in time to miss his swinging fist. The silent, brooding one came at me from the left, pistol drawn and aimed at my face. I shoved it out of the way, instinct making me duck at the exact moment to miss another blow from Beardy.

"Sel," Thor shouted from the cell, but I couldn't focus on him. I had to pay attention to the fight.

Broody didn't like my hit and tried to take aim again, but Baldy was in his way, still trying to grab at me. If it were three on one or even two on one, I might have had a fighting chance. But in the chaos, I'd hadn't accounted for the fourth guard, lurking in the shadows by the door. Taller and bigger than the others, he threw his massive arms around me from behind, circling my torso in an attempt to stop me.

"Give him to me," Thor said. I understood what he wanted. I used Big Guy's momentum to jump up and kick out at Broody with both feet, sending him careening into the door of Thor's cell. My mentor caught him around the neck in a headlock, yanking him back against the bars while he fought for purchase.

I had to trust that Thor had that fight as I whipped my head back on Big Guy, a satisfying crack letting me know I'd broken his nose. He groaned and dropped my body to the floor, so I grabbed one of the chairs around the table and flung it at him, breaking it across his back and forcing him to the ground. Baldy was already next to me, his massive hand gripping his gun. It came down on my face again so hard I saw stars, and this time, I dropped to the ground, dizzy and blindsided by the attack.

Fuck.

I clenched my eyes shut, hoping for a reprieve that never came. Something hard collided with my stomach and all the air whooshed out of my body as I collapsed to the side, struggling for oxygen. The hit came again and again, and I wheezed, attempting to curl into a ball to protect myself. It did no good. When Baldy kicked the next time, I grabbed onto his foot, holding it against myself to offset his balance. He tried to yank it away but couldn't and ultimately lost his footing. One of them kicked me in the back, and I ignored the jolt of sharp, agonizing torture so I could bite down on Baldy's Achilles tendon, ripping flesh and tendons with my teeth.

"You fucking bitch!" he shouted, wilting at the knees.

Hot, sticky metal filled my mouth as he cried out, and I kicked him in the face, sending him toppling toward the table. He hit his temple against the edge and went limp.

A gunshot echoed, and jolts of scalding torment burned up my leg into my hip and spine. Big Guy had shot me right through the thigh, likely hitting my femoral artery from the way it spurted blood, and before I could process that, another boot careened at my face. My head whipped back from the contact, blinding pain echoing through my skull and down my neck.

My vision went black.

My ears rang.

My jaw snapped shut.

I thought there was another gunshot, but I couldn't be sure. Face screaming and vision darkening, I attempted to retreat to my mental library, my safe space, but the shelves had crumbled in the fight. My books lay open and flayed, the boundaries between my past and present blurred to the point where I couldn't be sure what was what.

My head sank and swam at the same time. The world had tilted on its axis. I lay on that concrete floor and blinked against my swirling reality, my entire body in wretched despair, my muscles unbearably clenched, and no matter how many times I tried to force air back into my lungs, they simply wouldn't expand.

That fucker had kicked my shit into next Tuesday, and without a CAT scan to be sure, I risked a much more serious injury if I tried to stand, only to fall on my face again. Instead, I stayed still and welcomed whatever further attack might come. More gunshots echoed in the distance, and some small part of me worried that it might be headed for me soon.

Get up, Montgomery, the cold voice in the back of my head said.

I'm bleeding out, another voice argued. My doctor voice. The one that told me what to do to save lives, the opposite of my monster. My muscles wouldn't move, and my brain had turned to mush in my head like chunky soup, sloshing around in my skull. Swish...Slosh... Swish...Slosh.

Every few seconds, my vision cleared enough for me to make eye contact with Nikki, who lay on the floor two feet away, her wide, lifeless eyes staring at me. In the mess of my mental library, her book shook to life, vibrating as its pages flipped forward and backward. Another wave of pain and anguish skidded across my nerve endings as I remembered the girl she'd once been, back before she dated Jer, before she'd fucked everything up—back when she had braces and wore her hair in braids. How innocent life had seemed, neither of us knowing how this story would end.

"Do you want to play mud pies with me?" she had asked, her eyes glimmering with childlike wonder.

Both Jer and I had looked at each other for only a moment before agreeing and running out into the fields behind the clubhouse, weaving in between the sheds, shouts from brothers about not going too far behind us.

More gunshots got my attention, and I remembered I was lying on the concrete floor in a bunker. Nausea rolled through my gut, inching up my esophagus, and I turned on my stomach, holding myself up on my hands and knees while I retched, but I couldn't move my left leg and anytime I tried, another bout of anguish made me want to vomit.

I was fucked up. Bad.

"All right," said a deep voice, rolling me onto my back again. Thor's blurry form came into view, and I smiled, knowing the gunshots I'd heard had been him storming the place and executing anyone in his path. "Let me see."

"My leg," I tried to say, but my mouth wouldn't work the way I wanted.

"We gotta go." Thor whipped off a belt from one of the dead guys and wrapped it around my upper thigh, pulling it tight. But in the bottomless abyss of all the aches in my body, that barely registered. He put his arms under my knees and stood, and the pain was too much to bear. I screamed and wilted against him. My consciousness dipped in and out while he walked, but I caught glimpses of the bloodshed whenever I opened my eyes.

He'd taken everyone out, anyone who had stayed behind, everyone who had come to investigate. I counted at least ten, but it might have been more. He whispered to me while he moved, murmuring things I'd never heard him say before, things that made me think I looked worse than I felt.

"Don't you dare think about leaving me," he said, kissing my temple. "You were so fucking strong, so fucking deadly. You got 'em, Sel. You got 'em."

"I love you," I tried to tell him, knowing deep down it would always end like this. I'd come here alone because I thought it would. Light poured in through the square window of a doorway ten yards up ahead, and then that was it.

Ding, ding. Lights out.

End scene.

21

SELENE

I woke up again sometime later. Alarms beeped from either side of me, the familiar scent of hospital and chemicals assaulting my senses. My face throbbed as the world came into focus, revealing my left leg had been wrapped around the thigh and lay slightly elevated on the bed in front of me. Every muscle ached despite what must be an adequate supply of pain meds dripping through my IV.

I tried to move my hand, but a warm, heavy weight enveloped it, and when I glanced down, there was a head of dark hair so similar to my own.

"Jer," I tried to groan, but my throat scratched and my jaw twinged like it was broken. My teeth weren't splinted and set, so I assumed it was bruised and nothing worse.

He sat up, swinging his head around to face me, his puffy red eyes relieved and elated that I'd woken up. "Sel."

I smiled, warmth settling in my blood at the sight of my twin. Our mother used to say we were two halves of the moon, and for the longest time, we'd argue over which side was which. Being the boy, he always wanted to be the 'dark' side, thinking he had some kind of territory over the more sinister things in life because he would one day join the MC.

As we got older, we learned the truth. Jericho was the brightest thing in the night sky, reflecting his wife's sunshine out into the world. I had become the shadow, the monster, the fucked-up half no one else saw.

"I ought to throttle you," he said, his voice choking as tears flooded his eyes. He blinked them back and cleared his throat. "But I'm just so fucking happy you're gonna be okay."

I squeezed his hand and looked around the rest of the room, trying my best to ask, "Where are we?"

"Some shithole hospital in the middle of nowhere, New York. When Thor brought you here, you were unconscious and needed surgery to close your leg." He shifted in his seat, rubbing at his eyes again to hide his worry. I'd known him all our lives, so I saw it anyway. "You have a bad concussion and your face is busted all to hell, but you got lucky. Thor says a Caputi bastard shot you point blank. It should have shattered your femur, but the bullet missed the bone, thank God."

Thor.

My heart pounded as the past came crashing back around me. We'd fought off the Caputis together. I killed Nikki. I watched her die right in front of me.

"I took care of her," I garbled.

His features hardened, his eyes narrowing and jaw tensing, needing no further explanation to know what I was talking about. "I know, and I could fucking kill you for doing it."

I rolled my eyes and huffed as his frustration poured off him in thick, suffocating waves.

"You didn't even say goodbye," he told me. "You just left, knowing what the fuck could happen to you." My brother shook his head, looking so much like our father in that moment, a stab lanced through my heart and I almost sobbed. "Ru's furious, and I guess I would be too if I didn't think I'd do the same thing in your shoes."

That got my attention, and I raised my eyebrows in surprise.

"If one of your exes was compromising you, putting the club at risk, I wouldn't even think twice." He looked over his shoulder, pulling his lips into a wicked grin when he met my gaze again. "We shoulda gone after her months ago, and most of the guys in the club are on your side." He put a finger over his lips and made a "shh" sound, as if to tell me that was a secret.

"How's Pollux?" I managed to ask, trying to suck back the pain and shame.

"He's still in critical condition. Crow was so fucking pissed when he heard what you'd done. No one needed this right now, Sel," Jer said, rubbing tired eyes. "You shouldn't have gone off on your own without telling anyone where you were." His big puppy dog gaze met mine, and the look he gave me would have been endearing if it wasn't for the fact it was meant to make me feel guilty. "I almost lost Sunshine last year, and it nearly killed me. Please don't force me to face the day I lose you, too."

A sob tore from my chest for real this time and I nodded, lifting my hand so he'd grab it again. When he did, he gave me another smile before the look in his eyes shifted entirely.

"Thor was worried about you," he said, raising an eyebrow. "Like...really worried. I've never seen him so fucking ballistic."

That made sense. He'd just been held captive while four men that were bigger and stronger beat me within an inch of my life. We'd worked together to get out of there, but only one of us was lying in a hospital bed. It had all happened so quickly. Once he'd gotten out of his cuffs, I was already on the ground, and by the time he'd gotten free, I was bleeding out on the floor.

I thought back to what he'd told me that night in the cell, when he'd confessed he loved me and knew I was in love with him, too. We had been for a while. It was the worst possible time for him to admit such a thing, but the timing had never been right between the two of us. He was ten years older than me, already a widower by the time I turned eighteen. Things had been stuck for years. Now that it was out in the open, relief swelled in my chest and a heavy weight had been lifted off my shoulders.

"Maybe this isn't the right time to ask"—he shifted uncomfortably in his seat, wiping his free hand down his thigh—"and maybe it's none of my business, but are you two...like...together?"

Forcing a small laugh, I nodded, my heart beating even harder at the uncertain look in his eyes. "Is that all right?"

He eased and sank in his seat, wiping his mouth before pushing his fingers back through his hair and chuckling softly. "You know... now that I've been watching it happen for the last year or so, I think it makes a lot of sense."

That surprised me, too. I expected him to show some patriarchal display of masculinity, perhaps beat on his chest and declare no one could fuck his sister without his say so, especially not our sort-of uncle. But when Thor walked into the room and froze, obviously having intruded on us talking about him, the energy wasn't malicious. Jer stood and leaned over to give me a kiss on the cheek.

"I'll let you two catch up." He turned and patted Thor on the shoulder before leaving. I set my sights on my lover, my mentor, my everything—the one man I loved the most in the world, even more than my brother. After what we survived together, both in the distant and recent past, I could no longer deny it. I wouldn't go back to that life in stasis, not fully together but not willing to be apart. Thor wanted me, I wanted him, and nothing else mattered.

He stood there for a moment, raking his gunmetal gaze over me. It caught on the bruises on my face and the bandage on my thigh but ultimately landed back on my eyes. He looked the same as he always had, barely a scratch on him for all we had survived. Still beautiful. Still terrifying. Still my beast.

"Montgomery." He sounded rough, and his irises shimmered with either pride or tears, perhaps both. Dark circles hung under his eyes, hinting at the last few sleepless nights between us. It had only been four days, but it seemed like a month.

"Erickson."

"You look like shit." He raised an eyebrow and shook his hair back behind his shoulders, standing up straighter.

"You look worse."

He hesitated a moment before cracking a smile and walking

closer to me, leaning down so he could kiss my forehead, my nose, and finally, my lips. His mouth was soft and delicate against mine, which must have been a clue as to how fucked up my face looked. I laughed out a tiny sigh and held up a hand to grip his, tightening my fingers against his palm.

"For a moment," he said, sitting down in the chair Jer had vacated, "I thought I'd lost you...for real this time."

I tried to grin, but it pulled my cheeks, and they screamed at me for moving. "You nearly did."

He opened his mouth to talk, but the nurse chose that moment to come in. The doctor came in shortly after her, checking my pupils and rattling off a long list of things they'd had to fix. She eyed Thor skeptically, flicking her gaze between the two of us as she spoke. I'd seen people like me before in the emergency department. I knew what she was thinking. Thor must have done this to me somehow. I could only hope Jericho had explained the situation.

"You should be okay to be discharged later this afternoon if all goes well." The doctor gave us one last nod before turning to leave.

"Jer asked if we were together," I said once we were alone.

Thor sat up straighter and raised his eyebrows. "What did you tell him?"

"That you'd be an idiot to let me go." I shook my head as Thor chuckled. "I think everyone else has known for years."

"Well"—he huffed out an arrogant laugh—"you weren't great at hiding your obsession with me."

"Obsession?" I scoffed, this time pulling whatever had been done to my ribs and making me cough. Groaning, I leaned back to take a deep breath, soothing the agony. "Please. You could have moved out of my house years ago. Instead, you stuck around like a creeper. If anyone's obsessed, it's you."

The corners of his mouth pulled even higher, and a swell of warmth shot down the center of my body.

"You told me you loved me," I said.

He nodded. "I did."

"Did you mean it?" I swallowed, angry my throat hurt so much while I was trying to have this conversation with him. "Did you mean it the way I think you mean it?"

"Sel." He smiled and the metal in his eyes melted. "I would chase you to the edge of the earth and then over the damn side if I had to. I've wanted you for years."

I shivered, and I wasn't sure if that was from his words or the morphine withdrawal. Probably both.

"The real question is," he went on, "did you mean it? Have you gotten tired of this song and dance? When we go home tomorrow, when we face our family, are you going to want to sneak around in the shadows?"

"No." The words flew from my lips. "No hiding. I mean it."

He nodded and stood to lean in, kissing me once more. His clean masculine scent swelled around me, and I breathed it in deep, letting it relax me, letting it pull me under its spell again.

"Good," he said, his radiant smile sending a lick of heat between my legs. I was gross and covered in hospital germs, but that didn't stop my hormones from reminding me why I'd been so attracted to him for so very long.

22

———————

THOR

I hadn't slept since those few hours in the motel with Sel wrapped around me. I couldn't, not when Gabriella was still out there, not when we were still on Kings of Carnage territory. I imagined the rest of the Kings stumbling on the bunker and finding the blood I'd left behind. After I'd killed the fuckers that were beating on Selene, I stalked through the rest of the place with their guns, taking out anyone in my way. In the chaos of it all, I didn't stop to ask which side they were on or if they knew we were there. They hadn't helped us and they deserved to die.

By the time I got back to her, she was as pale as a fucking bedsheet, the crimson puddle around her body having grown breathtakingly huge. She'd barely made it.

I almost lost her. Again.

In all the terrible things we'd done, we'd never come this close to death. I'd lost brothers and best friends. I'd bled the life from enemies. But never her. Never me. It wasn't that I thought we were invincible; just that I'd hoped our luck would never run out.

By now, Gabriella would know we weren't dead, that we'd somehow defeated her men and escaped. She'd come for us. This wasn't over, and the longer we sat in that hospital, the more of a liability we were to everyone else in it.

KC had taken me back to get the Impala, which was surprisingly undisturbed, and after careful inspection to make sure no one followed us, we went back to the hospital to pick up Selene. A few of the other guys had come with him, expecting a full court press, but once they found us mostly unscathed at the hospital, the rest had turned back, leaving the two of us to wait for Selene's recovery.

Now a few hours on the road, my girl had fallen asleep in the back seat, leaving me and her twin brother alone for miles on end. He drove because I could barely see straight. I needed a bottle of whiskey and a month's worth of sleep.

She'd said he'd asked about our relationship, and if anyone were to immediately notice a difference between us, it didn't surprise me it had been the man that had lived with the two of us for over a decade. So far, he hadn't said anything, just filled me in on the few things I'd missed while we were gone.

"Pollux is still critical. No one knows if he'll make it. Crow is fucking pissed," KC said. "At her, at the Kings, at everyone. He wants blood. I've never seen him like this."

I sighed and pinched the bridge of my nose. "What the fuck is he thinking?"

KC shrugged. "Bear tried to talk him down, but the pressure is getting to him. Going after the Beacon was a low blow. It wasn't just Pollux that was injured. Prospects and civilians died, twenty more ended up in the hospital."

I pursed my lips, listening to what KC wasn't saying. Since the shootout last August, the Feds had been up our ass, and after Saint and Ru were nearly killed a few months ago, Detective Jordan hadn't let the man have a moment of peace. He couldn't leave the state. He could barely leave his house without a pig oinking up his shit.

"How bad is it?"

KC ran a hand back through his hair and sighed. "The media is blaming us, blaming the blood feud with the Caputis. The rest of Madison County is pissed."

"Fuck," I murmured. For the several decades that the Roses had operated out of Madison County, the rest of the city had tolerated our existence because we kept the mob away. Over time, the tenuous relationship had become more of the-devil-you-know-is-better-than-the-one-you-don't situation.

"We've been through worse," I said. "We'll make it through."

KC gave me a look that said he didn't quite believe me but wouldn't argue. I knew his concern. The Montgomerys had a notorious temper, and Crow could be the king fucking shit of throwing a tantrum. Sure, the man was levelheaded and calm most of the time, but I'd seen him tear through people with his bare hands. He had a mean streak, just like his kids, just like his niece and nephew.

"What about her?" He nodded toward the back. "You think she's okay?"

I wanted to tell him she'd been through worse, too. I wanted to tell him this whole experience hadn't changed her, hadn't done something irrevocable to her, but I didn't know. I'd seen the look in her eyes when she stabbed Nikki. It was echoed there when I'd come to get her after sweeping the place. It reminded me of the night I'd shot that extremist in Afghanistan, of the look in my eyes the first time I'd seen myself in the mirror after that little girl had stripped me down to the bone.

Selene had let the beast inside her take over. She had wanted to take out her vengeance so bad that I wasn't sure she understood the gravity of doing it until it was over. Killing Giuseppe Caputi was one thing; he was an old man with nothing else going for him. Killing the long line of strangers every time I took her on a raid meant little to someone who didn't know them personally. But Nikki? The two had grown up together. They'd known each other almost their entire lives.

Selene had hunted her down like an animal and stabbed her in the chest with a poison that Doc made using Gods only knew what. Nikki and Selene hadn't been close since they were kids, but that didn't mean this wouldn't haunt her.

"I'll take your silence as my answer," KC said, rubbing at a tight spot on the back of his neck. "You're watching out for her."

It wasn't a question, nor was it a command. It was a statement, something he was putting out there to test the waters.

"You got something to get off your chest, brother?"

Between us, KC and I had a lot of monikers for each other—nephew, uncle, brother, son, friend. I chose this one specifically because it reminded him we'd both sworn loyalty to the SRMC, that we were Roses, that we were family in more ways than one.

He laughed in that carefree way I'd always associated with him and scrubbed at his face, perhaps trying to bring himself back to reality. "No, I guess I don't. My sister's always been the smarter one. If she's with you, I assume you did right by her."

I shifted uncomfortably in my seat, trying not to think of the horrible things we'd done right by each other in just the last few days.

"This better be real. Don't get back to Madison and end it because you're worried about what the guys—"

"I wouldn't do that," I said, my tone steady and calm despite the rising outrage in his. "She's everything to me, KC."

He nodded and touched his collarbone where he had a tattoo of his wife's nickname. *Sunshine.* "Yeah, I get the feeling."

I bet he fucking did. Alba was his old lady, the light of his fucking world. I doubted Selene would agree with being referred to like that, but if there were something similar for us, I would say the same. She was the shadows my beast crept in, the only one that matched the dark side of my soul. Without her, I would be incomplete.

Had I instilled this darkness in her or had she reignited it within me? What the fuck did it matter anymore? She was mine and I was hers, and nothing was going to change that ever again.

"I approve, ya know," KC murmured, almost too low for me to hear, but I did, and my chest tightened, something warm and sappy zinging down my spine. I didn't need his acceptance. Sel and I would continue on even if he hated it, but it meant a lot that he'd said it, that he'd acknowledged he wouldn't stand in our way. "But Thor, she's one of the most important people in my life. You keep taking care of her, or I'll help her feed your body to the pigs."

At that, I barked out a laugh and clapped him on the shoulder. "Thank you for loving her enough to say that to my face. I appreciate the reality check."

"Yeah, you're welcome. Don't forget it."

The hours passed in comfortable companionship. KC and I had always gotten along. He'd inherited the more jovial side of the Montgomery line, the same as his cousins, Castor and Pollux. He was an easy conversationalist, quick to laugh and make others feel seen and accepted. It was times like these that I wished I'd known their parents when they were alive. Was Selene more like their father or their mother?

Eventually, she woke up in the back and groaned about food. "I'm a woman on the mend," she whined. "I need carbs."

"Fuck yeah," KC added, his stomach grumbling right as he said it.

We helped Sel into the restaurant and ate like the world wasn't a fucked-up place, made even more so by our continued existence in it. The three of us were bloodthirsty and terrible, but to look at us in that diner, no one would have known it. KC and Sel teased each other and laughed as loud as they could, occasionally trying to pull me into the revelry the way they always had.

It reminded me of simpler times, back before the war had escalated, back when we were younger, when I was a struggling young man in my twenties trying to figure out what to do with these two kids that had lost everyone that had cared for them before they graduated high school.

My attention caught on Sel, and even though her face was bruised and busted, she was still the most beautiful person I'd ever seen. I watched her joke with her brother and smile along with his attempt to cheer her up. But after the giggles faded, her eyebrows furrowed, her gaze turned distant, and when she thought we weren't looking, she blinked back tears. I recognized the deep, solemn loneliness filling her expression.

I wouldn't have thought twice about it if I didn't know it myself. It was an all-consuming darkness, one that would envelop what little remained of her soul if she let it.

And I wouldn't. I'd fight back even if she couldn't.

23

THOR

"Welcome back, brother," Crow said, clapping my outstretched palm to pull me into a hug. "It's damn good to see you."

He looked rough, deep purple bags hung under his eyes and his features had turned gaunt. He must have lost twenty pounds in the few days I'd been gone. Was he even eating? And what was he doing here if Pollux was still in the hospital?

I nodded and received the handshake, even though I sensed the reprimand coming. I had gone off plan. I'd helped Selene go after Nikki, even knowing I had orders to get her and bring her home. The rest of the club had eyed me when I walked in, some with apprehension and some with awe. I'd kept my head down and made my way to the back, knowing my fellow officers were already here for our weekly catch-up.

"It's good to be home," I said.

Aris pulled me in next, quickly followed by our road captain, Slip, and our treasurer, Coins. Once everyone had an opportunity to make sure I was still in one piece, I took my place next to the veep, pretending like the stares on me had nothing to do with the bunker in New York.

"Well?" Slip said, raking his hawkish blue eyes over me. He never missed a damn thing. "What the fuck happened up there?"

I shifted in my seat, knowing I'd have to explain myself sooner or later.

"You were told to come home," Crow said. "What went wrong?"

Clearing my throat, I leaned my elbows on the wooden table and told them the entire story, including how Selene wouldn't be talked into coming back. "She was going to do it anyway. I couldn't stop her. If I tried to bring her home, she'd keep escaping until she got what she was after. She's a grown woman, Prez, and a fucking Montgomery. I can't stop her from doing something once she's put her mind on it." It was one of the things I loved the most about her. "I never could."

Aris hummed a small sound, knowing it was true, but Crow sighed and rubbed a finger over his eyebrow in annoyed disapproval. I explained everything that happened after that, how we'd hid out in the woods, only to be tracked down by dogs. "We held our own for a while...until we couldn't." It spilled out of me, but I kept the more intimate parts to myself. They didn't need to know about the fucked-up shit we'd gotten into or how I loved her so much, it throbbed in my bones. They'd figure that out for themselves soon enough. By the time I got to the bunker, Aris held up his hand to add in a piece.

"The Kings have already reached out," he said. "Their president insists he didn't know. He says Cheese, Hooch, and the others were acting on their own, and he's glad they got what they deserved."

Crow hummed and crossed his arms over his chest. "Easy for him to say after the fact. Cheese still knew about the bombing."

"That's my point," Slip added. "No way the president didn't know they'd made a deal with the fucking Caputis."

I shook my head, remembering how terrified Hooch had been that the rest of their club would find out. "I don't know about that. Nikki's fuck buddy and his friend were thrilled about being able to split the payday only two ways. He could be telling the truth."

"He wants to stay out of it," Aris went on. "He's pissed Nikki had the audacity to hide out in his club, but even more so that we came on his territory to hunt her down without at least telling him we were there." A few eyes slid my way, but Crow only ran his hands back through his hair as a response.

I finished my story, making sure to describe how much of a badass Selene had been, going up against those fuckers by herself until I could get out of the cell. They smiled and clapped like a bunch of proud father figures, and to be fair, this group of devils might have been the only such people in her life. Then I shifted my focus back to Gabriella. "She said killing Benito was the worst thing you ever could have done. She wants you to be scared of her."

"By the time they get there, I'll already have my final move in place," she'd said. I repeated it to my fellow officers as a few gasped in alarm, raising their eyebrows in surprise.

"What do you suppose that is?" Coins asked, running his hands over his gray beard.

"Another attack," Slip said. "We'll run bomb sweeps again."

"They got away with that once," I said. "They know we won't let it happen again."

"Could be the IRA." Doc shook his head, pursing his lips in consideration. "She's got that deal with Kellan McMurphy." She'd spent the majority of this past summer in the Caribbean, securing a trade agreement with an ex-IRA drug smuggler who now lived in Cuba.

"The Feds are closing in," Aris added. "Detective Jordan is breathing down our neck."

"Since the bombing, she's been popping up every fucking where." Crow rubbed at his eyes, pinching the bridge of his nose with a weariness I hadn't seen on him in a long time. He'd been president since before I joined, but recently, the stress seemed to bring an extra heavy burden.

"Gabriella Caputi wouldn't work with the pigs," Slip said, clearly amused by the proposition. The silence stretched on. "Would she?"

Crow made a soft chuckling noise. "I think it's more unlikely that Detective Jordan would work with the Caputis."

I ignored the strange affection and pride in Crow's voice when he talked about Detective Jordan, choosing instead to focus on being logical. If I were in Gabriella's shoes, I'd feel like I had been backed into a corner. She'd tried to swipe our knees out from under us, and in return, we'd taken her nephew, the only other person in her vicinity capable of taking over the family business. I'd seen it in her eyes while she ordered Cigarettes to kill us in that bunker. She'd gotten desperate.

"I don't think we should underestimate her," I said. "She hasn't made her final move yet."

"Saint sent the picture of Leo to his source on the inside," Crow said, glancing around between us with wise, careful eyes. "She's working with us again. According to her, Gabriella has become unhinged. The people who supported Leo are rising up against her, and she's fighting a war inside her own family. She can't keep both up. That's why she's trying to lure us out in the open, so we're easier to pick off."

That made sense. It explained her search for Leo and why she'd been willing to torture us for his location.

"How is our favorite houseguest?" I looked at Doc, knowing he must have worked him over in the days since I'd been gone.

"He still hasn't said a fucking word." Doc lit a cigarette and shook his head. "I'm running out of nonpermanent ways to make him talk. His knee is a swollen mess, and eventually, he won't be able to use it. I bet he talks then."

"Doc," Crow snarled. "I told you to handle that."

"And I told you that as long as he isn't *dying,* he's capable of speech. If he's not talking, he's not in enough pain." Doc rolled his eyes and shook his head. "Honestly, it's like no one thinks I know how to do my job around here."

"Fix him," Crow said. "We need him."

"No," Doc replied. "If you want him healed, you get him a different doctor. I'm not wasting any of my med school debt on that piece of shit."

"We shoulda killed him already." Coins added, shaking his head. "He's a liability."

I wasn't so sure. When we'd first brought him home, I had agreed with the rest of the MC—he deserved to die. I had wanted to kill him when we found him. Now that I'd seen how much Gabriella wanted to find him, I was glad we'd spared him. Saint had no reason to show him mercy, and yet, that one kindness may end up being the thing that puts this war in a stalemate.

"What if we can turn him?" I raised an eyebrow and looked around at my fellow brothers. "Enemy of my enemy and all that." Shrugging, I waited to see if anyone would stop me before I went on. "What if we could end the blood feud?"

"That would require participation on his part." Doc tapped ash from his cigarette into the bowl at the center of the table. "Did you miss the part where I said he's been silent for two months?"

I mulled this over. "We just have to find the right spot to apply pressure."

"What would you suggest?" Crow raised his eyebrows.

"Who's the Caputi leak?" I asked. "If she's concerned about him, he must be concerned about her, too."

Crow didn't say anything for a long moment. "I'd rather not blow her cover."

"Maybe the threat alone is enough," I said. "Maybe if he knows we can hit him hard, right where it hurts, he'll start cooperating."

"Nah," Crow said, shaking his salt-and-pepper head. "I know how to get through to a violent man like Leo Caputi, and it ain't more violence. When you've been raised in the storm, you get used to the lightning and thunder."

"How do you do it, then?" Slip asked. "What are you thinking?"

Crow looked around at us before taking a deep breath and sighing. "You bring him out of the rain."

The room fell silent, the massive weight of what Crow suggested hanging between us. Leo Caputi wasn't just Gabriella's nephew and the heir apparent to the entire Caputi fortune. He was the one who'd tried to have four of our family members killed, Crow's daughter and Aris's daughter included. When he was in control, he was drugged out and unpredictable. At least Gabriella had an old school approach to politics...*or had.*

"Leave Leo Caputi to me," Crow said. "It's a gamble, keeping him around this long, but I stand by the decision. This is a good thing, brothers."

"And what about Nikki?" Slip said, eyeing me again.

"Technically, Selene is the one who killed her," Aris said. "The Roses did nothing."

"Agreed," I said at the same time as Doc.

"Then, it's settled." Crow nodded. "We keep working on Leo, and we wait for the right time to strike against Gabriella. It's nearing. She's growing more impatient. She's losing control."

"We just need to be there when it finally snaps." Aris's bright blue eyes nearly sparkled as he said it, but he looked like these past few weeks had worn on him as much as the rest of us. I didn't pry into his business, but he and Saint had a falling-out after the whole thing with Ru. My guess was they hadn't quite patched everything up, and it showed in how clearly Aris was breaking apart at the seams. Fuck, I'd known the prick for sixteen years, and I'd never seen him fuck a hang-around. Just last week, I'd had to throw three of them out for fighting over his old ass. What the fuck was going on with him?

I wanted to ask, and perhaps the mother hen in me wished I had, but I had enough of my own shit, so I left it alone and figured Aris or Saint would handle it before it got too bad.

"We need the club's support, no matter what we do," Crow added, pushing to his feet so we'd know the decision was final. "Let me think about it for a few days. We can discuss it at the next session."

"Sounds good, brothers," Aris said, giving the table a clap to signal our dismissal before standing so he could head to the back rooms again, yanking off his cut before he'd even gotten out the door. Coins, Doc, and Slip filed out front, seemingly not surprised by his behavior, but I eyed Crow with my best *what-the-fuck-is-his-deal* side-eye. He only held up a hand and shook his head, indicating he didn't know, but he was already well aware it was an issue.

Crow and Aris were the head of the MC leadership for a reason. For the most part, they were calm and levelheaded to the point of annoyance. Aside from Aris's affair with Alba's mother, Penny, there were very few things any of us could hold against them. Between the two, they set the tone for the rest of the club, especially the younger brothers like Bear, Hollywood, and KC. It wouldn't do to see Aris lose his fucking shit over a midlife crisis, especially not now. We needed his head in the game.

As sergeant at arms, it was my duty to keep these fuckers in line.

Silent communication aside, I had to ask. "Do I need to be worried?"

Crow only hummed a noncommittal noise. "Let me handle that, too."

I nodded and got to my feet, knowing I had an injured little monster to keep caged up at home.

24

SELENE

"I ought to tear out your guts and watch you choke on them," Verona said, crossing her arms and eyeing me skeptically with those rare deep indigo eyes, so blue they appeared violet. "Look at you! You could have at least *hinted* at what you were going to do."

I took a deep breath and let it out on a sigh, trying not to let the ache in my leg consume my whole attention. The hospital had given me a few pain pills, but I didn't like opioids, so I'd flushed them as soon as I'd gotten home. I took acetaminophen to help me sleep, but I dealt with it the rest of the time.

I'd been through worse.

"Go easy on her," Hollywood said, winking as he walked into my living room with a plate of leftover spaghetti. "Selene did us a favor."

"I'm not arguing that." Verona wrapped her blanket tighter around her shoulders as Hollywood lowered himself into the space next to me, as far from her as he could be. "I just wish I'd been a part of it."

"I didn't think it would be safe," I said. "I mean, look at me. I barely made it out alive."

"I should kick your fucking ass for that." Ru came into the living room next, her curly hair tied in a messy bun on top of her head. "How dare you take off without me? I mean...it's me."

She glared at me with puffy eyes, the only hint that what happened with the Beacon had worn her down. She'd spent the last six months getting the place renovated, and now it was a fucking rubble pile once again. This may have been the worst time to take off on my best friend, only to return looking like I'd been put through a meat grinder and hastily shoved back together.

"I mean, if *anyone* deserved to go with you—" Ru narrowed her gaze at me.

"Hey!" Verona scowled at her. "I got shot that night, too."

"We *all* got shot that night," Saint said, sitting down next to his girlfriend.

"And this was my problem before it was any of yours." Alba walked around the corner, having gone to the bathroom before this line of questioning. She gave me the same look as her sister, inscrutable and judgmental, like I'd stolen all the best cookies and licked them before putting them back in the jar.

"I mean..." Jer came out of the kitchen with his own pile of spaghetti, plopping down next to Hollywood and scooting closer, so Alba had space to curl in his lap. "If anyone has a reason to want Nikki's comeuppance, it's me, but not at the expense of anyone I love."

Suddenly, I'd been lined up against my family's firing squad, like my nearest and dearest had brought their finest ammunition to take me down for my crimes. Perhaps I deserved it. Perhaps I needed it.

"I didn't ask for any of your opinions," I said. "She was going to keep coming after us. I saw a problem and I took care of it. It's done now."

"Oh, and that's it, huh?" Verona raised her dark eyebrows at me, the diamond in her septum piercing shining in the dying afternoon light. "Didn't you say Gabriella promised Crow retribution? Do you think you took out all of those people and that's *not* gonna fall back on us somehow?"

Jer and Saint paused, exchanging a glance between them that I could only guess at. Being part of the SRMC, they knew a lot more about the consequences of this side quest than I probably ever would. Saint had always been silent and unreadable. The only person who could interpret his barely audible grunts was Ru. But I knew the fire in Jer's eyes.

Before I could reply, the back door opened and heavy boots sounded on the kitchen tile. Thor's boots. He came into the main room and paused, looking around at everyone sitting in our house, eating our food, and acting like it was a common occurrence.

"You give her the fifth degree?" Thor nodded in my direction.

"Not yet," Ru said. "We were getting to that."

Hollywood pointed at me, a stern expression forming between his brows. "No running away. No killing KC's ex-girlfriends, even if they're nasty two-faced snitches." He wagged his index finger like he was chiding a naughty dog. "Bad, bad Selene."

Alba and Ru erupted into laughter while I tried to hide the tiny bit of pride that shot through me. I had wanted to protect my family, and here they were, safe and sound and warm under my roof. Hadn't I done what I'd set out to do? Hadn't I completed my mission and made it back successfully?

I should be over the moon. I should be shouting my victory from the rooftops. But it didn't taste as sweet as I thought it would. I kept seeing that memory of Nikki from when we were children.

"Do you wanna make mud pies with me?"

I had nodded and grabbed her hand and my brother's. Together, the three of us raced out behind the clubhouse into the fields, disappearing into the forest until the sun went down. Her eyes had been so innocent then, so wide and clear and naive to the evils in this world. Jer and I hadn't lost our parents yet. We hadn't known the ways life would break our spirit. Nikki had giggled so loud, her smile so big, her cheeks so flushed with the happiness of a child enjoying the world. We thought we were safe. We thought nothing terrible would ever happen to us.

Countless more memories assaulted me—high school prom, when she'd fussed over Jer's hair until the moment they left, and the first morning I'd come downstairs to find her in one of Jer's old shirts and nothing else. I hadn't liked Nikki, but I hadn't despised her, either. At least, not then, not until she started breaking Jer's heart and acting like he meant nothing.

When I'd killed Giuseppe Caputi, I knew it was the right thing to do. He was a mass murderer, a man up to his ears in other people's blood. When I killed all the Caputi fucks after that, I never gave them a second thought. They were casualties of war, bodies on the wrong side of a trench. But Nikki sat like rotten sushi in my gut, like a two-ton lump of coal that wouldn't pressurize into anything shiny or invaluable no matter how hard I tried.

My mental library had been decimated in that bunker, and while I'd tried to pick up the pieces, to put it back together again, some books were irreparably damaged. Nikki's book had screamed at me for months, and I'd ignored it. Now that I couldn't anymore, it rattled on the burned-up pile, shaking against the scorched curling edges of other books, other memories, now lost. This wasn't like anything I'd done before.

Every time I closed my eyes, I saw her lifeless ones staring back at me. For those few heartbeats, while I'd been bleeding out on the floor, I thought that would be the last thing I'd ever see—her bruised purple lips, her haunting marble complexion, her glazed-over pastel-blue irises against millions of burst blood vessels painting the white a violent shade of crimson.

I'd destroyed her. I'd destroyed the little girl that once loved to play in the mud.

"Look at me," her corpse said, its head twisting unnaturally from the floor. Bent at this odd angle, she reminded me of a vampire in an old horror flick, some demon unfurling itself out of a television to choke the life from my lungs.

Heart pounding, I wasn't in the living room with my family anymore. I was back in that bunker. Everything else had disappeared —no Jimmy, no Thor, no Gabriella. Just me and her and the horrible things we had done to each other.

"Look at me," she snarled again, bending her arms backward to push herself off the floor. Foaming saliva dripping from her chin, she lumbered toward me as I scrambled to move away.

"No," I shouted, clenching my eyes shut. I couldn't see anymore. I couldn't watch her come closer. "No, no, no."

"Look at me!" Her icy breath coasted against my cheek, the stench of rotten eggs and metallic decaying blood filling my nose, coating my tongue, twisting down my throat to make me retch. "Look at me! Look at me! Look at me!" She screamed it over and over again, banging on the jail bars behind my head before sinking her claws into my shoulder to shake me. My skull slammed against the hard surface, sending jolts of blinding stabs through my brain and down my spine.

Oh fuck, I'd fallen asleep. This is a dream.

Despite that, I couldn't find the surface of my subconscious. I'd be trapped here forever with her, caged in this disgusting cell with those horrendous fluorescents and the knowledge that I'd never see my family again.

I deserved this. I'm a monster, and I always will be.

"Sel," came a deep voice. "Montgomery, wake up."

Fists wrapped around my forearms, and the line between reality and dreams blurred. A heavy weight sat on my chest, suffocating me, holding me down, keeping me captive. I punched out as hard as I could, shoving, clawing, scratching, anything to get her away, get her off me.

"No," I shouted. "You're dead. You're not real. You're not real."

"Selene," the voice came again, and this time, the scent of soap and warm, clean man hit me in the face. Soft tendrils of hair brushed against my cheek, and delicate lips dried the tears on my cheeks. "You're okay. You're here with me. Open your eyes."

I couldn't. No. I couldn't see her dead stare again.

"C'mon," Thor said, nudging my chin with his nose. "Open them for me."

Against every instinct I had, I forced my eyelids apart, gasping against the moonlit glow in my room. When had I fallen asleep? How had I gotten from the living room to my bedroom?

"You passed out on the couch," he said, wrapping his arms under my torso so he could roll us to the side. "I brought you in here. Everyone's gone. It's just us." He lay on his back, draping me across his broad, naked chest while he hugged me close.

I gasped for air, the room too hot, everything too close and yet, not close enough. Sobs racked the back of my throat, tearing from my lungs without my conscious effort. I didn't even know why I was crying. Was it Nikki? Did I feel that bad about killing her?

That was what I wanted, after all. She'd deserved it. She came after my family. She'd keep coming after us until someone did something. *It had to be me.*

I couldn't...I didn't regret it, did I?

"When I was in Afghanistan," he said, "they sent me to take out an extremist responsible for killing hundreds of thousands of people. It should have been an easy job, but when I got there, it turned out to be an ambush." He told me the story of his time in the SEALs and how he'd been forced between saving the life of two innocent people and killing the one responsible for murdering his best friend. "I killed that little girl's mother. I knew it. She knew it. My whole squadron knew it." Thor kissed my forehead, his lips lingering as he took deep inhales next to my hair. "Some kills haunt you for the rest of your life."

The heaviness in my chest snapped, sinking an icy-cold deluge into my heart. I couldn't hold back the tears now. They fell in earnest down my face, and I covered my eyes with my hands to keep my shame to myself. I didn't want him to see me like this, weak and terrorized over something I had brought on myself.

He'd told me to stay out of it. The club had told me to stay out of it.

Maybe I should have listened, maybe Thor had been right. Everything I'd ever done had been to try to fix what happened to my parents—going to med school, killing Giuseppe Caputi, going on raids with Thor, taking off after Nikki.

It was true. I thought I could handle it, and maybe if it had been anyone else, I could have. I learned a long time ago that the opposite of love wasn't hate; it was apathy. And therein laid the rub. The Caputis didn't sit like anvils on my conscience because I truly didn't care about them. I never had. But Nikki had been a member of my family. I'd known her for decades. Her betrayal sliced me open and turned that fraternal respect into raging abhorrence. I'd hunted her down from a place of emotional vulnerability, and now I paid the price.

I'd literally dug my own grave. Time for me to lie in it.

Flayed open and raw, I let the emotions have me. I couldn't stop them, even if I wanted to. Thor held me through it all, tightening his embrace when the worst of it came, whispering encouraging words of affirmation when he thought I'd been the most susceptible to hearing them.

Years passed by while we were tangled together in that bed, me processing what I'd done, him providing a rock for me to beat myself against. Sometime in the middle of it, I managed to fall asleep again. This time, the monster didn't come. This time, it let me have my peace.

25

SELENE

"Weren't you the one that told me to get extra rest when I got shot?" Jer eyed me skeptically from the other side of the counter as he wiped his oily hands on a rag before slinging it over his shoulder and raising an eyebrow at me.

It had only been ten days since I'd been released from the hospital, but sitting around the house and reading smutty novels could only entertain me for so long. I wanted to get back to my routine. I'd been by the hospital to visit Pollux a few times, but I still hadn't seen my uncle Crow since I'd been home. I had an ass whooping waiting for me. The sooner I got my strength back, the sooner I could prepare myself for that.

"I'm the doctor here," I told him, flipping a page in my trashy celebrity gossip magazine and blowing a big bubble with my gum, popping it before reeling it back into my mouth.

"Uh-uh."

"Don't fucking touch my socket wrenches," Bear shouted from inside the mechanic's bay, pointing a tire iron at Hollywood. "You leave them torqued, and it fucks up the springs."

"How did you grow up in a family with three other siblings and not learn to share?" Hollywood playfully smacked the iron with one of said wrenches, widening his grin when Bear's face turned beet red and his brown eyes flared.

"Don't fuck with me, Hollywood." He balled his fingers into fists as Hollywood reached out and playfully smacked Bear on the cheek. That was all it took to set Bear off after the beautiful brother, who raced out of the garage like his ass was on fire. He sprinted into the woods out behind the building, dodging through the rows of rehabilitated death traps and dissected junkers used for spare parts. "You fucking prick!"

I rolled my eyes and snorted, returning my attention to the latest celebrity A-lister who had fucked his nanny and cheated on his ridiculously gorgeous wife. *Fucking men.*

"I'm done for the day," Jer said. "Alba's making chicken parm if you're not doing anything."

I sighed and shook my head. "Thanks for the invite, but I'm just going to go home." *And hopefully fuck our uncle until I can't see.* "Like you said, I need to rest."

"Okay." He raked his eyes over me for one more moment before he took a step forward and put a hand on my shoulder. "I love you, Sel. You know that, right?"

"Yeah, of course." I looked up at him, trying to figure out what could prompt him to say that out of the blue. "Are you all right?"

He shrugged and kissed the side of my head. "Just happy you're here is all."

Great. Another unintended side effect of my ill-advised adventure. Everyone had faced the possibility that I might up and run away for good one day, so they went out of their way to make sure I understood my impact in their life, my brother especially.

The holidays usually made him sappy, and Christmas in particular could draw out the most altruistic side of people, but the way he looked at me then sent a stab right through my heart. Up until now, I suspected Jericho had never thought he could lose me. He never thought I'd do something that would put myself in so much danger. I'd broken a trust between us, one I wasn't sure I'd ever be able to fully rebuild.

"I love you, too, little brother."

He let out an indignant scoff, one so like my own, before rolling his eyes and shaking his head. "You're only older than me by thirty minutes."

"Hey, I learned a lot in that precious time. You'd be wise to listen to your elders."

He threw his head back and laughed before heading to the front door. "I'm taking off. Tell those idiots to get the fuck out of here whenever they're done beating the shit out of each other, all right?"

I chuckled and waved goodbye as he headed out to his truck and climbed in. A few moments later, Bear and Hollywood returned, flushed and sweaty, but otherwise laughing at each other. They said their goodbyes and headed home for the night, leaving me and Thor to close down the shop. We'd driven here together today, and if anyone thought anything about it, they kept it to themselves.

Our business wasn't any of theirs anyway, and I'd protect that with my dying breath.

When Thor came out of the back office, I sat up straighter, the molecules in my body so attuned to his that I could sense him approaching with my eyes closed. He raked his steel gaze over me, his hair loose over his shoulders, the tension in his gait alerting me to how close his beast was to the surface. My own monster perked up, bucking at the cage I kept her in, rattling the chains to be let out to play.

Thor hadn't touched me since that day in the woods before we were captured. He slept in my bed every night. He held me in his arms any time I woke up sobbing. But other than chaste kisses and soothing words, he kept his hands to himself.

This had started to irritate me.

Hadn't we said we weren't going to hide? Verona wasn't blind. She could see him going into my room every night and coming out again the next morning. Undoubtedly, she had told Hollywood by now, who would pass it around the club like a gossip blunt, not stopping until everyone had a puff-puff-pass.

"Montgomery," he purred. The low tone sent a shiver down my

spine, and I tensed my muscles to try to hide it. If he saw, he'd think it was weakness. He'd exploit it.

"Erickson." I tilted my chin up higher, refusing to back down, refusing to look away.

He moved closer, his hands linked behind his back as he circled around the desk, coming to stand in front of me. I turned the stool to the right, opening my legs into a V so he could step between them. With no warning, he grabbed me under the arms and lifted me to the desk, planting me on top of my magazine and the closing paperwork he needed to sign before I could count down the till. One eyebrow arched up his forehead and he took a step back, sharp gaze appraising me as I struggled not to move.

"You've been disobedient," he said, his tone dropping into a low snarl. "Reckless. Impulsive."

A playful lilt teased at the edge of his voice, but his stern gunmetal gaze rooted me to the spot, my heart pounding behind my ribs, surging blood to all the right places. I tried to clench my legs together, but the movement pulled at the healing wound on my thigh and I bit back a grimace.

"If you were one of my soldiers, I'd have you tied up and flogged for two whole days."

I flushed at the mental image, a racy lust surging in my veins. "Never say never."

He launched his hand out like a snake, wrapping around my throat, squeezing just enough to remind me who was in charge. I was a bad soldier, the one who had gone AWOL and returned home with an entirely new set of traumas to keep me up at night. When I looked into his eyes now, I saw the dark side of him peering back out at me. Thor was gone.

Now, I danced with his devil, his wolf, the one that had hunted me down for sport, the beast who had claimed me as his and would never let another person touch me again. My monster growled inside my mind, yearning to be a part of the conversation. Seeing no reason to hold back any longer, I slipped off the chains and set her free.

She was hungry. She had been starved of him this whole time, and now that he stood so close with his hand wrapped so possessively around my windpipe, she couldn't hold back any longer.

"Do you think I'm joking?" He came closer. "Do you think I chase everyone halfway across the fucking country?"

I recognized this battle of wills for what it was. He wanted me to resist. He wanted me to put up the same fight I always did because he liked to overpower me, and God help me, I loved the fact he could. I lifted my good leg, pressing the heel of my leather boot into his chest, reminding him he only touched when I allowed it.

"I think you love me so much, you don't know what to do with yourself." I bit my bottom lip and glanced down to the bulge behind his denim.

"That might have been true," he said, using his free hand to peel down the zipper on the side of my boot, "before you took off. But now?" He sucked in air through his teeth, tsking me like an insubordinate grunt as he grabbed the back of my shoe to guide it off my foot. "You have to rebuild my trust." After dropping it to the ground next to us, he lifted my bad leg to do the same. Just because I was in my jeans and socks now didn't mean I put down my defenses.

"Trust?" I ran the ball of my foot down his filthy white work shirt to his belt buckle, rubbing my toes along the metal before dipping lower. He was already hard, probably had been since the start of this game, and that fact sent another surge of fire right to my cunt. Underwear clinging to me uncomfortably, I ached for more. "Are you saying you don't trust me anymore?"

"I don't take kindly to disciplining my wildcat only to have her run off two days later." He canted his hips into my touch, stepping closer, moving the hand on my throat behind my head, twisting his fingers into my hair. "Even less so when she then gets me captured and nearly killed."

"A wildcat, am I?" I chuckled softly, the most evil parts of me delighting in being compared to such a creature. We were the wild things in the night, he and I. Dark. Twisted. Incapable of redemption. I wouldn't want it any other way. "What does that make you?"

He flashed me a toothy grin, yanking my hair back so I had to stare up at him while he talked. He completely owned me like this, and with very little resistance, I'd turned wanton and pliant with anticipation. I'd do whatever he asked. I'd worship every part of him. I'd make him feel so good every night. The scent of man and woods and motor oil slipped down my throat, intoxicating me, reminding me of what safety tasted like.

"Your willing plaything," he murmured against my lips, electric shocks of the almost touch radiating down to my curling toes and back up again. He was so fucking hot like this, absolutely feral for me and because of me. I loved it about him.

"You didn't have to chase me," I whispered, staring at his mouth while I took long, controlled breaths. I gripped his shoulders and dug my nails into his skin through his shirt, pulling him closer, needing him as close as possible. "You could have let me go."

He shook his head. "Never."

Our lips collided, hard and fast and sloppy, teeth slipping against each other, tongues wrestling for dominance. He explored the inside of my mouth like he'd never done it before, like he hadn't spent hours memorizing it. But that had never mattered to Thor, not when it came to me. Every time was like the first time, like he'd been gluttonous since he'd last dined on me and now that he got to have his fill again, he'd devour it as much as he could.

His hands were everywhere—in my hair, sliding down my back, kneading my ass and what he could get of my thighs before roaming back up to my breasts. He knew where to touch me, how to elicit those soft whimpers that made him chuckle and push for more.

I dragged my nails down his scalp and twisted them in his mane, tugging and pulling to make him growl in response. Heat hit me full blast when he rolled his pelvis against mine, massaging my clit with his cock through our jeans. The seam rubbed me just right, forcing me to break the kiss so I could gasp. He took the opportunity to nibble down my jaw to my neck, finding that sweet spot near my pulse point with his tongue, ramping up my needy want for more.

"Thor, please," I groaned, grinding myself against him, wrapping my good leg around his waist so I could pull him closer.

"Please what?" he mumbled against my collarbone, tugging my shirt down so he could lick more of my chest.

"Please take me. Fuck me." I moved my hands down his chest and over his stomach, going for his belt, but he grabbed my wrists to stop me, placing them at my sides, close to my hips.

"I said *you* needed to earn my trust again, not the other way around."

26

THOR

I grinned like a big, bad villain right before he stole the innocence from the sweet, demure princess. But perhaps there had never been innocence between us. We were both better in the shadows.

"Now, you sit still," I told her. "Don't fucking move."

I'd been fantasizing about this for years, much longer than I'd ever admit to anyone. I'd imagined doing this to her countless times, hundreds, every time I caught sight of these gorgeous long legs. I undid the button of her jeans, holding her gaze while I pushed the metal through the hole before tugging the zipper down. She shifted her hips to help me pull the denim to her ankles and off her feet, leaving her in her pink polka-dotted underwear.

Fucking adorable. I hummed in quiet approval before grabbing the stool behind me and scooting it closer so I could settle in for my meal. As much as a part of me wanted to rush this, the beast urged patience. He wanted to make this last, to wait for the right moment.

"Don't come," I said, running a knuckle down the obvious wet spot at the very center of her cunt. "This is mine to play with until I feel the trust has been restored."

It was mostly role-play of course. I trusted Selene down to my marrow, and I always would. I lifted her good leg over my shoulder, adjusting the other one in the most comfortable position before dragging my lips down the inside of her thigh, biting and licking at pieces I liked the most.

"And when will that be?" She nudged at the feral side of me, knowing one of these times, she'd push too far and I would snap. Maybe she wanted me to; she'd claimed to love the animal inside me, saying it matched her own. I couldn't disagree.

"When I fucking say so." I latched my lips on her most sensitive skin, sucking at her through her panties. She moaned and bucked against me, liking the roughness in contrast to the warmth and decadence of my mouth. I ran my tongue over her, lapping and swallowing her down. Gods, she tasted so fucking good—like woman and arousal and *mine*.

Forgetting anything related to instructions, she ran her fingers through the hair on the top of my head, angling her hips so I'd hit a certain spot. But that disobeyed my rules, and this whole thing had been about rebuilding "trust." How could we do that if she didn't even keep her word?

I grabbed her wrists with a punishing grip, making her wince as I twisted her arms behind her back. "I said don't fucking move," I growled, biting her earlobe for emphasis. "Do I need to tie you down?"

Thor, the human, was completely gone now, leaving only the beast in his place. If she were healed, I'd set her little ass to run through the woods out back. I'd revel in hunting her down and making her pay the old-fashioned way. But, being injured, she was easy enough prey on top of my front desk.

"Would you?" She raised an eyebrow, and I let out a disbelieving laugh at how she lived to stomp on my thin ice.

"Don't tease." I hooked my index and middle finger under the crotch of her underwear, yanking it back before letting it go with a loud *thwap*.

She let out a whimper at the sting, and the sound reverberated through me, etching itself in my molecules. I'd never forget it. Her head fell back on her shoulders, her mouth open and her eyes closed —a fucking vision-made manifest.

"C'mon, Montgomery," I whispered, pulling the panties to the side so I could spear my tongue through her overheated skin, taking my time to savor her, every single note. "You have more self-control than that."

She huffed out a laugh because, let's be real, neither of us had much discipline when it came to the other person, not anymore. For years, I had held back, telling myself she was Gemma's niece and I shouldn't touch her. I had wasted so much time.

But for my tongue between her legs, I would move mountains. So despite my shaking biceps and sweating palms, I peeled her underwear off her body, careful not to hurt her wound. She'd referred to it as an ugly, disgusting thing, but I thought it added character. Chicks weren't the only ones into scars. I'd seen it a thousand times by this point, and just now, I was more focused on other parts of her anatomy.

My pulse raced and the rest of the world faded away while I took my fill, licking and sucking and nibbling in all the places that made her moan. I fucked her cunt with my face, but she'd always been a quick trigger. She didn't last long, and as soon as I nudged a second finger inside, curling to find the spot that sent her into a frenzy, she lost it.

Tension snapped through her body, tightening her muscles, forcing moans and sighs out of her mouth louder than I'd ever heard her make before. I'd told her not to come, but she didn't listen. She never did, and I suspected she might do that anyway, so I kept going, kept licking, kept sucking, kept fingering her while she fell apart.

But then, maybe just to fuck with her...I didn't stop. She'd come, her pussy probably far too sensitive for my ministrations, but I kept going.

"No," she whined, trying to wrestle away, but I draped my heavy arm over her hips to keep her in place, clawing my fingernails into the flesh on her waist. "No, stop. Stop."

She didn't want me to stop, not really, and if she did, she would have been able to use her safe word. But she liked to play into this as much as I did. She was mine to do with what I would, my plaything, my little kitten. She bucked and tried to scramble away, but I held her firmer, fucked her harder, driving her toward another agonizing climax.

"Thor," she groaned, and I hummed in response, making her melt into the touch, her shoulders hunched near her ears, her thighs spreading farther on their own.

"Oh, did we like that?" I looked up, grinned, and latched my lips around her clit, sucking and humming at the same time. She collapsed, a second climax yanking her under its wave. Gods, it fucking set me off, making me hard, sparking through my bloodstream. I loved turning her to mush like this. No one knew her as well as I did and never would. She was mine...truly mine.

After she'd turned to fucking putty in my hands, I stood and lifted her, putting her down on the stool and lowering the height so she was face-to-face with the bulge in my jeans. She tried to lift her arms to help me undo the button, but she could barely move. I chuckled and pushed her hands away, reaching inside so I could pull my throbbing cock out.

"Open up, Montgomery," I said, and she did, sticking her tongue out so I could slot myself on top of it. Fuuucckking hell, she enveloped me in a hot, sucking embrace, lapping that talented tongue over my shaft the way I liked. She swallowed me down, breathing through her nose so she didn't gag, and the feel of her tight little mouth working me so good sent tingles down my legs and back up again. I grabbed the top of her head and the back of her neck, fucking her skull the way I wanted, the way we both wanted. She liked it rough, she liked being a mess afterward, and fuck me, I couldn't stop the filthy words as they tumbled over my lips.

"You're such a dirty slut for me, aren't you? Letting me fuck your face after a long day at work. But you like it, don't you?" My head fell back on my shoulders, euphoria erupting in every molecule, the anticipation of my orgasm surging through my muscles. She grabbed my balls with one hand and used the other to work me while she sucked harder, lapped faster, driving right where she wanted me.

My release built, my cock twitching and thigh muscles growing more strained the longer it went on. But that wasn't what I wanted. Right before I would have exploded, I pulled back and gripped the base of my cock so hard, the tip turned purple.

"Stand up," I snarled. She complied, and I gingerly turned her toward the counter, bent her over it, and put a giant palm between her shoulder blades to pin her in place. My beast had a hold of me now, and I couldn't contain him. He needed to be inside her, to fill her to the fucking brim, to claim her hard and rough, the way we both liked. "Brace yourself. This isn't going to be nice."

I shoved inside her so hard and fast that we both gasped at the intrusion, and she gripped the other side of the counter to hold herself in place. Normally, I would have taken a moment to let her adjust. At almost ten inches, it wasn't like I was easy to take. But I didn't this time. I put one hand on her shoulder, the other around her throat, palming her windpipe to use for leverage. I pulled out for only a heartbeat before shoving back in harsher and meaner.

"Tell me you won't run again," I said, the desperation in my voice coming from some guttural part of my soul—the beast's soul. "Tell me you're mine forever."

"I'm yours," she said, with no hesitation.

"Tell me you love me." I needed to hear it. I yearned to hear it.

"I love you." Her voice cracked while she said it, whimpers mixing with mewls as her body gave in to my violent treatment. I relished in it, in the rush of her bucking back on me as fervently as I rutted into her. The space between our slapping thighs was drenched, a decadent display of her orgasm dripping down our legs, likely making a mess on the standing mat, but that fucking delighted me and spurred me on.

I grabbed the hair at the base of her head and yanked her head up, arching her back into me, her palms sliding across the granite to keep herself up. I nipped at her earlobe before moving down the side of her neck to her shoulders and back up again.

"Tell me how bad you want me. Tell me I'm yours. Tell me—" My forehead went to her crown, my thrusts firmer now, more possessive, more like a claiming. "Tell me—"

Suddenly, the words weren't about role-play anymore. They weren't about a forgone trust between us. I didn't care about the blatant displays of adoration. I already knew she loved me and had for years. No, this had suddenly become about so much more. I wanted this forever. I wanted...I wanted her to be my old lady, to marry me, to be my partner for life. And the fact she might reject me, despite how unlikely that was, terrified both me and my inner beast.

"You're mine, Thor," she said, softening her tone, seeming to recognize this without me having to say it. "And if you even so much as think about touching someone else, I will hunt you down and tear your heart from your chest. Do you understand? You belong to me." She fucked me now, focusing her territorial rage into marking me the way I'd marked her. "You think you're capable of sadistic things to find me?" She scoffed and rolled against me, making me hit a spot inside her that had me sucking in a gasp and tightening my fingers on her throat. "You'll never be able to hide from me, Thor. I would burn the fucking world down to get to you."

That was all it took. I unleashed hell on her cunt, rutting against her like a brute, scratching and clawing her right over the edge of her next release. I came with her, growling into her ear, sinking my teeth into her trapezius muscle so hard, I almost broke the skin.

In the aftermath of whatever that was, she lay limp on the counter, me barely holding myself up behind her, both of us sated down to our marrow. I panted on top of her, and the heat of her body under me unraveled warmth in my chest like a protective alpha. As long as I was here, nothing could hurt her. And almost as important, as long as she was here, nothing could hurt me.

27

—————

SELENE

Crow summoned me to the clubhouse three days later. I figured it was time I owned up to what I'd done. The MC had every right to ask me to leave and never come back, even though I stood by my justification. Nikki wasn't in the club. Neither was I. Technically, me tracking her down wasn't any of Crow's business.

"There she is," he said from his spot at the head of the table in the back room. It had the SRMC crest burned into the center, a rose with a dagger going through the middle. "The hero of the hour." His tone dripped with sarcasm and judgment.

"Uncle." I pursed my lips and glanced around at the empty space. At this time of the day, only the hang-arounds and the old ladies were milling about, doing whatever it was they did with their lives of leisure. He gestured at the spot to his right, normally Aris's seat, and I limped to it, pulling out the chair and lowering myself into it as best as I could.

"How are you feeling?" He nodded to one of the hang-arounds in the corner, who quickly brought us two cups of ice water. He sipped at his, and I ignored mine.

"Much better, thank you." It wasn't necessarily a lie. True, the wound was healing. But on the inside, the muscle pained me more every day. I understood what Verona was talking about a few weeks ago. It wasn't like the injury itself still hurt, but it wasn't getting better, either.

He nodded and narrowed his eyes, the scolding look of a patriarch about to deliver his ruling. "And you know how you've done wrong?"

I cleared my throat and shifted in my seat. "Uncle, I'd like to start my three-part defense by first stating I am not, nor have I ever been, a member of the Steel Roses Motorcycle Club. Neither has Nikki McNally. As you are the president of such club, you know your jurisdiction does not apply—"

He held up a hand to cut me off. "You're just like your old man, you know that? Jee-sus Christ. He could argue his way out of anything, ever since we were kids."

I laughed softly, shaking my head. My father had been nicknamed Esquire because he'd been a lawyer by trade, a damned good one. "I should have gone to law school instead, huh?"

"He'd be proud of you no matter what." Crow's ancient eyes assessed me, the wrinkles at the corners telling the story of the long life he'd lived. It wasn't in years, either. It was in the two siblings he had lost, the son currently on life support at the hospital, the members of his club he'd seen maimed and brutalized, the MC princesses he'd tried and failed to protect from danger. "Look, you're a grown woman. I can't ground you or command you not to do idiotic shit. As long as you know that what you did was stupid as fuck."

I shook my head. "I don't see it that way."

"Oh?" He raised his eyebrows. "You've possibly started a feud with the Kings of Carnage. Do you think we have enough brothers to fight two wars?"

I swallowed against the dread threatening to rise in my throat. "They helped bomb the Beacon. If it comes to that, they deserve it."

He paused and narrowed his gaze, taking a slow deep breath to indicate he did not feel that same way. "Despite this, Gabriella showed her hand that day in the bunker. She's scared. She's acting impulsively." Crow gave me a fatherly grin. "She's scrambling. That alone is worth its weight in gold."

I ran my tongue over my lips and agreed. "Nikki is dead. She can't harm us anymore."

He remained silent for a moment, tapping his fingers on the table until he finally gave me one solemn nod. "You have my thanks."

That, at least, I could drink to. I held up my glass and took a swallow.

"But," he said, "I need a favor from you in return."

And so quickly, he sucked the joy right out of the room.

"Oh?"

"I need you to check on Leo Caputi."

I sneered, suddenly remembering the conversation Bear and I had before I left. His leg had been fucked up in the scramble to capture him, and it hadn't healed correctly. "How is his knee?"

Crow pursed his lips. "He's not doing well. Doc is..." He cleared his throat and shifted in his seat. "Doc doesn't have the same bedside manner."

"Yeah, no shit." He would rather slit his throat and bleed him dry. "What do you want me to do?"

"Heal him. Get on his good side. Get him talking."

I laughed because I thought he was joking. When he didn't respond with his own guffaw, my grin dropped. "What? Me? You think *I* can get to him?"

He took another sip of his water but said nothing.

"Have you met me? You'd have better luck getting Jericho—"

"KC wants him dead. As does half the club." Crow sighed and rolled his eyes.

"Then you should kill him and get it over with."

"You're not thinking big enough." He used his thumb to spin the ring on his index finger, a tick he did when he was about to drop something heavy on his audience. "What if we could partner with him?"

I raised my eyebrows, stifling down the shock as it bubbled in my chest.

"What if we could use him against Gabriella?" Crow shrugged. "She's the real threat. She's the reason the whole war started."

"He tried to kill your daughter. He tried to kill Saint and Ru."

Crow nodded. "And KC killed his uncle and his brother. You, yourself, have killed how many of his family members? Nobody's hands are clean."

I couldn't believe what I was hearing. "Why the fuck would we ally with him? He's scum. He's a piece of shit—"

"The enemy of my enemy can be my friend." Crow eyed me with a knowing stare, the wise sage here to dispense wisdom on the insolent pupil.

Fuck that.

"No," I said. "I'm not the right person. You need someone with charm, someone with charisma, someone willing to play the game. That's not me. I *hate* him, and I always will."

"Fair enough. Thank you for being honest." Crow furrowed his eyebrows, seeming to consider that for a moment, before coming to some silent conclusion. "I'd still like you to check in on him, if you wouldn't mind. Consider it a personal favor to your dear favorite uncle."

I pursed my lips and ignored his wording, ultimately deciding to give in. "Okay, I'll heal his stupid leg, and then I'm done. You and me, we're square."

"We're square." This time when he said it, the sincerity echoed in his dark eyes. There could be no denying he was Verona's father, especially not when they shared that same expression of skeptical acceptance.

I nodded. "Anything else?"

He smirked and tilted his head, taking another drink of water. "You seem happier."

I chuckled. "I always feel this great after getting the shit kicked out of me." Not to mention the nightmares and PTSD and constant ache in my quadricep. Was that not happiness?

"That's not what I meant."

I took a deep breath, preparing myself for the *talk*—the one where he told me he had heard about the evolution of my relationship with Thor, his brother-in-law, my *other* favorite uncle.

"It's not any of my fucking business, and Lord knows you two deserve your peace." He let the suggestion hang there, perhaps waiting to see if I'd take the bait and talk to him about it. But I didn't want to. The thing between me and Thor was precious and dearly held; it always had been. It didn't matter what Crow thought or felt about it.

"I hope you're doing what you want." He gave me a soft smile. "You're too young to have lived so long."

Between me and Jericho, my brother had always been the one that wore his heart on his sleeve. He had a short fuse that burned bright and fast. Me, on the other hand, I held everything inside, bottling it up until I could use it for a purpose. My uncle's words broke me, and tears welled in the corners of my eyes before I could blink them back. My cheeks burned as a sob clogged my throat and I tried to choke it down. Nodding and trying to bury all these wretched hormones he'd evoked in my chest, I took another drink of water and forced myself to swallow.

"Thank you, Uncle," I said. Sensing he'd said his piece, I stood to leave, but he reached out to grab my hand, stopping me.

"You do anything like this again, and I won't be able to be so understanding." He said it on a whisper, as if he didn't want the hang-around or anyone else to hear.

I narrowed my eyes, waiting for him to release me, but he seemed to want my acknowledgment before he did. I nodded and tugged my arm away to head back out front. "Have a nice night. Thanks for the chat."

Things would get rowdy soon. The brothers would get out of their day jobs and come here to blow off steam, just as they did every night. Two weeks ago, I would have posted up behind the bar and slung them back until the wee hours of the morning. But now, I ached for something different, something more intimate. So I figured I'd fulfill my uncle's request and see what other trouble I could find.

IT REEKED like old blood and shit inside the barn where they kept Leo Caputi, and I grimaced at the immediate drop in temperature as soon as I stepped inside. The only heat source was the fireplace, and they refused to turn that on unless they were tearing someone apart and burning the bits they took. My heart pounded behind my ribs as I moved down the center aisle and took a deep breath, filing my raging fury away so it didn't distract me. Lightbulbs hung from overhead, guiding the way to the main cell, but they didn't light up the entire space, so it still had that creepy glow that spoke of the lives that had been wiped out within its walls.

The prospects on duty shut the barn doors behind me, and I stopped, glancing over my shoulder to see Hollywood following closely behind.

"Cozy, huh?" He flashed me a grin, revealing the dimples in his cheeks and his beautiful, glittering eyes. Not only was he attractive in that traditional masculine way, six five and covered in muscles, but he had an easygoing radiance that instantly made everyone feel at ease. Even if I'd always related to him more like a brother, I understood how people could fall so effortlessly into his bed.

"If he's been living here the whole time, I know why his leg isn't healing." Gripping the leather handle on my bag tighter, I forced myself to move closer to the cell, stopping when I finally took in the sight.

It was far worse than I imagined.

Leo Caputi sat on the far edge of the rectangular stall, one leg bent, the other outstretched in front of him. He'd been imprisoned for over two months and looked like it. His hair had grown out, now dark and curling around his shoulders, and his clothes were tattered, gaping holes in the knees and elbows hinting at his mistreatment. Dirt and blood smeared his skin, and aside from a small bowl of water and a bucket to shit in, he hadn't been given any other amenities.

For the first week or two, he had refused to eat as he detoxed from whatever he'd been binging when we'd taken him. Now, dried out and sober, he'd resigned himself to our food but hadn't uttered a word since he'd been here. The brothers were running out of ideas, and Leo was quickly losing his potential usefulness.

He looked up when I moved closer, his scowl visible even from the cover of darkness.

"How are you?" I asked.

He didn't answer, just tilted his head back so it rested against the wall behind him. Objectively, he was an attractive man, despite the withdrawal and the grime and the guts. I'd seen pictures of him in his prime, surrounded by the women who agreed with me. Now, he looked pitiful, like a dog that should have been put of his misery weeks ago.

"I hear your knee is still fucked up."

No answer, just more angry glares.

"Are you able to put weight on it?"

Still no response.

Hollywood chuffed a laugh from next to me. "Trust me. It's like talking to a wall."

I nodded to the door. "Unlock it. I need to get in there."

My accomplice hesitated, shoving his hands in his pockets while he stared at our captive. "You're not gonna do anything stupid, right?"

Leo shifted his attention to Hollywood and let out a long, slow sigh through his nose, clearly annoyed by our presence. He was chained to the wall with a fucked-up knee and barely any weight on his bones. I doubted he could do much more than sit there and brood.

"Let's just get this over with, okay? Neither one of us is looking forward to it." I nodded to the lock, raising my eyebrows as I waited for Hollywood to pull out the keys. I shoved all the memories of Ru in a hospital bed and V with her scar into a book inside my mind. This motherfucker had been the one responsible for that night, had sent his fucking cronies after my family. He'd be lucky if I didn't shove a dagger into his heart myself.

Grumbling curses under his breath, Hollywood unlocked the

door and yanked it to the side so I could slip through. Leo stared at me while I approached, his jaw set, his lips curled into a thin line. I had expected to see hatred in those eyes, just as he must have seen the animosity in mine. However, the only thing behind Leo's chestnut-colored irises was pain, and when I kneeled at his side so I could assess his injury, I understood why.

Leo's knee had swollen to double its size, and while the wound had healed on the surface, I suspected it was a tangle of misshapen bone and scar tissue underneath. It likely needed to be drained, reset, and recast in order for him to walk on it again, and even then, I couldn't be sure. Doc should have handled this weeks ago.

"Does it hurt here?" I squeezed down his shin, watching as he curled his fingers into a ball and yanked on the chains. "On a scale of one to ten, what would you say?"

Still nothing.

"It'll be much harder to treat you if you don't help me." I raised an eyebrow when I moved up his thigh, pinching a sensitive area that made him gasp and let out an involuntary whine. "It didn't heal correctly. He needs surgery."

"Meaning?" Hollywood crossed his arms over his chest, his gaze concentrated on Leo's limb.

"I have to cut it open, break the bone, and put it back together the right way. He'll need recovery time and physical therapy. It could be months until he can walk again."

"No," came the sharp sound from Leo.

Both Hollywood and I glanced at him, shaken by the sudden deep baritone. He darted his frantic eyes between the two of us like we could somehow save him from his fate.

"If I don't, you won't be able to use it." I grimaced because it might already be too late, but with a decent recovery plan and access to a clean environment, it *could* heal up nicely. "I might as well cut it off."

"Just give me medicine," he said. "No more knives."

I narrowed my eyes at him, suddenly curious how much time he'd spent with Doc before I agreed to see him. Ignoring his request, I turned back to Hollywood.

"He can't stay here."

Hollywood dropped his jaw, his eyes going wide like I'd asked him to recite the Greek alphabet forward and backward. "What?"

I shrugged, remembering what Crow had said. Leo might be a way to work against Gabriella. If we could ally with him, maybe he could help us take her out. Maybe we could end the war, end the bloodshed. It could start with this one act of kindness, this one olive branch across an enemy trench.

"He needs to be somewhere clean with access to heat and fresh water. Or it'll just get fucked up again."

Leo popped his head up, his eyes wide and his eyebrows raised. Whatever he thought I was going to suggest, it wasn't that, and it nearly had him pissing himself with excitement. After two months in this shithole, I imagined he was desperate for a warm shower.

"What do you want me to do with him?" Hollywood blinked, still dumbfounded. "Book him a room at the Ritz? He's fucking Leo Caputi."

"I don't know, Hollywood." I stood and clapped his shoulder. "But he needs a bath before I can operate on him, and if he ever wants to use this leg again, I'll need to do that as soon as possible."

Hollywood looked like I'd slapped him, like I'd hauled off and kicked him in the nuts right here in front of our mortal enemy. "And who's supposed to do that?"

"Guess it's your lucky day, huh?" I laughed, turning back to my medical bag for a bottle of antibiotic pills and a syringe.

"This is fucking torture," Hollywood said, pulling out his phone from his back pocket. "I'm not going to bathe the son of a bitch. Get a goddamned prospect to do it." He wandered out of the cell, muttering as he pressed the rectangle to his ear.

"How do you want to do this?" I said to Leo, holding up the pills and the needle. "I could give you the pills only if you promise you'll take them without trouble." I shook the orange item in question, making a rattling sound with the amoxicillin. When he went to reach for them, I held them out, giving him a skeptical eye. "Fair warning, I'm not as nice as Doc. If you spit them out or hide them in your cheek or some stupid shit, I'll come back here every eight hours to personally stab you in the ass."

Leo gave me a solemn nod and held his hand out so I could dump two pills into his palm before handing him a bottle of water and an energy bar. He washed them down, sticking his tongue out afterward in some dramatic display to show me he *had* in fact taken his medication before opening the package so he could eat.

"Prez, respectfully, this is bullshit." Hollywood paused while Crow responded, and judging by the way his tone echoed over the enclosure, I got the sense he was on the losing end of this argument. "The son of a bitch tried to kill me."

Leo attempted to hide a smile by ducking his head down toward his chest, but I saw it. I thought about kicking him in the knee to knock that smirk off his face, but that might make things more difficult for me in the long run. I needed Leo to get better. Crow and the MC needed Leo to get better.

And maybe...just maybe...if he felt grateful enough, we'd convince him to help us.

"Yeah...Yeah..." Hollywood pinched the bridge of his nose and wandered back into the cell, staring down at Leo like he was literal shit on his boots. "Yeah, okay. You got it, Prez." He lowered his phone, pressed end, and glared at our captive.

"Guess it's time for my sponge bath, is it?" Leo curled his lips into a filthy devil's grin, and for the first time since Crow had told me his plan, I had a faint flicker of hope it might actually work.

28

THOR

Selene liked the chase. For fifteen years, she had loved to run from me, and I had lived to seek her little ass out. Her being shot in the leg put a damper on that game for now, but I had a few other ideas based on the things we'd agreed were fair game between us. I parked my truck farther down on the mountain so she wouldn't see me coming. When I got to the house after my shift at the garage, I scoped the place for a few moments to confirm where she was inside. The lights were off downstairs, but the windows in her room glowed with a soft amber haze.

After I decided on the quietest route, I sneaked in through the back door, careful to make as little noise as possible. Heart pounding and fingers twitching with excitement, I stalked down the hallway, attempting to step in places where I knew the wood wouldn't squeak. Her door had been closed, but not shut all the way, so I planned to charge in and grab her quickly, "forcing" myself on her before she had a chance to "stop" me.

But I should have known better. I thrust the door open...to an empty room. Her bed lay unmade, covers shoved haphazardly around, and a quick search of her bathroom revealed no one in there, either. I didn't think there was enough room in her closet for her to hide, but I checked anyway.

Empty.

I chuckled, a sick thrill shooting down the center of my chest when I realized I'd have to search the rest of the house. She'd been in here moments ago when I peered in through the window, so she must have heard me coming, must have known the game was on, must have hid to play along.

Trying to force my breaths out in slow, measured exhales, I swept the first floor. *Nothing.* Which meant she was in the basement, my old room.

"Kitten..." My boots echoed off the stairs as I descended into the dark, dank space, but I no longer cared about trying to remain quiet. This would be the only place left for her to hide. "Come out, come out, wherever you are."

A scuff in the far left-hand corner got my attention, but between the shadows and the boxes of old junk piled up down here, I couldn't tell where she was. The thrill of the hunt pumped through my blood as I took slow, deliberate steps in that direction, my vision sharpening in the dark, my audio response honing to her unique frequency. I slowed my breathing, taking measured inhales and pausing so I could hear over my own body.

A hushed breath came from my right.

I turned and snapped my arm out at just the right time to grab her waist as she passed, and I wrapped her struggling body into mine, her back to my chest, her mouth under my palm, her head on my shoulder.

"Got you," I snarled.

She laughed as cold metal teased my windpipe, the sharp blade of a knife digging into the skin near my jugular. She knocked her other hand into the inside of my thigh, near my groin, no doubt fisting another sizable weapon.

"Let me go or I'll slice you open." She mumbled it behind my hand, but I understood her words anyway. Fuck yeah, my girl knew how to get my pulse pounding. I wanted to be her villain as much as she wanted to be my damsel in distress. But in this fairy tale, she could kick my ass nearly as hard as I could hers.

I gripped her tighter, digging my fingers into her jaw. "I'd like to see you try."

A sharp zing shot down the left side of my throat, smarting like a paper cut, and I let out a sigh, physically unable to stop it. Warm, sticky liquid oozed down my windpipe, pooling in the dip between my collarbones. The fucking minx had sliced me.

"You'll pay for that." I twisted her in my hold, disarming her and trapping her wrists between us in a quick move. The knives clinked to the floor at our feet, but Selene stared up at me with that moonlight gaze, iridescent and shimmering in the faint glow of the basement. Down here in the dark, she looked like the wildcat I'd teased her about a few days ago. She could be the creature hiding in the woods, waiting for the perfect moment to pounce and sink claws into my throat.

"What are you going to do?" Her grin said it all—her lack of respect for my authority, how she planned to fight this the whole night, how much she hoped I'd hold her down through it. "Spank me? Beat me?" That smile widened, and she tucked her bottom lip between her teeth, making me wish I could bite that flesh myself. "Stab me?"

"You should be so lucky." Shaking my hair out of my face, I advanced on her, pleased when she backed up and stared at me like she couldn't wait to see what I'd do next. "I bet you'd get on your knees if I told you to, wouldn't you?" Grinning, I waited for her to sneer before continuing. "Tell me I'm right."

She growled and snapped her teeth at me, the wind brushing my beard before I yanked my face out of the way. I tightened my grip on her wrists and tugged her toward me, leaning down so I could use my height to intimidate her. I loved how much bigger I was than her, how much I could toss her ass around like she weighed nothing.

"Go on," I said, relishing in the delicious perversion of watching her cheeks turn pink.

She took a deep breath, her gaze falling to the trickle of blood trailing down my neck and under my shirt. Without responding, she leaned forward and dragged her silky, wet tongue across the length of the wound, and the sparks from that touch sizzled down the back of my legs and up again, gathering in my balls.

Fuck, she was so Gods damned hot like this—savage and rabid and addictive. I didn't normally have a blood kink, but when she leaned back to reveal crimson staining her lips and teeth, I almost keeled over for how fucking hard my lower gut clenched. I let go of her to grab the back of her neck with one hand and force her mouth to mine. She tasted like metal and whiskey and girl, and the concoction unleashed the beast inside. I forced my tongue into her mouth, sucking and licking to get more of her, desperate for all that she could offer.

I knew, even then, it wouldn't be enough. Nothing would ever be enough. I'd become insatiable for her, and I thought back to earlier in the day when all I'd wanted was to make her mine. With my blood smeared across her lips, the possessive monster that lived in the dark pit of my heart reared up in a toxic, territorial rampage.

I had to have her. I could waste no time.

Breaking away, I hauled her up on my shoulder, holding behind her knees to keep her there. She squealed and laughed, digging into my lower back to keep herself upright while I raced back up the stairs and into our bedroom. I tossed her down onto the mattress, stripping off my shirt while she scrambled to her knees, peeling her tank top off her chest. Using my shirt, I wiped the rest of my blood away and tossed it to the side, taking a moment to stare at my spoils.

Her brown hair tangled around her head in a messy halo, and her nipples were already pebbled, pointing at me, begging me to suck one into my mouth. Pale skin flushed in the night air, her shoulders trembling with nerves.

Fuck, that got me even more turned up. She was the most dangerous person in this room, possibly in a hundred-mile radius, and I reduced her to shivers.

"You didn't answer me," I said, taking a step toward her as I slid the leather of my belt through the metal buckle, whipping it out of the denim loops in a whoosh that could only mean one thing. I planned to use it to tie her razor-sharp claws down so I could have my way with her. "Tell me how submissive you are. Tell me how little I have to say to get you to do what I want."

Her eyebrows shot up her forehead and her grin vanished at the accusation, but we both knew how true it was. She'd fight and sneer and swipe out at me only for me to overpower her. She *wanted* it as much as I did, and I was the sick fucker that wanted to hear her admit to it.

"Submissive, am I?" She curled her tongue around one of her canines as she eyed me like a fucking vixen, like she knew all the right buttons to push.

I laughed and kneeled on the bed in front of her, nodding as I crowded her back. "Submissive as a little kitten. My kitten."

She gasped and tried to claw at my face, which was exactly the reaction I wanted. I grabbed her wrists and held them together while she thrashed. As strong and capable as she was, I still outweighed her, and she wasn't fighting me nearly as hard as she could. Once the leather was secured around her arms, I shoved them over her head and held her there while she wiggled under me, pretending to try to get free, her legs naturally spreading wider.

Now that she was only in her underwear, that hot cunt slid right up against my growing cock, sending a rush of euphoria straight to my balls, and I moaned, nearly melting into her while she struggled.

"Fuck," I whimpered, slamming a hand into the mattress next to her ribs to hold myself upright as I rolled into her again. She turned her head to the side, exposing her neck and the bite marks I'd left there yesterday. Gods, I loved the sight of them. I leaned down to lick across the sensitive purple skin, causing her to suck in a harsh breath. She always tasted so fucking delicious, like flowers and female, and her mewling sounds made me feel so damned powerful.

"Now, who's the submissive one?" She giggled, soft and feminine, reminding me she wasn't all hard edges and jagged pieces. Deep down, Selene had a soft side that needed to be soothed and coaxed into coming out. "You look like a lost puppy that just discovered what it's like to be pet—"

I kissed her to shut her up because if she kept going down that road, I was going to lose my shit before I had a chance to take her the way I wanted. She moaned into my mouth, and I rutted against her again, rolling that hard part of me over the soft part of her, driving us both into a frenzy.

"Stay here," I said, breaking the kiss to drag my mouth down her jaw to her neck, licking and sucking at those delicate spots again. "Don't make a move. If you do, I swear to the Gods, Montgomery, I will make this last all night."

She laughed and looked down at me, her stare glittering as I kissed my way down her chest. Ignoring the throb in my dick, I gripped her tits and bit into the tops of them, relishing in how soft and beautiful they were.

"What if that's what I want, huh?" She rolled against me, urging me on. "What if I want this to last forever?"

I rolled one nipple into my mouth, lapping at it like it could give me the secret to eternal life. She arched into me, throwing her head back as I continued my torture. Those little sounds she made coasted down the center of my body, etching themselves into my molecules, physically becoming a part of me.

"I could make that happen." I went to the other breast, giving it the same torture as the first one, sucking and biting until I had her panting.

"What do you mean?" It was nearly a silent whisper, her tone more serious.

"That's enough out of you." I went lower, dragging her panties down her thighs and off her ankles, crumbling them into a ball and rising back over her, hovering the fabric over her mouth. "Open your fucking lips."

She glared at me for a moment, seeming to debate whether she would do it. If she didn't, I'd force her, and she knew it. So she kept her gaze on me and slowly dropped her jaw, pleasing me in all those lovely, rotten ways. I stuffed them inside and grinned, wishing I could memorize everything about this moment—the look of disgusted pleasure in her eyes, the bead of sweat sliding down her temple to her hair, the way her perfect pink mouth wrapped around her girly lace underwear.

"I said you were mine." I kissed her stomach, moving to her hips, biting the fleshy bits I liked the most, marking them so she knew they were my favorite. She wasn't skin and bones, and that was one of my most favorite parts. Her curves matched everything else wild about her. "Did you think I was fucking around?"

I stared up her body from between her legs, her throat bobbing as she swallowed and tried to digest what I was saying. But I couldn't stop. I had to say more, do more, touch more. I pulled her legs over my shoulders, kneading my hands down her thighs to her ass, scooping it into my palms so I could hold her exactly how I wanted when I said the next part. She needed to know how I truly felt, what I'd been thinking since earlier in the day...perhaps since I'd met her.

"We should get our own place." I dragged my teeth down the inside of her thigh, teasing and biting harder. "I want something that's ours...that's *only* ours."

Her legs shook against the sides of my face, her inhale caught in her throat, and I knew I had her.

"I want your name in my skin." I speared through her cunt with my tongue, savoring her taste like it was the first time again, her distinct taste appealing to every animalistic urge I had. She got me so fucking riled, I couldn't stand it. I wanted more of her, always more. "I want my marks on you every day. I want your name on my cut. I want you in my blood, in my fucking bones..."

She perked her head and looked down at me, that curiosity in her eyes turning to apprehension and confusion. Furrowing her brows, she mumbled something unintelligible around her panties, making me laugh as I wrapped my lips around her clit.

Selene groaned and tossed her head back, rubbing her pelvis against me, seeking more friction that I was all to happy to give her.

"Will you marry me?" I kissed her pussy, worshipping the most sacred part of her, the part that she only gave to me from now on.

"Will you be mine for real? In all the ways I want you?" To accentuate my point, I dragged my tongue over her again, from the entrance to her tight pussy up to her perfect, hard clit.

She couldn't talk, not bound up and gagged like this, but her chest caved in a sob and she closed her eyes, perhaps trying to hide the tears that streamed down either side of her head. But I saw them.

Are those happy tears?

"Sel?" Using her real name made her glance down at me, and when she did, she nodded.

With fabric sticking out from between her lips and a flush painting her cheeks, she grumbled an affirmative noise that sounded like, "Yes, I will."

That really set me off. If I thought I was desperate for her before, I was fucking insatiable after that. I had no ring. I had no public declaration of promise to her, but I would put one on her finger soon. I hadn't planned on doing it like this, but now that I had, it seemed right.

We were wild things, her and I, and lying there between her legs, petting her and kissing her into a soaking, limp mess, nothing could have ever been more perfect. We had found each other, and we'd have each other, no matter what came for us.

I fucked her with my face and my fingers until she came, grumbling and crying around my makeshift gag, straining her arms against the leather belt. But I didn't let her go, oh no. I kept at her, dining on that delicious cunt while it clenched and quivered around me, until she squirmed and tried to close her legs around my head. I wouldn't let her, my shoulders blocking her path, and eventually, she got tired of fighting it and relented, sinking into the mattress again. Her muscles tensed, another orgasm yanking her under so close to the last one, and this time, I pressed down on the top of her pelvis, curling my fingers just right, yanking on that trigger deep inside her, the one that only a good lover knew how to find.

"There it is," I said, laughing as warm fluid soaked my hand and upper arm. She squirted fucking everywhere, all over the sheets and my chest, and I fucking reveled in it, rubbing her clit hard now, extending it as much as I could.

And when she was done, she collapsed back into the bed, her body a heavy pile of limbs. I sat back and took my jeans off before hovering over her body long enough to pull the panties from her mouth so I could steal her lips for my own.

She smiled against my mouth, whispering in between kisses. "I can't believe you proposed to me when I had my own underwear in my mouth. You fucking brute."

It should have pleased me, how much I could horrify and arouse her at the same time, but I had other ideas for my own euphoria. I unfastened the belt, checking that her fingers were still flesh colored and working. When I was satisfied she wasn't damaged, I rolled us so that she sat on top of me, her wet cunt practically scalding against my now bare cock. I held her up for a moment, just long enough to angle my tip at her entrance, and then I yanked her home, all the way down, all at once.

"Fuucckkk," I moaned, the noise barreling out of me from the depths of my poor, pathetic heart. She was so fucking wet and tight, like she'd been ready for me all damned night. Fuck knew I had. She reached down and grabbed the back of my thighs, tracing her nails up to my ass. When I pulled out, she used those talons to shove me back in hard and rough.

"You like it like that, huh?" She grinned, the feral side of her now completely in control, peering out at me from behind those devilish baby blues. "When I scratch and mark as much as you?"

"You better fucking believe it, kitten." She sank her teeth into the other side of my neck, leaving bruises that would last for days, and after she reached another climax, I used it as my launching pad to seek my own.

It hit me behind the eyes, blinding and piercing, as it exploded down my spine and into my soul. I emptied myself inside her, the thought of filling her up with come fueling that sick beast inside. It kept going, reeling me under again and again. I groaned and fucked up into her, and once it was over, she collapsed on top of me, her legs on either side of my hips, her head tucked under my chin.

"You're so beautiful when you come." Her chest vibrated while she chuckled softly to herself. "And you got blood everywhere. You're gonna have to cut me, too, ya know?" She ran her fingers through my hair, softly untangling pieces as she encountered knots. "Otherwise, it's not fair."

I groaned and shifted my face so I could look up at her. "Be careful. You're gonna get me hard again."

She laughed and pulled me in for another kiss.

29

SELENE

"When did the nightmares start?" my therapist, Rosa, asked, furrowing her brows and tilting her head to the side while she assessed me.

I shook my head, running my hands over my face as I tried to remember. Certainly before Billy, but that had escalated it. "Maybe when my parents died. Maybe when Gemma died."

"What was your relationship with your parents like?"

"Mostly good." I shifted in my seat. "I was a daddy's girl, and my mom liked to say I was her little twin." The memory warmed me, the thought of her big smile and the way she'd wrap her arms around my waist to give the best hugs. "It would piss Jericho off because he's my *only* twin." I went into more detail about the day Crow told us they'd died and how we'd went to live with Gemma. "And then she died, and I..."

I didn't handle it well.

I wasn't handling any of this well.

Running my hands down the tops of my thighs, I took a deep breath and prayed for tears to fall. We'd been talking emotional baggage for the better part of an hour, and still, no physical release came. Rosa had an explanation for that, too.

"Everyone expresses emotions differently," she said. "I have some clients who cry the whole hour. I have some that never cry at all." Then she wanted to know why I thought my lack of tears said anything about me, and I realized Alba may have had an ulterior motive for suggesting I go to therapy. Rosa had a more analytical mind than I did. She wanted to talk about the *why* of everything and dissect where I felt it in my body.

And fuck Alba, because the more I saw my therapist, the better I handled the icy inferno inside. The more the world became manageable. Not that I couldn't manage it before, but I'd done a psych rotation, and I had enough self-awareness to consider the fact that taking off on a solo revenge mission to kill my brother's ex-girlfriend might have meant I needed some professional assistance with sorting out my emotional state.

Rosa had been recommended to me by Alba's therapist, and the moment I met the no bullshit Cubano-American, I knew we'd get along just fine. She didn't mince words, and neither did I.

"I'm marrying her husband," I murmured. "I love him. It's a good match, but...he *is* my uncle."

Rosa pursed her lips. "Labels like that do no one any good. It sounds like he's been protecting you...loving you...for a long time."

"And Pollux is still in the hospital. At least he's off life support now."

"That must be really difficult," Rosa said.

"I'm the reason he's there," I said. "I'm the reason the bombing happened at all. If I had gone after Nikki earlier, I could have prevented it."

"You'll never be able to know that for certain," she argued.

"How can I be happy with Thor when so many people are suffering?" I cleared my throat, wincing against the burning shame in my gut. "How can I deserve happiness?"

"You know what I think?" She gave me a rare warm smile, her dark eyes glimmering as she continued. "I think you've been telling yourself the reasons you can't be happy for so long, you think it makes you some sort of evil person when you want a little bit for yourself."

Fucking. Ouch.

"It's okay to want joy in your life, Selene," she continued. "It's okay to find peace with another human while healing from guilt and remorse."

"But the things I've done..." I wanted the tears to fall. I wanted to feel the release that came with them. "And I don't feel any regret."

"*No* regret? None at all?" Rosa eyed me with that knowing stare, the one that said she believed I was lying to myself.

Nikki.

"She deserved it," I said.

Rosa didn't comment, just narrowed her eyes and let me go on.

"Someone else should have taken her out." I cleared my throat. "It shouldn't have been up to me." At her knowing smile, I continued. "Maybe it isn't as black or white as I'm making it out to be."

"Ah, there it is," she said, nodding. "Both can be true. The world exists in shades of gray. Does that not make you worthy of happiness?"

I knew what she was trying to do. I needed a perspective shift, and God help us all, but Rosa was the queen of seeing things in a new light.

"Perhaps," I said. "Perhaps that means I deserve even worse."

She seemed to consider that. "Do you think your brother deserves worse?"

"No," I said immediately. "Jer always does what he has to. He has a fucked-up sense of honor, but it *is* honor."

"And you see yourself differently?"

"Of course. I'm the—" I stopped myself before I said *smarter one.* Because that was also a lie I'd been telling myself for too long. I wasn't the brains of anything, and just because he was stronger didn't mean he was the brawn. Jer and I were twins. We were the same. If he deserved Alba, then I deserved Thor. It was one thing to say it, but quite another to believe it deep down inside. "Oh."

Rosa nodded, remaining silent so I could drink from the enormous firehose she'd led me to. I wasn't better or worse than any of those fuckers in the MC, and definitely not my brother. We were all a bunch of fucked-up monsters, but we lived in a fucked-up world...a world that had forced us to be this way in order to survive it.

"Thank you, Rosa," I said.

"Give yourself some grace, Doctor Montgomery. The world isn't on your shoulders, and it never has to be again."

With that in my heart, I went to the garage to put in a day's work. KC and Hollywood were already fucking around with a beat-up Ford Ranger that had been dropped off overnight. My brother spotted me when I arrived and walked into the office to greet me.

"Hey, your limp is getting better." He grinned, his eyes lighting up. "How's the leg today?"

It always hurt more after therapy, but it was like lancing an infection. Every time I sat through an agonizing cleansing, I came away better for it.

"It's okay," I said, returning his smile. I remembered what Rosa said, how if he deserved Alba, then I deserved Thor. If I didn't think Jer was a monster, perhaps I wasn't one, either. Or perhaps if we were both monsters, then there wasn't anything wrong with that to begin with.

"I wanted to say I'm sorry," I said, meeting his gaze. "Truly. I should've done a lot of things different, and while I don't regret going after her, I feel the worst about leaving you behind."

Jer paused and stared at me while I confessed my apology.

"It was always you and me against the world. I guess you've got Alba now, and I've got Thor, but that doesn't mean I get to ghost you whenever I want. That was fucked up, and I'm sorry."

He cracked a smile and pulled me into a hug, kissing the top of my head the way we'd done to each other since we were kids. "Yeah, you bitch."

I laughed and hugged him tighter, blinking back the tears in my eyes. "We're still gonna grow old together, right?"

"You fucking know it." He stepped back and chucked my chin

with his fist, shooting me a wink before returning to the mechanic's bay to bust Hollywood's chops.

I went to find Thor in the back office, peering around the corner to spy on him before I went inside.

He sat behind his desk, shuffling through paperwork and writing something down in the notebook he had open. He'd pulled his hair back into a knot at the back of his head, and paired with the dirty white T-shirt and the leather boots, I had to restrain myself from climbing into his lap right there in the office. He squinted at the paper before leaning in to see it better.

"You need glasses," I said, taking a few steps inside. "You're getting old."

He looked up at me and grinned, scooting back from the desk. "Bet I could still outshoot you."

"That's a wager you don't wanna take." I circled around the desk, eyeing the work orders he'd been sorting through before standing in between his legs so I could grip his jaw and give him a kiss.

"How was therapy?"

I groaned and shook my head. "Brutal and gut-wrenching...so you know, it was a good session." He laughed at my misery before I added, "Rosa is a cruel mistress."

Thor leaned in and kissed the side of my neck before nibbling on my ear, sending a shiver down that entire side of my body.

"I've been thinking," I started, turning to face him so I could put my knees on either side of his hips and sit across both of his legs. "Let's go do it. Let's go get married."

He furrowed his brows, assessing me for a moment before speaking. "I thought you wanted to wait until things settle down."

I shrugged, remembering my conversation with Rosa. I was holding myself back because some part of me thought I didn't deserve this, or maybe that I would never deserve this. But I couldn't do that anymore.

"We've waited too long. Make me yours and chase me every night."

His answering grin eased the tension in my gut, making me shake harder with anticipation, shocking me down to my core.

"I'll give you anything, kitten. Anything you want." He kissed me, and that too I felt everywhere at once.

"WHAT THE FUCK IS THAT?" Ru gawked at the ring on my left hand, pointing at it like she'd never seen jewelry before. Thor had given it to me this morning while we were still in bed, a simple princess-cut moonstone, nothing too outlandish. I didn't like gaudy, and the moment I saw it, I nearly sobbed at its perfection. Damn him for making me emotional on Christmas morning.

Ru's eyes narrowed, her stare hardening. "Is that what I think it is?"

I looked around, checking to make sure it was just the two of us behind the bar. The brothers were in the back, doing whatever the SRMC did to celebrate Christmas, while the old ladies and MC princesses stayed out here.

Dinner was almost done, and the scent of ham and vegetables floated around the space, masking the normal musk of old cigarette smoke and bad life choices. It had been a rough celebration, considering Pollux was still in a coma. We didn't know when he would wake up, if ever, and after everything I'd seen from his medical records, even I had to admit, the prognosis wasn't good. Even if he did wake up, he'd been on the ventilator so long now, he might never be able to come off it. The entire family had been a mess, not wanting to celebrate Christmas but also not wanting to sully Pollux's memory by changing anything about our routine.

"Would you shut the fuck up?" I whisper hissed, trying and failing to keep my voice low. "I'm not trying to steal the Christmas spotlight."

"And *why* would you being stealing the spotlight?" Ru blinked and raised her eyebrows up her forehead, staring at me as if I'd suddenly grown a horn between my eyes. Those ice-colored eyes always saw entirely too much. Which, unfortunately, was a family trait. Ru, Alba, and Aris all had the same annoying superhuman ability to pierce a person's armor with their stare, and no one was capable of standing against it, least of all me.

"Exactly." I grabbed a beer out of the fridge and used the opener to crack off the top before pouring it into a glass.

"No, I'm serious, Sel." Ru took another step closer. "Are you and Thor getting married?"

I cleared my throat and ran a hand over the back of my neck, refusing to meet her gaze, opting instead to refill the peanuts bowl from a jar on the shelf in the back. "We're not hiding it."

It wasn't a confirmation, but it also wasn't a denial.

Ru stared at me, dropping her jaw and curling her lips into a mischievous grin. Paired with all that dark curly hair piled on top of her head and the excitement in her gaze, she looked like a little kid that had woken up to a pile of gifts under the Christmas tree. "Is this real? Is this happening?"

I cleared my throat and looked around for Verona. I didn't want her to overhear because we hadn't talked about it with her yet, and I'd rather face that conversation head-on.

"We're looking at getting our own place, somewhere out in the woods." Somewhere we could run free without the fear of neighbors thinking we were killing each other. When I'd first agreed to have Verona move in, it had been to break up the tension between Thor and me. Obviously, the circumstances had changed. Now, I agreed with my fiancé. Having her around all the time, having her *brothers* around all the time, put a damper on the way Thor and I liked to play with each other.

We were going to let her stay there. The house was paid for, and she could do whatever she wanted with the extra space. Knowing her, she'd turn it into a dungeon to torture all her submissives on her camming feed.

"Sel." Ru's eyes welled with tears and she waved at her face, her cheeks flushing. "I'm so happy for you."

"Why are we so happy?" Alba came to stand next to Ru while

Verona huddled in on the other side, narrowing her eyes at my left hand.

"Oh, thank God," Verona said. "Can I tell everyone now?"

"Tell us what?" Alba looked between Verona and Ru before coming back to me. "What's going on?"

I stared at Ru, grimacing my way through the extra attention. I hadn't wanted everyone to find out today. It was fucking Christmas. But Ru wouldn't be discouraged.

"Thor and Selene are getting married."

"Wait, what?" Hollywood had just come out of the back room, and I ran my palm over my face, groaning because now that he knew, everyone would find out in seconds.

True to brand, he threw an arm over Ru's shoulders and shouted, "A round of shots for Thor and Selene!" He threw his head back and howled into the air like a wolf at the moon, laughing when Bear pretended to hit him in the gut. After an announcement like that, Christmas had long been forgotten. Hollywood lined up twenty shot glasses, pouring damn near a whole bottle of whiskey across them to fill them up.

"So much for keeping the wedding small and private, huh?" Thor pulled me into a hug, wrapping his arms around my shoulders as he leaned down to kiss me in front of everyone.

"Christ, it's about damn time." Verona held up her glass, clinking it against Ru's when she did the same thing. Jericho and Saint crowded closer, followed by Crow and Aris and the rest of the brothers. They said a round of cheers to our happiness, and the whole thing was so damned overwhelming, I couldn't stop blushing.

But this had been what I'd almost died for, hadn't it? This had been what I'd sacrificed a leg for, what I'd spend the rest of my life limping for. Love. Family. People who stood by my side to celebrate my wins and help me up after my losses.

"Congratulations to you both," Crow said, and everyone around us echoed it before shooting back their shots, me included. It warmed me on the way down, itching my throat in all the right places.

Thor tightened his arms around me, finding the curve of my ear before he whispered, "Make your rounds, kitten, and then I'm taking you home. I have my own Christmas gifts to give."

I laughed and gave him another kiss that tasted like whiskey before nodding at Lore, sitting in the far corner all by himself. To his credit, he hadn't taken a hunting knife to Leo Caputi yet, despite what the bastard stole from him, and that showed a massive amount of restraint on his part.

"How are you feeling?" I asked, after taking another shot over to him and placing it down in front of his closed fists. "Are the headaches still coming?"

He looked up at me and smiled, his dark beard longer now than the last time I'd seen him. Like everyone in the club, he'd aged so much in the short time since he'd joined. Wrinkles around his eyes told the tale of how poorly life had treated him, not to mention the jagged scar he kept hidden under a black eyepatch. Still, he tried to seem happy, putting on the fake grin while passing out fake pleas-antries.

"Right as rain, Doc. How are you?" He nodded to my thigh, where I still sported a brace to help me walk while the muscle repaired itself around the broken tissue. "That looks nasty. Bet it'll leave a wicked scar."

"You're the one to talk."

He sighed and rolled his good eye, taking a long pull from the shot of amber liquor. "It's horrifying, I know."

"Hey," I cut in. "Don't sell yourself short. Chicks...*and dicks*...dig scars." I'd heard rumors about Lore's sex life from some of the brothers in the New England SRMC. He didn't limit his exploits to the ladies. Despite the relatively homophobic background of *some* MCs in America, no one in the Roses gave a shit about sexual orienta-tion or gender identity. When life could literally be snatched away any second, things like that were so fucking trivial. If you were a Rose, you were family, no matter whose dick you liked to suck.

"Thanks, Selene." He chuckled and nodded to my ring. "Congrats on the engagement. It's about damned time y'all got together."

My cheeks burned and I glanced away, suddenly unable to hold the eye contact. "Thanks, Lore."

I headed toward the bar, biting back a smile when I approached Verona playing a round of poker with Hollywood, Jer, and Bear. Judging by the size of her pile, she could hold her own.

"Read 'em and weep, gentlemen," she said, biting her cigar as she placed her cards down on the table. It was good to see her in livelier spirits, all things considered.

"Jesus Christ, V," Bear groaned. "Again?"

"I told you not to bet against me, big brother," she said, giving him a smile. "I'll rob ya blind every time."

Hollywood grinned, but remained uncharacteristically quiet while Jer pushed his chips toward our little cousin. When she saw me standing there, she put her cigar down and pushed to her feet.

"I need fifteen minutes for a checkup, guys," she said. "And no touching my chips."

I followed her to the same back room we'd met in a month ago, locking the door behind me after it shut.

"How's the pain?" I limped toward her, gesturing at her to pull her cropped band tee higher on her chest.

"It's okay," she said. "It's still really sore." Her chest wound looked the same as it had last month, healing in its early stages of turning into a scar. She still had the bullet fragment hanging in a glass bottle between her breasts, and this time, I couldn't resist.

"What are you doing with that?" I flicked it and stepped back so she could pull her shirt down.

"It's a souvenir." Verona kept her eyes on the ground and pursed her lips, crossing her arms over her chest. "It reminds me how precious life is, how quickly it can be taken away." She cleared her throat, her shoulders deflating for a moment, just enough for me to see through the tough veneer she kept up as a front. "It reminds me there are people that would sacrifice themselves for me, that I'm not alone."

Hollywood.

I didn't pry, and when she turned to leave, I gave her a solemn nod as my goodbye. It was none of my business, and I appreciated that Verona had mostly minded her own despite living with me and Thor all this time.

But the thought did intrigue me...

Hollywood had always been a charismatic guy with a big, open heart and a smile for anyone who needed it. He'd been voted class clown in high school, and now that he was a full-fledged adult, only two years younger than me and my brother, he knew what to do with all that personality. And his appeal wasn't *just* how great of a person he was. He'd hit puberty going a thousand miles an hour, and now he towered over the rest of us like a Greek God, his body and his jawline carved from marble. The club had nicknamed him Hollywood because of those good looks.

Verona, on the other hand, had a tough outer shell that was nearly impenetrable on her best days and diamond encrusted on her worst. She barely smiled, and she was more likely to cut you down to size with the honest truth than give you fake niceties that meant nothing to no one. Ru referred to it as Verona's "black cat" energy, and considering the dark makeup and clothing she wore, I couldn't disagree with that assessment.

She loved to hate everyone, and Hollywood loved to be loved.

I thought about his reaction to her performance that night at the Beacon, how he'd seemed turned on and horrified and confused at the same time. She was Bear's little sister, the president's daughter, off-limits in a thousand different ways. Showing any interest in her would be a good way for him to lose his favorite part of his anatomy. And then, I laughed and laughed and laughed all the way back out front.

EPILOGUE

SELENE

Six months later

The light from the full moon crept in through the trees overhead, the humidity of late August sticking to my neck and face despite being almost midnight. I took a hesitant step, my heart pounding, tracing down the hard scratchy bark on the nearest tree.

He was around here somewhere. He'd promised he would be.

We'd spent the better part of this week talking about this scene—how we wanted it to go, what we both wanted to feel, what we'd do if it all suddenly went wrong. We had a safe word should either of us need to stop at any time. But I didn't think I would. I had been wanting this since the first time I'd run away, since the first time he'd tracked me down.

A twig cracked from my right and I took off again, racing through the forest, jumping over logs, laughing as heavy steps barreled after me. He was onto me now, having figured out where I was and what direction I planned to head. Adrenaline burned through my blood, fueling me on, making me lighter on my toes than I normally would have been.

My thigh ached and protested the whole time, but I could put a few miles on the treadmill these days with little issue, so I ignored its warm-up pangs and kept going until I found a huge maple to hide behind.

"I can smell you, kitten," he growled. "I can smell how bad you want me."

We'd been teasing each other all day, every casual brush and accidental touch a type of foreplay. I'd look up and catch him staring at me in the same way he did right before he pounced, and my cunt would clench, soaking my vulva and my panties combined.

After all this prey-play, though, I had a fucking ocean between my legs and the earthy scent of feminine desire followed me around like that cat in that fucked-up skunk cartoon from the nineties. When I stopped, I could practically taste it in the air.

He came closer, his heavy footfalls rustling in the undergrowth, and just when he'd gotten within arm's reach of me, I took off again. Legs pumping and arms swinging, I sprinted as hard as I could, dodging trees and shrubs. I'd almost made it to the riverbank when strong arms grabbed me around the midsection and tackled me to the ground.

"Got you," he growled, pinning my wrists above my head and flipping me in one movement so I lay on my stomach. I tried to struggle, twisting and yanking my arms away, but he held them tighter. "Stop fighting. That's only going to make this worse for you."

"You're a sick fucker, you know that?" Again, I tried to buck his hold, but he gripped me tighter. "I can't believe you like chasing women through the woods. You're a fucking beast, an animal."

"You're right about that." He scooped one hand under my waist and hoisted my hips up so I could get my knees under me. "Now shut the fuck up and let me enjoy my prize."

The press of cold metal at the base of my spine made me arch into the touch, and I shivered as the cut of fabric echoed out into the air. He'd used his hunting knife to slice my leggings open. Then I remembered the game and tried to get away from him again, scrambling forward on my hands and knees.

"Oh no, you don't." He clambered after me, using his weight to hold me down this time, one giant palm in between my shoulder blades keeping me still. "Stop fucking moving."

He didn't give me any time to gather my strength. He lined his cock up and shoved inside me in a rough thrust, damn near splitting me in two. How I fucking loved it. He put one hand around my throat, arching me farther into him, and used the other to hold himself up so he could rail me as hard as he wanted.

It was brutal and twisted and so fucking hot. I fell apart in seconds, my euphoria almost too much for me to handle.

"That's right," he snarled, letting me go so he could use my back as leverage to fuck me harder, deeper, as rough as he could. "You fucking love it like this. You love letting some wild thing rut inside you because you're a filthy little beast, too, aren't you?"

"I am," I whimpered. "I am, I am."

But only for Thor, only for him. He brought this side out of me, and whether it was because I had learned it from him all those years ago or because it had been there all along, I didn't know and I didn't care. I had spent so many years trying to deny it, trying to deny the similarities that existed between us, it was fucking exhausting.

Life was too damned short, and the love between us too damned beautiful to deny. Two weeks after that conversation with my therapist, we were married in a private ceremony with just Jer, Alba, Ru, and Saint in attendance. I didn't want anything big, and Thor believed he had waited far too long to do this already.

Now husband and wife, MC brother and old lady, the primal kink between us had ramped up to eleven.

I was his, he was mine, and I had the marks in my skin to prove it.

THOR

EVERY TIME with Selene was like the first time, and every morning that I woke up by her side, I counted myself one lucky fuck. We matched each other in ways that should have been obvious to me from the beginning, and the more deeply she wove herself into my soul, the more I realized there would never be a way to undo it.

I loved her more than I'd ever loved anything in my life, and spending my nights like this, chasing her through our woods, holding her down while I did wonderfully perverse things to her body, making her come over and over again, it made life worth living.

I'd seen horrible things in my life and done even worse. I'd lost damn near everyone who ever meant anything to me, and a year ago, I woulda decked anyone who told me I'd be married to Selene Montgomery one day.

But here we were, and I was damned determined to never let her go.

She gave me one last moan, and I pulled back to toss her over like she weighed nothing, pushing inside her again before she could protest. I knew what she wanted next, and fuck, how badly I'd wanted to give it to her when she asked.

I grabbed my knife from where I'd dropped it nearby and pressed the cold steel edge to the side of her neck, the beast inside me fully awake now, desperate to do all the deliciously horrible things we'd planned. I put my free hand on her pelvis to hold her still so I could keep fucking her slow...so slow that my trembling hand didn't accidentally slip.

It was terrifying, yes, but it fucking turned her on so much that she couldn't stand it, and that sent me into a frenzy.

I paused to drag the knife delicately down the center of her chest, careful not to break the skin, pushing just enough to threaten.

"Where do you want it?" I asked, though I knew already. I wanted to check in with her, to make sure she was still in the game.

She arched into the touch, biting her lip and succeeding in being the sexiest and most adorable thing I'd ever seen.

"Tell me," I said. "Beg me for it."

"Please," she said, pulling her shirt up to reveal those breasts and aching round nipples I loved to mark. "Please, Thor."

"Hmm." I liked the pleading the most. Unable to stand it any longer, I reared up onto my haunches so I had complete control when I dragged the edge of the blade across the underside of her tit. It was barely more than a paper cut, the nick so clean and tiny, but it was enough to satisfy that masochistic side of her, the one that loved when I ducked my head and licked over the wound, the metallic taste of her lifeblood spilling over my tongue and down my throat.

Her blood was in mine, and mine was in hers, and all of it was so fucked up that the monster in my head laughed as loud as it could while she pulled me down for a deep, resounding kiss. I fucked her into the forest floor. I fucked her until I couldn't think anymore and we were both a messy pile of sweat and hormones and come.

And then we lay there and stared at the stars with nothing but comfortable, sated silence between us.

WANNA JOIN THE ROSES?

Thank you for reading! If you enjoyed this book, please consider leaving a review They help other readers find my work, and because of that, they enable me to keep writing.

If you want more **STEEL ROSES** content, check out the prequel novella, **THEY CALLED HIM SAINT,** for *free* when you sign up for my newsletter.

https://jenadoyle.com/join/

(No spam, only smut. I promise.)

But wait! There's more! The next book in the Steel Roses is July 30. 2024. Keep reading for a sneak peek at **HOLLYWOOD** and **VERONA's** story, **MISCHIEF MAYHEM.**

MISCHIEF MAYHEM

CHAPTER ONE
VERONA

"Do you believe in soul mates?" Ru, my friend and fellow MC princess, asked as she leaned over the pool table so she could sink her four ball into the corner pocket.

"I suppose." I cleared my throat and winced as the familiar ache shot down the center of my chest. Instinct had me clutching the glass jar necklace that hung under my shirt, the one I wore at all times, the one that reminded me I was still alive for better or worse. "Like twin flames? That kind of thing?"

"Sure." Ru took a sip of her beer and nodded, her curly brown hair bouncing around her face as she moved. When she failed to put her next ball into a pocket, I took my turn, easily sinking my nine in the center.

"Maybe." Taking a drink of my own beer, I ignored my throbbing scar that ran in between my breasts like I'd had a heart transplant. "What about you?"

"I used to think it was bullshit." She grinned, her icy-blue eyes sparkling under the shitty fluorescent lighting in the club as they sought out her fiancé, Saint, across the room. The dark-haired brother sat with some of the other motorcycle club members, drinking and laughing as my cousin, KC, talked. "But after everything that's happened, I can't deny it."

"Please." I rolled my eyes and sank another ball in the far left. "You're twenty-three, same as me. Don't you think you're a little young to be talking soul-mates and happily ever afters?"

She laughed, her cheeks flushing despite how open we were with each other. Once upon a time, Ru and I had been best friends. I was the president's daughter, the proverbial princess of the Steel Roses Motorcycle Club, and she'd been born to the VP two months after me. We were raised in this chaos together, and even if we lost touch after high school, I'd never discounted her friendship.

"You don't know what it's like," she said, nodding toward the rest of the brothers, "to have one of them devoted to you, those alpha assholes."

"I grew up in a house with four of them. I think I have an idea." Being the youngest sister to three older biker brothers combined with having the president as my father meant I'd had to be tough, much tougher than the rest of the princesses and hang-arounds. Bear was the eldest, Castor and Pollux were the twins in the middle, and I came last. Our mom died when I was nine, leaving me as the sole girl, someone to be protected, the apple of their fucking eye. It had been fifteen years and my father hadn't moved on. I'd never even seen him with a hang-around.

"What about fate?" Ru brought the topic back as she tried to make another pocket, missing it.

"Maybe. My mom was a witch. She used to believe in magic." I lined up to pocket another ball, but it bounced off the edge and scattered the others around it.

"You believe in magic but not soul-mates?" Ru raised an eyebrow and moved around the table, tilting her head to the side.

No, that wasn't true. I did believe in magic, the kind that linked two people based on spilt blood and experience, the kind that gave me an undeniable link to my found family. But soul-mates might be pushing it.

"I don't know what I believe," I said because that seemed easier to explain. "But I do know that settling down and getting married at twenty-three is stupid."

"Hey," she grumbled with a laugh. "I'm not married."

"Uh huh." I chuckled and swallowed the rest of my beer, deciding to change the subject. "How's the construction going at the Beacon?"

Her features dropped, and she ran her palm over her face. "We're almost there, thank fucking God. Hopefully, by St. Patty's Day, we can be back in the space."

This past Thanksgiving, a former hang-around turned traitor had bombed the BDSM club where Ru and I worked. Technically, the MC owned the place, but Ru had been given a partial stake and a loan to renovate it. On the night of our grand reopening, the whole place exploded, nearly killing my brother, Pollux, and putting dozens more in the hospital. He'd been in ICU for weeks afterward, and only just recently started talking again after being taken off the ventilator. After that, the Beacon had been confiscated by the Feds, and once they returned the property to us, Ru had filed the insurance claim to rebuild. She had the stamina of a fucking Olympic athlete. I would have thrown in the towel and sold the place by now.

"But with the extra cash, I can finally get those marble countertops I wanted for the bathrooms, so... silver lining, I guess?" She smiled and sat down her stick when Saint approached, wrapping his arms around her waist from behind before whispering in her ear. The public display of affection would have grossed me out if it wasn't such an everyday occurrence around the clubhouse.

She, of course, had been right. These alpha assholes loved their women, and the more they loved them, the more obsessive they were about them. Ru turned in Saint's embrace to wrap her arms around his neck while he grabbed her ass and nodded toward the exit with a devilish grin.

"See ya, V!" Ru gave me a wave before giggling and stumbling out into the frigid February air.

With Valentine's Day tomorrow, the normally grungy clubhouse looked like love had vomited everywhere. My cousin, Selene, grinned at her husband, Thor, by the bar while Ru's sister, Alba, walked over to sit on KC's lap, leaning into her husband so she could kiss his cheek. Some of the other old ladies mingled around, laughing with the old timers, the ones that had been in the club since I was a child. Red hearts hung from the rafters and streamers weaved from corner to corner. It was tacky as hell, but at least no one was getting shot or murdered... so there's that.

I stood by the pool table, knowing I'd be alone for the first Valentine's Day in years. I was fucking proud of that fact. This year, I celebrated my single status. I'd gotten away from an abusive ex-stalker, I was back with my family, and... my gaze caught on a dark stare across the clubhouse.

Hollywood — my eldest brother's best friend and the club's resident man-whore. He'd gotten his road name because of how beautiful he was. At six-foot-five and corded with muscle, Hollywood had the traditional square jaw and chiseled features that made both women and men swoon. I, on the other hand, lived to push men like him to their knees and hear them beg.

As soon as I made eye contact with him, he darted his gaze away, going back to his conversation with Bear and another brother, Wheels. Had he been staring at me?

I snorted and took another drink of my beer, relishing the fact that Hollywood had never been interested in me, not like that. Pick any number of the female notches on his bedpost and put them in a lineup, they'd all fit a profile: paper thin, traditionally beautiful, hopelessly devoted to inflating his ego. None of that included me. Sure, I was tall with legs for days, but my thighs had been built for crushing men's souls, not appeasing a their fantasies. I preferred my tattooed skin and raven hair with matching make up. I liked people to know who I was as soon as they saw me, lest they form any incorrect opinions of their own.

Besides, it wasn't like Hollywood was *my* type, either. He was probably a dominant biker badass in bed — holding his women down, growling dirty words in their ears, choking them until they begged for air. While I loved a good rough fuck, I preferred to be the one doing the growling and choking.

Despite his namesake and the rumors floating around about his sexual prowess, I wasn't susceptible to his charms. Sure, his dimples complimented his perfect teeth, and the fact that his biceps were bigger than my thighs meant he could probably bench press me, but that changed nothing about how I treated him.

He was my brother's idiot best friend, and except for one time... a long time ago... nothing had ever happened between us. He didn't even know it was me, and I planned to keep it that way until I died.

"Hey, let me know when you're ready to roll," Wheels said, shooting me a smile as he passed me to head outside. Right after I'd gotten back from college, Hollywood had been assigned to be my bodyguard, but shortly after the bombing at the Beacon, Wheels had taken over. I never asked why, but I didn't mind. The younger brother had an easy-going personality and mostly kept to himself. I appreciated that because while things were still being renovated during my day job, I relied a lot on my income from Alba's website, *Crimson*.

I nodded and glanced over to Hollywood again, watching as a hang-around approached him and put her arms around his neck. That would be it for the two of them. It couldn't have been a more open invitation. He shook his head and smiled, whispering something to her that made her pout and back away from him.

"Are you sure?" she whimpered.

He chuckled and tapped the end of her nose. "Don't be like that, beautiful. It's only a few more weeks."

"But I want you now," she whined.

He ran the back of his knuckle down the side of her cheek, clearly uncomfortably but doing his best to appease her. "I'm sure you'll survive."

Christ, take no for an answer, lady.

I furrowed my brows and finished my beer while she crossed her arms over her chest, giving him puppy dog eyes. "You're no fun after you've taken a vow of chastity—"

Surprise choked me and bubbles flew up the back of my windpipe into my nose. My eyes burned, and I coughed, tapping myself on my chest to clear my throat, but that aggravated my chest wound, and I gasped, struggling to breathe.

Focus. Slow down. Inhale.

"You okay?" Bear asked, suddenly at my side with his hand on my shoulder.

I nodded and wheezed a quiet, "Yes," before hacking again.

"You sure?" My brother's dark brown eyes radiated concern, his curly hair falling in his face as he assessed me.

Giving him another nod, I grabbed the glass of water out of his hand and took a few swigs to settle my esophagus before handing it back to him. "Yeah, just... it went down the wrong pipe."

"Listen, I already have one sibling in the hospital, I don't need a second one." He smiled, and the movement lit up his entire face, making him look so much like our mother that it clenched my heart.

My scar burned again, racing up the center of my chest with the same agony that it had the night I'd been shot. I'd been in the backseat of Saint's truck when my family's enemies attacked, and a bullet had gone through Hollywood's torso into my sternum, where it lodged in my bone until I had surgery to remove most of it. I'd never get rid of it all. Fragments of that bullet, of that night, would be permanently embedded inside my skeleton until I croaked.

"Did you hear they're discharging him next week?" I grinned. "I've got the space at my house to take him if you and Castor can't."

Thor and Selene had moved out a few weeks ago, leaving the whole place for me. When Wheels started babysitting me, he'd moved into the basement, but he mostly kept to himself. Having Pollux around wouldn't be a total hardship.

"No, Castor swears he's got it. You know they have that twin telepathy thing." Bear chuckled and shook his head before giving me a more serious stare. "You probably ought to check in on them from time to time."

I laughed and agreed. Where Bear always had his head on straight, the twins had the luxury of living like carefree teenagers...at least until the Beacon. When Pollux got out of the hospital, the three of us would take on the brunt of caring for him until he was self-sufficient again. With third degree burns on fifty percent of his body and a healing wound from shoulder to groin, he should have died that night. I thanked whatever Goddess watching out for us that he hadn't.

"Sure," I said, nodding to our father in the far corner, whispering to the MC's vice president, Aris, and road captain, Slip. "How's he doing?"

Pollux's injury had worn him down on top of being the patriarch of this fucked up found family. His hair had turned nearly gray and heavy bags sat under his eyes, a hint as to the last time he'd had a full night's sleep. Being the president of the SRMC meant the crown lay on his head, and every casualty, every ounce of blood spilled, was the direct result of his action or inaction.

Imagine the pressure.

Bear sighed and took another drink. "He'll be better once Pollux is moving around again."

"Are you coming to the Valentine's Day party tomorrow?"

My brother barked out a laugh and shook his head. "No, I've got guard duty, thank fucking God." Before he could elaborate, our father caught his stare and nodded his head, gesturing Bear over. Pushing himself upright, he clinked his beer glass against mine and moved to walk away. "Take it easy, V."

"You, too." I watched Bear make his way to Dad and the other MC officers, and by the time I glanced back at Hollywood, he'd already disappeared without saying goodbye.

Want more? Click here to preorder MISCHIEF MAYHEM

ACKNOWLEDGMENTS

Dear Reader,

Thank you for checking out Selene and Thor's taboo romance. If you got Elena / Alaric *The Vampire Diaries* crack!ship vibes from this, you were onto something. In another life, I might have written such a fanfic if I had the time. Instead, I took the pieces I liked the best and incorporated them here. I wish I could say this will be the last time I do that, but... I must not tell lies.

To my ARC reviewers, y'all are the best. Thank you for your continued support and enthusiasm. Every time you give a new author a chance, you change their lives for the better. I will never be thankful enough for you.

Leslie Grace - You are my savior. You literally read the shittiest version of everything I write and fix it with your amazing literary magic.

Maggie Sims - Your input has become invaluable to me, and I look forward to continuing this indie publishing journey side by side.

To my editors, Misha and Kim, I am forever grateful to have you on my team. Thank you, thank you, thank you. I bow to your humble and generous wisdom.

Lastly, and most importantly, I once saw a quote on tumblr that said "I don't make characters, I break myself into pieces and give the pieces names." I've never related to something more, especially with this story.

If you've ever thought yourself a monster, if you've ever looked in the mirror and hated your reflection, I see you. You are valid. You are still breathing. You've fought those demons off this long because you're a fucking badass. I am so proud of you.

Keep. Fucking. Fighting.

If you're in the States, you can always dial 988 for crisis support.

Cheers!

-Jena

PS - Sorry for the sharp tangent but it needs to be said. I don't, nor will I ever, use AI in my work. Every word I write comes from my heart and soul, having been honed through years of dissociating from my trauma by escaping to fictional worlds built by masters of the craft. I don't use AI in my writing, and I don't use it in my graphics. In my best Archer voice, "Do you want Terminator? Because this is how you get Terminator." I live to make Sarah Connor proud.

ALSO BY JENA DOYLE

<u>**STEEL ROSES MC**</u>

They Called Him Saint (prequel novella)

Crimson Chaos

Savage Saint

Oleander Oaths

Mischief Mayhem (July 2024)

Ruthless Reign (February 2025)

<u>**MIDSUMMER**</u>

Midsummer (June 2024)

Samhain (October 2024)

Solstice (November 2024)

Beltane (March 2025)